REPUBLICS
of the MIND

Also by James Robertson

The Fanatic
Joseph Knight
The Testament of Gideon Mack
And the Land Lay Still

REPUBLICS of the MIND

New and Selected Stories

JAMES
ROBERTSON

BLACK & WHITE PUBLISHING

First published 2012
by Black & White Publishing Ltd
29 Ocean Drive, Edinburgh EH6 6JL

1 3 5 7 9 10 8 6 4 2   12 13 14 15

ISBN: 978 1 84502 491 8

New stories © James Robertson 2012

Selected stories from *The Ragged Man's Complaint*
© James Robertson, B&W Publishing 1993, 2012

The right of James Robertson to be identified as the author
of this work has been asserted by him in accordance with the
Copyright, Designs and Patents Act 1988.

All rights reserved. No part of this publication may be reproduced,
stored in a retrieval system, or transmitted in any form, or by any
means, electronic, mechanical, photocopying, recording or otherwise,
without permission in writing from the publisher.

A CIP catalogue record for this book is available from the British Library.

ALBA | CHRUTHACHAIL

Typeset by RefineCatch Limited, Bungay, Suffolk
Printed and bound by Nørhaven, Denmark

For Michael Marra,
who *really* knows how to make less more

Acknowledgements

The first eleven stories in this collection were originally published in *The Ragged Man's Complaint* by B&W Publishing in 1993. They reappear here with some minor editorial and orthographical changes.

The remaining stories have either not been published before or have appeared in earlier forms in a number of different outlets.

Acknowledgements are due to the following:

'The Dictionary' was first published in an earlier form in *Stepping into the Avalanche* (Brownsbank Press, Biggar 2003).

'Don't Start Me Talkin' (I'll Tell Everything I Know)' was first published in an earlier form in *Friends and Kangaroos: New Writing Scotland 17* (ASLS 1999).

'Old Mortality' was first published in *The Sunday Herald* in October 2006.

'MacTaggart's Shed' was first published in Stuart Kelly (ed.), *Headshook* (Hachette Scotland 2009).

'The Future According to Luke' was originally commissioned by the Edinburgh International Book Festival with the support of Creative Scotland and the Scottish Government's Edinburgh Festivals Expo Fund.

Contents

Giraffe	11
The Plagues	31
Screen Lives	41
The Jonah	51
The Claw	68
Bastards	79
Facing It	91
What Love Is	93
Tilt	106
Republic of the Mind	131
Pretending to Sleep	152
Opportunities	155
The Shelf	167
The Dictionary	179
The Dayshift	184
Don't Start Me Talkin' (I'll Tell Everything I Know)	194
Willie Masson's Miracle	205
The Rock Cake Incident	215
Old Mortality	227
MacTaggart's Shed	240
The Future According to Luke	259
Sixes and Sevens	271

Giraffe

The day Eilidh died. It started with a hangover and got worse. That's how Jimmy Sanderson minds it.

He minds doing the meat-run that day, feeling like shite, him and Eck down at the mink farm loading up the dead beasts. 'There's a wee treat for the cats in the horsebox,' Murray had said, but he hadn't said what. Jimmy can still picture himself, clear as anything, flicking up the snecks to let down the back of the box. It was full of horses' heads – twenty or thirty of them – and pathetic wee bundles of dead lambs in plastic bags.

'Fuck's sake,' said Eck.

It was May, and very hot. The heads had been lying for days and some of the eyes were out on their stalks. Up until that moment Jimmy'd always thought that only happened in cartoons.

Still feeling rough with the drink, he grabbed a couple of heads by the lugs and swung them up into the meat-trailer where they landed with a thud. 'Right,' he said. 'May as well get this ower wi.'

After a few seconds Eck stamped out his fag and joined

him. 'Need tae pit these oot o sight,' he said. 'Where the punters canna see them.'

First there was the hangover, then getting a roasting from Murray for being late in, then the meat-run with those heads from the knackers, then Eilidh dying. And the dead monkey, don't forget the dead monkey. That was a lot of bad things for one day, even for the Park.

Jimmy had been out on the bevvy with Eck the night before and he'd stayed over at Eck's because he couldn't ride his bike home in the state he was in. Eck's ma was supposed to wake them at half-seven but she must have been drunker than both of them because she never did; the first thing Jimmy knew about the morning was the sun hitting him in the eyes through a gap in the living-room curtains and himself swimming off the couch with a full bladder and a burst skull. Eck's ma was still snoring when they left the house ten minutes after they should have been at work. Jimmy got the bike started (at least he'd had the sense to leave it at Eck's before they hit the pubs) and Eck jumped on behind and somehow Jimmy managed to get them to the Park without putting the bike in the sheuch, the bevvy sloshing around in his head every time they leaned into a curve.

They were only half an hour late but Murray gave them a bollocking just the same. 'This isna a fuckin holiday camp by the way.' Jimmy was going to say, 'Well, it is, kinda,' but thought better of it. 'I'm dockin an hour aff your wages, the pair o yous,' said Murray. 'Ye're lucky ye're no gettin your books.' He'd already sent Dave Maxton to let out the giraffes and camels. That would be all that he'd done, you could bet on it. Maxton was one lazy bad bastard. Jimmy and Eck got given the meat-run, which didn't exactly help the queasy feeling in Jimmy's belly. A couple of sheep for the tigers, an old cow and some heads for the female lions, some more heads and the lambs for the males. Eck had gutted the big beasts the day before, but Murray had forgotten to tell him about the stuff in the horsebox till that morning. Jimmy said, 'Are we gonnae huv tae gut the lambs an aw?' but Eck shook his head. 'They can hae the fuckin lot.' In the lion sections they dropped the heads behind fallen tree-trunks so as not to upset the public when they drove by.

They were back at the office an hour later, waiting on orders, which was when Murray exploded off the phone about the monkey. The second one in a week. Apparently it was lying on the hard shoulder of the motorway, about four miles across country from the Park. 'That's quite a hike for a wee Injun bandit in hostile fermin territory,' Eck commented. (He was a great man for the Westerns.) Some concerned motorist had phoned in to complain. Murray was not a happy man.

'How dae the fuckers get oot, that's whit I want tae ken. We've been roon that perimeter fence three fuckin times. An how come they ayewis end up on the fuckin roads? I mean, could they no jist disappear intae the hills or somethin, for fuck's sake?'

It was embarrassing. For the Park, that is. Personally, it didn't put Jimmy up nor down. He wasn't even that bothered about the thing getting squashed; truth was, he wasn't fond of the monkeys and his head was killing him.

'It must be a hole but,' said Eck. 'There's nae wey these

monkeys can get ower the tap, no wi the electric strands and the wey it angles in.'

Murray gave him a look. 'I don't need you tae tell me that,' he said. That wasn't what was bothering him, it was the publicity.

'I'm jist sayin,' said Eck.

'Aye, aw right,' said Murray. 'Away and check the bloody fence again. Jimmy, you go doon an kick Dave Maxton's erse. I better go and pick the bugger up afore the Salvation Army get on the phone.'

As Murray drove away, the first cars of the day were just going through the lock-gates into the tiger section. Jimmy headed off to the giraffe-house to see what Maxton hadn't got up to, and to have a look at Eilidh.

Rhesus monkeys. The Park only had them because they were easier to manage than the baboons. The baboons were before Jimmy's time, and they'd had to go. They were maladjusted. They systematically ripped people's cars to pieces. They weren't intimidated by human beings or human devices at all. Somebody had to stand at the section exit with a long bamboo pole and knock them off from under the cars to stop them escaping. After closing time they went over the fence anyway – using the shock from the electrified strands to give themselves an extra boost – and roamed through the woods at the back of the Park, jumping out at evening joggers and strollers. Drunk men arrived home to their wives with tales of hairy old Satanists scampering naked through the undergrowth. The baboons came back to the Park before dawn so that they wouldn't miss out on any food that was going. The final straw was when half the troop turned up at a funeral in the nearest village. Uninvited. Whenever Jimmy thought of that it was the uninvited bit that made him laugh. He could see the baboons sitting po-faced and blue-arsed on the gravestones, wearing tall black hats and stroking their chins, being cold-shouldered by the other mourners. The local paper had made a fuss and they'd had to go, back to Africa or Longleat or wherever they'd come from.

But then, as Eck said, nobody could be sure they'd caught them all. Baboons weren't daft – some of them might have opted to stay out. They might be out there yet.

It was a rat that killed Eilidh, Jimmy's pretty sure of it. Not in the long term of course. He has a theory about that too, about captivity and exploitation and living conditions. But in the short term, as an immediate cause of death, he'd put his money on a rat.

She didn't mind about the rats if she had company. She could deal with them if the other giraffes were in the stall with her. But in the period before her death she'd been on her own a lot. They'd had to keep her in the yard, or sometimes in the stall, when the others went out each morning. Some days the vet was coming to see her, or she had to be put in the crush to get the wound treated, or she was stumbling around so much she was a danger to herself and to the people having their picnics. Towards the end it was the smell of the wound as much as anything. Murray had enough complaints on his hands what with the squashed monkeys. Some do-gooder was always trying to spot animals in poor condition. So Eilidh was stuck inside all day, stretching her neck out into the sunlight through the top half-doors, on her own, not coping with the rats. She was a sad case.

Nobody knew quite how the wound on her front left leg had started, but probably it was from a sharp point on one of the fences. Jimmy felt a bit guilty because he should have spotted it sooner. Either the metal was rusty or the wound had got septic some other way, but before long it was weeping and expanding in a big oval patch that Eilidh made worse by rubbing it against the trees and fences all day. Murray and Jimmy got her into the crush and cleaned it up and sprayed it with purple disinfectant but it didn't improve. Then she started limping with it.

The vet came and told them to treat it daily. It fell to Jimmy to organise this. It would take two or three of them to coax her into the crush, tempting her with food and prodding her in the oxters with the bamboo poles, but after a while she associated the crush with the pain of disinfecting the wound and it became harder to get her in. Food no longer tempted her as she was eating virtually nothing. She became more and more difficult; you couldn't help getting impatient with her.

Maxton said the only thing the animals understood was pain, if you hit the bastards hard enough they would do what you wanted. He demonstrated this by giving the male camel a flying kick in the bollocks to prove he could get it into its shed at night when nobody else could. The camel went – spitting and gurgling, but it went. Maxton also tried his theory out on Stumpy, a wee elephant without its tail that had been dumped on the Park from one of the Company's places in England. Maxton regularly battered Stumpy across the head and trunk with an old table-leg, to show who was boss. It worked. Whenever he saw Maxton coming, Stumpy backed into a corner of the yard, watching him warily.

'That's great, Dave,' said Jimmy. 'If the rest o us take turns tae beat him senseless he'll respect us all.'

'He's fuckin dangerous,' Maxton retorted. 'Ye've tae fuckin watch him.'

'Aye, nae fuckin wunner,' said Jimmy. One of his fantasies was that Stumpy would grow tusks overnight and staple the bastard to a tree. Around that time he hated having his day off if Maxton was working it, he didn't like to think what he might be doing to Eilidh. It was a relief coming back and finding her still limping and thrawn, still stinking of gangrene.

One morning – this was a week or so before she died – Jimmy was up on the walk in the giraffe-house checking the feed in the troughs. Eilidh didn't hear him coming. Even before he reached the stall he could tell something was wrong. Up there he was on a level with Eilidh's head, but she didn't notice him at all. She was wedged into one corner, her flanks quivering, her big soft eyes fixed in terror on the opposite corner of the stall, where a huge wet rat was scuffling around in the straw. The rat wasn't paying Eilidh a blind bit of notice. One well-aimed kick from her would have splattered it all over the walls. But she couldn't move. Jimmy'd seen her nervous often enough – the giraffes were skeerie, easily spooked – but he'd never seen fear like that in her before. That's how, later, he was certain it was a rat, maybe even the same rat, that finished her off.

There were two stalls, each big enough to take four giraffes at night. One of the things that had to be done every second day was move Eilidh from one stall to the other so they could be mucked out. For several days before she died Jimmy had tried to shift her and failed, she was getting that stubborn. So this morning he arrived at the giraffe-house with his head pounding, knowing she would have to be moved. Maxton was propped up on some sacks of feed in the store-room, drinking tea and smoking. 'Did ye shift Eilidh?' He might as well have asked if he'd been up Ben Ledi before breakfast, the look Maxton gave him.

'Did I fuck. Fuckin bitch willna fuckin shift.' Jimmy had a sore head, he wasn't in the mood to take Maxton on. He was trouble, everybody knew that. Of course he hadn't mucked out the empty stall either. Jimmy just went on and did it himself.

It was while he was in there that the crash came in the other stall. A terrible thumping crash followed by a scrabbling, thrashing sound. He tried to jump up onto the walk from the floor but it was too high, so he had to run all the way back across the yard and in through the store-room. Maxton was still lounging around. 'Whit's the fuckin hurry?'

When Jimmy got to Eilidh's stall it was almost over. She was backed into that same corner, but this time she'd gone down with all her legs tangled up underneath her. When she saw the rat she must have slipped in her panic on the sharn that hadn't been mucked out, and she was too weak to stop herself falling. She was struggling to keep her neck upright against the wall, but it was no good, what strength she had was going into the useless flailing of her legs. Jimmy couldn't get near her. For all that she was weakened and timid she still had enough power in those legs to kill him if she connected a kick. He couldn't even reach over to support her head, and all the time he could hear her breathing becoming more desperate. The giraffes were odd like that. They never made a noise, and they could only sit down with a special folding arrangement of the legs. Any other way and they couldn't get up again, and what was more the length of their necks made it impossible for them to breathe properly if they weren't upright. He shouted on Maxton to get Murray on the radio but then he minded he was away for the dead monkey, out of range, so all he could do was hunker down on the walk and watch the life ebb out of Eilidh. That's how he sees it now: sitting watching her, thinking, 'This is a crime, this is not the way a giraffe should die.' But she died anyway. He never even saw the rat, but for days after that if he caught one in the open he would go after it with a spade and batter it to bits.

Maxton appeared on the walk beside him. He took a drag on his cigarette and flicked ash in the direction of Eilidh's corpse. 'Aboot fuckin time,' he said. 'Least we'll no hae tae bother wi thon fuckin crush ony mair.' Maxton hadn't helped with the crush for a week at least. Jimmy pushed past him.

'Fuck off, Maxton. Jist fuck off, right?' He went out into the fresh air. Behind him he heard Maxton saying, 'Away and fuckin greet then.'

Jimmy thought only people in the *Sunday Post* were called Eck until he met Eck Galbraith. His ma in a moment of insanity (not the first or last by a long stroke, according to Eck) had named him and his twin brother Hector and Lysander, and they'd had to go through life disguising themselves as Eck and Sandy.

Eck had been at the Park longer than Murray, and even though Murray was the boss, Eck had a way of getting round him. He could give him lip and get away with it when anybody else would have got a smack in the face. It was as if he had something on Murray. He always managed to get the easy work, or at least the work that was most out of the way and least supervised. Like, for example, he'd persuaded Murray that he knew all about butchering and could therefore be entrusted with preparing the meat for the cats. This was crap – he'd never cut up anything bigger than an ashet pie – but he learned by trial and error before Murray was wise to him, and nobody else got near the meat-room after that. Also he was one of the few workers whose driving licences were still unmarked, so he could be allowed out on the public roads with a tractor and trailer, going round the neighbouring farms to pick up the cheap cows, sheep, horses and other corpses that the Park fed to its beasts.

Eck was left pretty much to his own devices, and early on Jimmy had seen it was a good ploy to get in with him and get a share in some of the cushy numbers. Not that he minded working with the giraffes and camels. They were easy, most of the time. But it was good to get away from the crowds once in a while, down the back road to the old mink farm which was where all the fruit, feed, hay and straw was stored. The stink of bananas down there – he couldn't eat a banana for years after he worked at the Park. Next to the stores was the meat-room, where Eck got to practise with his big knives, gutting the beasts and freezing what couldn't be used straightaway. The freezer was something out of a horror picture: whole beasts – mostly sheep – gutted and flung on the heap where they froze with their legs all twisted

20

and sticking out at grotesque angles. Nobody was quite sure if everything in there was 100 per cent safe, so they tended to use fresh meat whenever possible. So long as the vet had given it the nod. No point in introducing foot-and-mouth or something into the Scottish lion population. (This was years ago, of course. Mad cow disease wasn't even invented in these days.)

Eck knew everything there was to know about working in the Park. When Jimmy first started, Eck filled him in on all the characters. He warned him about Dave Maxton. 'That bastart's gonnae end up back in the jyle.' Then there was old John, one of the gatekeepers, who'd been three years in a POW camp in the war and had never got over it. He used to shout abuse and wave his shotgun around at any carload of Japanese that came through. But they couldn't understand what he was on about, they probably thought he was part of the show. Another old guy, Wull Telfer, used to take the chimp island boat across the artificial river and set snares for rabbits on the edge of the farmland there. Sometimes he'd take one of the Park's guns, load up with his own cartridges, and try for a pheasant or two. A fierce auld bugger, was Wull. But when he got home on a Friday he had to hand over his wage packet unopened or his wife would batter him, and if he wanted a smoke he had to get out of the house and do it in the toolshed.

There was Gav, who when he got married they stripped him naked, sprayed his balls with purple dye and drove him through the tiger section tied to the bonnet of a Land Rover. There was Annie up at the restaurant who stood up on a table at a Park disco one night and challenged all the white hunters to arm-wrestling. 'White hunters!' she snorted, meaning the guys who drove the zebra-striped Land Rovers in the cat sections. 'Think ye're in the fuckin Serengeti or somethin.' Nobody took up the challenge.

Once there were two year-old lion cubs that had been taken off their mother to be trained for the circus. They turned on a guy called Andy who'd gone into their cage to play with them, to impress Annie, and Annie went in after him and dragged him out, beating the cubs off with her handbag. Andy had an artificial hand because he'd lost the real one years before in some accident. Eck claimed he'd blown it off making a bomb. 'Whit wis he daein that for?' Jimmy asked. 'Dinna ken,' said Eck. 'Maybe he wis gonnae blaw up the oil pipeline tae England or somethin. He doesna like fowk talkin aboot his haun by the way.'

Eck and Jimmy were out on the randan and Eck was playing pool with a guy he knew called Iain. Jimmy was chatting to this lassie that was with Iain, he'd seen her around before and quite fancied her. She was impressed by the fact that he worked at the Park.

'It must be brilliant, workin wi the animals and that. I love animals.'

'Aye, it's aw right,' said Jimmy casually. You didn't want to be too enthusiastic, sound like a wee boy. Anyway, it wasn't that great. 'The pay's shite,' he said. 'Thirty-nine pound for a fifty-four hour week. I could maybe get somethin else but I'd miss bein ootside.'

'Is it no dangerous?' she said. Her name was Carol. She worked in Boots in the new shopping centre. She had short dark hair and bright red lips and Jimmy bet she'd look great in one of those white chemist's coats.

'Naw, no really,' he said, playing it dead casual still. 'No unless ye're stupit.' He thought of the game he and Gav had been playing the week before. You parked your Land Rover behind the male lions and let them sit dozing for a while, forgetting you were there. Then when there were no punters about one of you had to run out and boot the nearest lion up the arse and get back to the Land Rover before it woke up and came after you. Gav did it first. Then Jimmy had to do it. As soon as he kicked the lion he heard Gav starting up the motor and backing away at top speed. Jimmy nearly shat himself catching up with him, then they couldn't stop laughing for half an hour. The funniest thing was the lion never even stirred. They'd have been in more danger from Murray if he'd seen them at it.

'These lions are fucked,' said Gav. 'There's nae fuckin lion left in them.'

Jimmy said, 'Did ye ever see that film about the Stones at Altamont? When they hired the Hell's Angels tae act as security and peyed them in beer?'

'That wis responsible,' said Gav.

'Aye,' said Jimmy. 'Well, things are gettin a bit oot o haun, and Mick's up on the stage tryin tae cool it, he's gaun, "'Ere, which cats wanna fite?" I tell ye, it wisna these yins onywey.'

'These cats widna fight wi fuckin dugs,' said Gav.

'Aye, it's pretty safe,' Jimmy said to Carol, 'if ye're no daft.' She was looking at him admiringly. He glanced over at Iain and Eck at the pool table. Iain was a big bugger. Jimmy said quietly, 'I could take ye roon some time. I could say ye're ma sister and get ye in for free. Take ye aff the road, right up close tae the lions and that.'

'Could ye?' Her eyes were wide open. 'I'd love that.'

Later, when he went for a piss, Iain followed him into the gents. 'Listen,' he said, 'jist in case ye wis thinkin aboot it, keep your fuckin paws aff Carol, aw right?'

'Hey, I'm jist oot for a bevvy,' said Jimmy.

'Ye think ye're somethin special, you and Eck,' said Iain. 'Workin oot at that glorified zoo. Carol said ye were gonnae show her roon. Well, ye might fool her but ye dinna fool me. Tae me ye're jist a pair o jumped-up sheepshaggers.'

'Hell, man,' said Jimmy as he went to wash his hands, 'I ken ye lost at pool but dinna tak it oot on me, aw right?'

Behind him he heard Iain moving. He turned round quickly, expecting to have to fight, but Iain was heading for the door. Probably going to check on what Eck was up to with Carol. Jimmy shook his hands dry. Time for them to move on to the next pub. The lassie must not have a brain, telling Iain that. He'd be as well staying clear of her.

Jimmy understood that the Park was a charade, but he resented a guy like Iain who knew fuck all about it criticising it. You shouldn't criticise things you knew nothing about. What was it he'd said? A glorified zoo? What would that be? A zoo without cages. Ah, well, he would know about that right enough. They all would.

When Murray came back with the monkey he found he had a bigger problem on his hands. Eilidh had to lie crumpled up in the stall all day – there was no way she could be moved with the public around. After the Park closed, Murray got Jimmy and Eck and a couple of others to stay on so they could shift her.

'Where's she gaun?' asked Jimmy.

'Doon tae the mink ferm,' said Murray, 'where else? Eck, you can get on tae it the morn's morn.'

While Gav was backing the trailer in Jimmy said to Eck, 'Whit's he on aboot? He's surely no wantin ye tae cut her up?'

'Dinna ken, Jim,' said Eck. He wouldn't look Jimmy in the eye.

'Christ, man, she's fuckin rife wi gangrene. She should be gaun in the incinerator, no bein fed tae the lions.'

'I'll tak a look at her the morn,' said Eck. 'Noo piss aff. I've things tae think aboot.'

That was odd. Eck had never deliberately had a thought in his life, to Jimmy's knowledge. Now apparently he was having several at once.

Jimmy never saw him all the next morning, which meant he was probably at the mink farm. On his dinner hour Jimmy jumped on the bike and hammered it down there. He found Eck in the big rubber apron, holding a long knife and surveying Eilidh, who was stretched out on the concrete floor of the meat-room. But it wasn't the Eilidh Jimmy knew. This was Eilidh in her socks just. All the skin was stripped off her, apart from four wee socks above her hooves. Her severed head lay on the floor a few feet away. The flayed corpse was bloody and stinking, parts of the meat were a grey-green colour. 'You were right,' said Eck, 'there's nae wey the cats can eat this. We'd kill the lot o them.'

'So whit's the idea?'

'The idea *wis*,' said Eck, 'tae sell the skin. It's worth quite a few bob if ye can tak it aff in a oner. Trouble is, wi that wound she had, there a fuckin great hole in it. Nae bloody use at aw.' He had the skin stretched out on the floor, and had been scraping bits of meat and gunge off it. Now he began to cover the inner side of it with handfuls of salt from a big sack, rolling the skin up and rubbing the salt well into it, packing the skin into a tight bundle.

'So whit's aw this for?'

'Murray wants it.'

'Murray wants it?'

'Aye. How? It's nae big deal.'

'It's obscene.'

'How? She's deid. Nae sense in wastin it. Canna sell it wi thon big hole in it, so Murray says he'll hae it.'

'Whit for?'

'How dae I ken? For his hoose, probably. For his front room. Hey, imagine his new chat-up line: "Right, doll, want tae come back tae ma place and make love in front o a big roarin fire on ma giraffe?"'

Jimmy laughed. 'He could have one end at the fire and the ither ablow the jawbox in his kitchen. So they could wash up efter and no get their feet cauld.'

'It'd be great for a lobby-runner,' said Eck.

Eilidh's guts were piled up in a heap on a big flat board. Eck said, 'Here, this stuff weighs a ton. Gonnae gie me a haun tae lift it in the skip?'

Between them they dragged the board out of the meat-room and over to the skip which doubled as an incinerator. Getting it up to shoulder-level was hard, the guts shifting their bulk around on the board. But they managed to heave it over the edge and let Eilidh's entrails slide down into the bottom of the skip. They landed on top of a wee monkey corpse.

The smell was very bad. Eck chucked in some diesel and half an old bale of straw and put a match to it. 'I fun a deid dug in here last week,' he said as they backed away from the stench. 'Some fowk've nae respect.'

Then he said, 'Listen, Murray doesna ken this yet. He's gonnae go mental when he finds out, in case onybody else does and he gets the blame for no lookin efter her properly. Eilidh wis pregnant.'

He took Jimmy through the meat-room to a second, smaller room at the back. On the concrete floor lay a miniature version of the skinless Eilidh, eighteen perfect inches from head to tail. The neck was curved and graceful even in death. There were two round swellings which would have been the eyes. The delicate, tiny trotters – they weren't big enough to be called hooves – were already formed. The pink skin had a pattern of red lines beneath it, outlining just where the brown and white patches of the coat would have grown.

'A while tae go yet,' said Eck. 'I cut it away frae the sack. It might no hae lived – wi Eilidh bein how she wis – but it looks healthy enough tae me. Funny, did ye ever see the male shaggin her? If we'd kent aboot this the vet might hae wantit Eilidh treated different.'

'I didna think the male had a shag left in him,' said Jimmy. 'Murray should hae kent, but. The fuckin vet inspected her – *he* should hae noticed.'

'Murray kens fuck aw aboot animals,' said Eck. 'He's nae fuckin empathy wi them at aw. If he could get away wi it he'd be as bad as fuckin Maxton. And the vet's a fuckin waster. I tell ye, Jimmy, you and me are mair in tune wi the fuckin animals in this Park, you and me feedin them ither animals, than the fuckin so-called management.'

★ ★ ★

Jimmy always thought Eck had something on Murray, some kind of hold on him. It just shows how wrong you can be. Eck must have tried it on too hard with the Eilidh thing – maybe Murray felt threatened with what Eck knew about it. Well, anyway, he called Eck's bluff. Two weeks after the skinning of Eilidh, Murray drove down the mink farm road one afternoon, switched off his motor two hundred yards short, coasted in and caught Eck kipping in the hay with a Louis L'Amour book over his face. First warning. Eck should have realised then that Murray was after him, he should have been on his guard. But Eck wasn't like that, he couldn't wise up. Within the week Murray had hauled him up for not cleaning out the meat-room properly, being late in for work again, and taking an extra ten minutes on his dinner. That was the one that finished it.

'I'm sittin on the pan,' says Eck to Jimmy in the pub that weekend, 'I'm sittin there evacuatin the premises afore gettin back tae ma work,' – he was covering for Jimmy that day at the giraffe-house, it being Jimmy's day off – 'and the cunt comes in and hammers on the door. "Is that you in there, Eck?" "Aye, Murray," I says, "I'm jist digestin ma dinner." "Well," he says, "when ye've digested that, digest this: ye're fired. Ye can get your books at the office." "Aw come on, Murray," I says but he jist batters on, "Dinna fuckin argue wi me, Eck Galbraith, I've had enough o your fuckin mooth." Then I hear him on his radio calling the office, so every other bastart with a radio can hear him. "Mary," he says, "Mary, will you make up Hector Galbraith's wages, whatever he's due, he's finishing up the day. He'll be along for them in twenty minutes." The bastart. He says,

28

"Oh, Mary, mind and take off the ten-pound sub he owes us." I'm stuck on the pan cursin him for aw I'm worth an he jist goes, "Wipe your erse, Eck. I doot I've wiped the smirk aff your face awready." '

And that was Eck. He'd been there as long as anyone could mind. Jimmy still sees him when he goes for a beer sometimes, but it's different: Eck works behind the bar in the Red Lion. He doesn't take a drink when he's on duty and he doesn't like talking about the Park. Jimmy left of his own accord, a year later, and got a job with the Post Office. One time in the pub Jimmy said, 'D'ye mind the day Eilidh died?' but Eck just looked at him and said, 'Whit aboot it?' so Jimmy said, 'Doesna maitter, Eck.' But Jimmy minds it all right, and so does Eck.

Four days after Eck was fired, Murray remembered about the meat-room, how there was nobody looking after it anymore. The lions and tigers were needing fed again. This time they'd no choice – they had to haul some sheep out of the freezer and hope for the best. This was because of the state of the meat-room – nobody had touched it since Eck went, and it was near the end of May. That summer was a hot one – not as hot as '76, but it was doing its damnedest. Murray sent Jimmy Sanderson and Dave Maxton down to clean up.

When they pulled the big sliding door back at first they didn't understand what it was falling on their heads. Then the smell hit them and they understood. The floor, the walls, the door were crawling with maggots, big fat white bastards like polystyrene chips that exploded when you stepped on them. In the middle of the floor, where it dipped down towards the drain, lay a heap of wool and decomposing meat that had once been three or maybe four sheep, it was hard to tell. It was oozing black blood and heaving with maggots and cockroaches. The pair of them backed out gagging, shaking and slapping at their heads.

'I'm no fuckin daein this,' said Maxton. 'Get on the radio tae Murray and tell him we're no fuckin daein it.'

Jimmy held the radio out to him. 'On ye go, Dave,' he said. 'You tell him.' He knew they'd be doing it. They both knew. If Murray could get rid of Eck he could get rid of anybody. That was it really. They were stuck. They didn't have great prospects in front of them. They had to take what they were given.

The Plagues

This is a dream Leonard once had:

Seven fat cows come up out of the river to graze. Then come seven lean cows, all skin stretched on bone. They come out of the river and they eat up the fat cows.

What did it mean?

It was odd because it was a boss's dream, a rich man's dream, and Leonard was not rich. It was someone else's dream that had somehow found its way into Leonard's head. There was fear in the dream, and guilt.

Also, it was a warning, which a rich man would probably ignore.

Years later. Leonard had a job but not because he could interpret the boss's dreams. He worked in a bookshop, behind the till. But he didn't do dreams, the boss's or anybody else's. It was enough to cope with his own. That is, if they were dreams at all, which he doubted.

It was this problem with the frogs. In the past they had never bothered him because he couldn't see them, but lately they'd been appearing everywhere. It wasn't as if he hadn't always known they were there, waiting, but for a long time they were quite invisible to him. If he spent the evening at home, they stayed out of sight. He knew they were moving behind the plaster of the walls, or down in the street, or congregating in unimaginable numbers in the canal, but they were impossible to see. If he went out, though, well – as soon as his back was turned they would emerge. He would be walking down the street on his way to the pub, and a black taxi, seemingly empty but with its For Hire light off, would pass him before he had gone four hundred yards. Below the level of its windows it would be loaded with frogs, ready to pour out and occupy the flat until his return. Parked cars that he passed would be teeming with the buggers, but if he looked through their windows he would see nothing, all would be still.

He remembered a poem from his childhood about walking the pavement and how the bears would get you if you stepped on the lines. Walking to the pub was like that, only with frogs. They were too quick and too numerous for him, but he knew they were there. And now, lately, they'd been getting bolder. They didn't hide from him as they once had. He'd hoped he would get used to them, but it was impossible when they were in such numbers. He couldn't help being anxious about them. Anyone would be, in his position.

Not that he had anything against frogs in themselves. Until recently, when they'd become such an overwhelming presence, he would have gone so far as to say that the idea of them always appealed to him. He remembered something else from his childhood. Every spring and summer he would go to a loch in the hills behind the town where his family stayed, in search of frogs. It might take two or three visits, but he always found them. Year after year they would be there – and so would he.

Thinking back, he reckoned the loch must have been an important breeding ground. At a certain time in the spring hundreds of frogs gathered under the banks in a kind of mass orgy. For a while after that, there would be nothing except the spawn filled with black life-dots, sago lapping in the weeds. Then, one day, he would go up there and find that the spawn had turned to tadpoles, and that the tadpoles were changing too, and all around the loch tiny frogs, no bigger than his thumbnail, were leaving the water. Thousands upon thousands of them. The track around the loch was so thickly covered that he could not avoid treading on them with every step he took. And if the sun was out and the day hot, hundreds of their tiny bodies, dehydrated and blackened, would be stretched on the grass and rocks. It was suicide for them to be moving away from the water on such a day, but it seemed that they could not help themselves, they moved away relentlessly, driven by something of which they had no knowledge or understanding.

These were the circumstances of his youth. He would even say he loved the frogs then. They were helpless, fragile, and yet their numbers seemed a source of strength. Enough would survive to return the following year and participate in a fresh orgy of procreation. Yes, he loved the frogs, and the other creatures of the loch; the heron, the pair of swans which returned every spring to breed, the ducks, the rabbits, the stoats. There was a sense of unison, of reassurance in the inevitable circles of nature, and he could sit for hours, or wander slowly around the water, and feel a great energy surrounding him even though he himself might be lazy and listless. But now it was different. Now he was disturbed by frogs. Not those ones, the long vanished amphibians of his childhood. Those were good frogs, country frogs. It was the others that were the trouble, the ones that had come to the city, that were always with him, ever present.

Leonard's job also caused him anxiety. All day long people kept coming to him with these packages. They handed him the packages and he put them in bags and they gave him money for them. He put the money in the till and gave them their bag and their change and a receipt and they went away. It kept happening.

The packages were all very similar. They were rectangular, full of little black squiggles and lines. Most of them were about six inches by four, and about half an inch thick. Some were much bigger and some smaller, some were hard, others flexible, but really they were all much alike. Although they had different pictures on the front and lines on the back explaining what the packages contained, inside they looked the same. Usually there was some truth in the explanations, sometimes they were utter lies. Leonard knew this because he himself had inspected many of the packages, every sheet that was in them and, what was more, in the right order.

Sometimes he thought – perhaps I need my head examined. A person undertaking such an examination would say, how can you be a bookseller and have such an attitude to books? (That, plus the frogs nonsense.) This is not soap-powder you are selling, it is Literature. Ah, he would retort, you literati always turn snooty when it comes to soap-powder. And yet it serves a definite and worthy function. You don't find people buying a packet of soap-powder and taking it home and staring at it for hours on end in front of the fire. The people who came into the bookshop, they did this with the packages they selected. They sought enlightenment or reassurance or excitement from the conglomeration of wood-pulp and glue and ink in their lap. Leonard knew, he used to do it himself. These days he didn't believe the packages contained anything as useful as soap-powder.

One thing about the frogs. It wasn't just him. He used to think it was, but then he began to see it in other people's eyes. That haunted, nervous look. You didn't get like that unless the frogs were bothering you. Of course people tried to stay calm, pretend everything was normal. That was what he did. But sometimes he looked into another face and he knew it was happening there too. Well, it stood to reason really. All these frogs and only being seen by the one person, it just wasn't credible. Sooner or later, he supposed, somebody was going to have the courage to mention them, and then they'd all start. What do you think's causing it? We must be doing something bad, that's why it's happening. We're going against nature. We're holding people under duress. He'd have said something himself but he didn't like to be the first. It might be dangerous. If the frogs thought you were about to squeal they might make a move on you, take you out. And he didn't want to speak too soon and find that nobody else had got that worried. Yet. He didn't want to jump the gun.

* * *

This Literature business. In order to disabuse yourself of the notion that the art of writing is somehow elevated, refined or otherwordly, visit a printer's or the distribution centre of a large publisher. Leonard went to such a place once in connection with his work in the bookshop. There he did indeed see Literature reduced and diminished. Cursing drivers fork-lifted pallets of Shakespeare as though it were dog food; men covered in sweat and tattoos, their arms dipped to the elbows in grease, operated machines that cut, mashed and pummelled the packages, with not a thought as to their contents. Ernest Hemingway was ruthlessly shrink-wrapped, Virginia Woolf glued and bound; yesterday's hopeful new writers were dispatched *en masse* to the pulp chambers. It became evident to him there that against violence all those squiggles and lines were quite powerless.

Things got out of control one afternoon in May, in the shop. He wasn't feeling too well – slightly nauseous and light-headed. Outside it was raining and the trouble came from there, in out of the wet. He didn't see it come in but that was the logical source. Also there was a thin pallid young man carrying a large empty sports-bag. He had to be watched. And a middle-aged, well-to-do woman shaking her umbrella and demanding attention.

She came up to the till and said, 'Do you have that new one by the Balmoral chambermaid?'

Leonard was shaping a reply to her in his head when everything started happening at once. The thin man, who had gone to the horror section, unzipped his sports-bag and began to load it with paperback packages. The woman said, 'Because if you have I should warn you that I shall never shop here again.' And a sudden green movement at the edge of his vision caused Leonard to look over at the fiction shelves, where round about the Wilbur Smiths a small single frog perched for a fleeting moment before disappearing with a sideways spring.

'Excuse me one moment,' he said to the woman, keeping his eyes fixed on the spot. He didn't feel under an obligation to her anyway as she'd asked a trick question. 'A slight emergency has arisen.' This was an under-statement. It was the first time he had ever seen a frog in the shop. He took a magazine from the counter and rolled it up to make a weapon. The weapon he made was a *knobkerrie*, a round-headed stick used as a club and missile by natives of southern Africa. He began to move cautiously towards the shelves.

'Whatever is the matter?' the woman demanded. 'Will you answer my question?'

'Please be quiet,' Leonard said. 'You'll disturb it.' He could cope with them at home – just about – and on the outside. But here, in his place of work – this was a new development. He took a risk and glanced at the woman. It was obvious from her eyes that the frogs had not yet entered her life.

It was tricky. The thief was stacking the horror packages into his bag very neatly and efficiently, as if they were small bricks. But the priority was definitely the frog.

He was halfway to the fiction shelves when the woman said very loudly, 'Where is the manager?'

'A good question,' said Leonard. 'I should like to know. I think it went in behind the Ps.'

'This is deplorable,' said the woman. 'I refuse to wait a minute longer.'

'Be patient,' he said to her, still advancing step by step. 'They're not like mice, you know. You can't just set traps for them.'

Possibly she might have responded, but at this point things took a turn for the worse. The thief, who was returning from the horror shelves with a further selection, let out a cry and dropped the pile he was holding. His open-mouthed stare swung back and forth between Leonard and his *knobkerrie* and the half-filled bag. From where Leonard was, it was possible to see the sides of the bag rippling and bulging. The thief backed away with his hand to his mouth.

'Oh my God,' said Leonard. It was a trap. He started to shout, holding his weapon aloft. 'Get back! Everybody back!' The woman retreated. Leonard could feel the sweat breaking out on his face. He wasn't sure what was happening, if the damage could be limited. He wanted to say something reassuring like, 'Everybody please leave the premises in an orderly fashion,' but both the angry woman and the frightened thief had already gone.

Leonard made it back to the counter and pressed the buzzer for assistance. He was breathing heavily and felt very hot. The manager arrived in a hurry. 'What happened?' he asked. 'You look dreadful.'

Leonard tried to explain. 'This woman didn't want to buy a package if we had it,' he said. 'I don't feel well. And look, there's a bag over there but you mustn't touch it. You'll have to phone for the frog disposal squad.'

'I don't know what you're talking about,' said the manager. This was only to be expected. He reached for the *knobkerrie*. 'Stop waving that about before you do yourself an injury, poke your eye out or something.' The manager came to a decision. 'Leonard, I'm calling a taxi to take you home.' Appalling! He couldn't possibly get in a taxi. 'It's fine,' he said. 'I mean, I'm fine. No I'm not. I'll walk. Get a bus, I mean. Honestly, the fresh air will help.'

Outside the sun was coming out. The pavements were beginning to steam. Leonard walked along briskly, determined to get home before the next attack. Black cabs swept past him. He tried to get his mind around the possibilities.

What was it all about? This was what people were bound to ask: what was it about? This was what they were always asking. But what did they want to know? Did they want him to tell them what it meant, or what he thought it meant? How could he do that? It might not mean anything. He could tell them only what he believed.

He believed that all the margins of his life were smitten with frogs. They came out of the rivers and drains and out of the old canal beside the street where he lived, and they got everywhere – in the house, in the bedroom, in the bed itself. He opened the oven and they were there, and they sat green and sullen in the saucepans and baking trays in the cupboard below the sink. They were in the fridge and the washing machine and there were a couple of dead ones in the toaster and they got down the sides of the armchairs and into the cupboard where he kept his videos and they sat like little green ornaments on the window ledges. And in the bathroom, that was the worst, it was overrun with them, they climbed the shower curtain and squatted on the soap and left their traces all over the surface of the bath and basin, and they came in clusters up through the toilet. And he dreaded that they would come upon his person, into his clothes and hair, whether he was asleep or awake. This was an awful anticipation.

But, more than this, he feared the aftermath, when the summer came and the sun burnt them up and he would be able to sweep them into the street and reclaim his own territory. He could already see the piles of corpses in the streets, he could catch the first whiff of their stench. And this was only the frogs. He knew there was worse, much worse, to come.

Screen Lives

She was home.

Her clothes still smelt of suntan oil. Her hair retained the thick heavy feel of swimming in the sea, drying in the sun, and with her nail she could still pick a few grains of sand from her scalp. Other parts of her body also, even after a couple of days, retained that salt scent and texture. For example, she loved to nuzzle deep into the crook of her arm and breathe in the beach and the sea, gently rub the soft brown crease with the tip of her nose and let her eye rest, unfocused, on the bleached hairs of her arm, her mind away.

But she was home. Dark Shona beginning to fade again, until next year. There was no escaping that.

Her first morning back at work she chose to wear dark colours. She had toyed with the idea of white, but she didn't want the others to think she was showing off her tan. Of course she wanted them to comment on it – she was almost black in places – but she didn't want them thinking that was all her holiday consisted of, just soaking up the sun for two weeks, thoughtless.

On her way to the bus stop some men putting up scaffolding on a block of flats whistled and cheered at her. She kept her head down, angry and embarrassed. She knew she was supposed also to be secretly pleased, but she wasn't. She had never felt flattered by the attentions of such men; the stupidity and crudeness depressed and frightened her. These ones were putting in a lot of effort. It must be the tan, showing on her legs beneath her short skirt. That was all she was showing.

In Crete she had gone topless on the beach, and if anyone had been eyeing her up they didn't let on by shouting and whistling. Most of the women were topless. In fact, it was the few who weren't that you noticed. All sizes and shapes of breast acquired a normality that was, after all, only normal. Even the men didn't seem to bother. Sometimes, though, she found herself looking at the other women, comparing. She liked her own breasts best. Lying with her back to the sun and resting on her elbows while she read a book, she cradled them between her arms, moving herself forward so that the nipples brushed against her forearms. Then she would find that she hadn't been reading the words in the book at all, and that her nipples were hard and wanting, and she would have to lie flat for a while, pressing her body into the towel and the beach below, blanking the ache from her mind.

A hook had lain in the pit of her stomach, gently goading her, sickening her, but now she thought she could feel it beginning to unbend and soften. For months her life had been in limbo. She had become aware of her dissatisfaction, but instead of trying to identify the source she had waited, as if for inspiration. She was waiting for her life to change.

Then one day she woke up and realised it would not happen. Something could come over your life, a mood, a feeling, but it had to be acted upon. Otherwise it simply weighed you down, daring you and subduing you at once.

She would never know what came first – this mood of disenchantment, or Devlin. Devlin had crept up on her too – he was no vision appearing suddenly, blinding her with love. In fact she hadn't even liked him much, to begin with. When she started working there she remarked upon his name – was it Irish, she wondered – and he said, 'It's after the character in *Notorious* – you know, the old Hitchcock film?' She nodded, of course she knew it, and he went on, 'My mother loved Cary Grant and my father loved Ingrid Bergman, so I suppose if I'd been a girl I'd be Alicia. It could be worse, I could have been a football team.' But he said it in such a practised manner that she thought, you think you are Cary Grant, don't you, you smug bastard. Even though he didn't look in the least bit like him, he was fair and a little ungainly, not smooth at all.

So probably it started not with Devlin but with the mood, within herself. But she could never be sure.

Or it might have been George. She was not so self-centred as to assume that change came only to her alone. George too was changing. They'd been going out for a year, long enough to breed boredom, not so long that she was afraid to let go.

So this day came when she woke up and decided to act. In the evening she phoned George. It was cowardly but she

43

didn't want to face him. She didn't want a scene. 'George, I want to stop seeing you.' 'George, I don't want to go on seeing you.' She rehearsed the two lines, wondering which was better, more truthful.

It didn't matter. She didn't use either, and he didn't fight about it. She said, 'George, I feel things have changed. I don't think there's much point in us going on with each other.' He agreed. This made her more certain that she was doing the right thing, that he too was changing. If he had fought to keep her, she might have had doubts. But he just said, 'All right.' It would have been hurtful if she had felt differently: she wasn't important to him after all. And so he passed out of her life, almost as if he had never been there.

But what if one person changed and the other didn't? That was when things became truly awful. What if this happened to married people – as it did – people who had grown so accustomed to one another that if one changed it was like tearing a chunk out of the other? The very thought of such trouble made her feel sick and weak.

And then she got over thinking he was too smart. Devlin. They made each other laugh. There was a cheap reissue of *Notorious* on video, and she bought a copy and watched it through. The lines and the shots came back to her just before they happened, so that they arrived like old friends. She watched it again the next night, understanding what a great, almost perfect film it was. In the morning she wanted to show off her appreciation to him, so when he came on the internal phone to her she contrived to interrupt him: 'What's your name? What's your name?' She heard his voice, surprised, a little offended perhaps, say, 'It's Devlin,

Shona,' and then she hit him with it: 'Well, you showed that cop something and he saluted you . . . Why, you double-crossing buzzard, you're a cop!' The joke was over-constructed but he got it, he laughed.

After that they both began to work it into every conversation, trying to outdo one another. He'd come to her office and say, 'We've got a problem here,' and she'd break into it, saying, 'What's the matter? Don't look so tense,' and he wouldn't say anything, just stare moodily out of the window, so she'd go on, 'Look, I'll make it easy for you: the time has come when you must tell me that you have a wife and two adorable children and this madness between us can't go on any longer.' Then, he'd say, 'I bet you've heard that line often enough,' and she'd say, 'Right below the belt every time,' and he'd break it off saying, 'Actually, it's this contract, it needs to be redrafted.' Or she'd be coming down with the flu and he'd say, 'You don't look so hot. Sick?' And she'd muster a smile even though she felt dreadful, and say, 'No. Hangover,' and he'd say, 'That's news. Back on the bottle again.' It was funny, and nobody else could join in, because it was just them, Cary and Ingrid. It was romantic. They both laughed but it was romantic. They were living out the movie.

After she had spoken to George she phoned her sister Louise. For the last three years they had gone on holiday together. She had been going to break the habit this year – she had been going to go with George – but now she phoned her to discuss destinations. They settled on Crete. They had always gone for islands: the Canaries, Corfu, Corsica, and now Crete.

★   ★   ★

She felt weak at the thought of trouble between lovers, yet she was not weak. She was deliberately reshaping her life, and she was pushing herself into a phase of it that might very well involve pain and more frustration. For she did not really know if Devlin would respond to her or if she would dare to make a move. Her change was not necessarily his at all. It would be like self-inflicted torture to have him in her thoughts all the time like this, if in fact he was not changing with her, to her. But surely he was – there were too many looks and smiles for her to have misread? And all the time he *was* in her thoughts. She imagined herself doing the most outrageous, beautiful things to him, her body to his, her mouth on him, his hands on her. She shocked herself with what she would do. There was in fact nothing she would *not* do!

Was it wrong to think of someone like that? It wasn't guilt that made her ask that question, but real concern. It was like an invasion, using someone against their will, or at least without their knowledge. There were social rules as to how you should treat another person, how you had to have their consent – but in your imagination these rules did not apply. You could do anything to them, anything. You could make love to them, or you could hurt them. If you hated them enough, you could even kill them. But mostly, she thought, it must be love. A person had one life, but in the minds of other people they could have more. Dozens, perhaps. Thousands, in the case of someone famous. How many lovers did Cary Grant and Ingrid Bergman have, that they knew nothing about?

Someone you knew. You knew them at your work, or as a

friend of a friend. And you made love to them without their knowledge. Did you take something from them when this happened? Could you capture a part of them as they had captured you?

In Crete she slept with a waiter from the hotel, a beautiful boy who was always in a loose white shirt, on duty or off, cool in his white shirt and moving with the grace of a cat and with soft thick black hair like a cat's. Probably he had a different girl every two weeks, as often as the package flights arrived and departed, but she didn't care. (She was careful, but she didn't care.) It was as if he were part of the holiday, an extra hidden in the small print of the brochure. Louise scoffed at her – going with a waiter was so *naff* – but he took them both to the best clubs and introduced them to the barmen so that they got their drinks cheap or even free, so she didn't complain too much. All Louise wanted to do was dance, dance, dance – with Shona, with guys, it didn't matter – it was as if she was dancing to push everything else in her life to the edges of her consciousness. The dancing was all. Shona's waiter said he could fix Louise up with one of his friends but Shona said, no, she's happy, she only wants to dance. *Her* life wasn't changing, at least it didn't look like it. She lived constantly in the present, never thinking either side of whatever three-minute song was playing. All day on the beach she slept. She didn't even go in the sea.

Ingrid: 'I'm practically on the wagon, that's quite a change.'

Cary: 'It's a phase.'

Ingrid: 'You don't think a woman can change?'
Cary: 'Sure. A change is fun. For a while.'
Ingrid: 'For a while.'

The trouble was, Devlin was attached. He lived with someone. She knew this of course but she couldn't help herself. Maybe that was where he and her change of mood came together, because she would hardly have begun to think of him in that way, the way that brought on the ache, if he had not one day, in one of their good conversations together, taken her into his confidence and talked about the relationship, explained that it was all but over. So he too was experiencing change. And they *did* have good conversations at work – but mostly *about* work, or about the news, or flippant, jokey banter about anything at all – good conversations that suggested even better ones, deep serious ones in other places and long into the night in which they could come to know each other completely. Conversations which would perhaps eventually die away because there would no longer be any need to speak, only to touch, only this deep need to touch.

'It's good to see you,' he said, halfway through the morning. 'And you're looking fantastic. That's some tan!'

'Did you miss me, then?' she said. She asked it lightly, but there was just so much weight in it.

'Of course I missed you,' he replied, and it seemed to her that he balanced the weight exactly.

'How are things?' Again, she asked it as casually as she could, but he looked at her in just such a way, and it was obvious he knew what she meant. Things at home. He said,

'Pretty bad still, I suppose.' And she said, 'But you're sorting something out, aren't you? You're doing something about it?' And he said, 'Yes, but it's not easy.'

'It won't happen itself,' she said. She was certain about this now, and certain that he would understand. She had this new knowledge inside her, from her own experience. She wanted to set him free too. 'I know,' he said.

Later she said, 'Let's go for a drink after work. Come out and talk to me?' The way she looked at him. She could hardly believe she was being so forward. And neither, apparently, could he. She saw that she had pushed too hard, that he shied away from her, wincing as if she had touched a wound.

'Better not,' he said. 'Not tonight. Maybe some other time. Sorry. I just wouldn't be good company.'

It was an awkward moment. She said, to cover it over, 'It's stuffy in here, isn't it?' Her Bergman voice.

'Might be,' he said, mustering Cary. She slurred the next line:

'What about . . . we have a picnic.'

'Outside?'

'It's too stuffy in here for a picnic.'

He smiled at her, that wounded smile that seemed to be conceding victory to her in some game, and left her at her desk, the cursor on her screen flashing impatiently, midway through a sentence. She sat and stared at the thing flashing faster than the seconds going by, hating its insistent demand on her time.

And yes, time was passing. It seemed now that it was going by very fast indeed. Suddenly she was afraid. She was fading away – more, much more than just her stupid tan. She looked at the screen, half-expecting to see the text vanish in front of her eyes. She put her fingers to her throat and found a fold of skin under her jaw, slack like the skin of an old woman. She plucked at it, filled with a terrible dread of being old, of not having done all these things. It was not death that she feared, but waiting for death. All she wanted, all she had ever wanted, was to be alive.

The Jonah

Billy was on the road, at the edge of it. Shoulders hunched, he waited for something to come out of the mist at him. The rain crept cold fingers down his back. Every so often he sneaked a look over his upturned collar, hoping for a car, lorry, tractor, pushchair – anything that might move them on a few miles. He had been doing this for a long time. It was hard to stay philosophical about it.

A few feet away Sean hawked and gobbed on the tarmac. Billy heard the splat even through the rain. He heard Sean swear at the weather. If he was expecting sympathy he could forget it. It was Sean's fault they were stuck where they were and cursing the rain wasn't going to get them out. Only some total stranger with space in his motor for two men and their rucksacks was going to do that.

They'd been waiting long enough – nearly two hours since the last cup of tea – and Sean's patience was exhausted, but Billy's trust still clung to the cliff-face of fate. Fate would have someone organised. Even now they'd be tootling along, oblivious to their role in Billy's life, maybe just a few miles to the south. In all the years Billy had hitch-hiked around, home or abroad, he had never not got a lift eventually. He might have been stuck for whole days in some places but he'd always escaped in the end, and this was going to be no exception. Not unless Sean turned out to be some kind of hitch-hiker's Jonah. Billy had never hitched with him before so he couldn't tell. But his attitude was all wrong, and attitude was important if you were going to hitch successfully. You had to do it with optimism, and faith in human nature. You had to have a belief in the logic of coincidences. Positive fatalism. That wasn't Sean at all. He didn't think on the big scale like Billy. He didn't see connections. He just stumbled around life, banging his head and treading on toes. Sean all over.

And yet he had something, Billy had to concede that. He had the power of persuasion. For example, he'd managed to persuade Billy off course into this vehicle-forsaken hole in darkest Perthshire – or was it still Stirlingshire? – and Billy, the one supposedly with the plan, had fallen for it. He might never have hitched with Sean before but he'd been around him off and on for years and he still hadn't learned his lesson: it was very hard to say no to him. Correction: saying no to him didn't make any difference.

They were headed for pastures new. Forests new. That was the idea. Their old forestry pal Kenny McPhail had beckoned them. He'd phoned Billy at his ma's house one night from somewhere in the northwest. Billy imagined him there, digging for coins in his jeans pocket, he could see the solitary phone box at the junction of two single-track roads.

'Get your arses up here fast,' Kenny said. 'I've spoken to the gaffer about yous and if you can get here for Tuesday there's a good chance of a whole summer's work.' A whole summer taking out a semi-mature plantation. Billy smelt the foustiness of old rucksacks, the dampness of mouse-ridden caravans. He said, 'The both of us?' and Kenny said, 'Aye, but tell that bawheid Sean he's got to behave himself this time. Nae skiving on the job and that.'

'I'll tell him,' said Billy.

'Listen,' said Kenny, 'better hurry before every other bastard and his dog turns up. That's my money gone now. I've put the word in for yous so you'll be all right, but try and get here by Tuesday. Wednesday at the –'

That was Saturday and this was Monday. Two whole days just to go three hundred miles and they'd only managed about sixty so far. Sean was to blame, chasing non-existent women all over the country and dragging Billy along with him. He had no idea about responsibility, and as for urgency, the only time he ever felt a sense of it was if he was taking his breeks off to get his end away.

They'd got in a carry-out on the Saturday night – it was cheaper than going to the pub – and decided what to do. Billy's mind was already made up – he was going after Kenny. He'd been taking it easy for too long, signing on, picking up a few bob on the side working for a guy who did house removals. 'I need to make some real money,' he said.

'I'm no sure,' said Sean. 'I mean, if you're going up there anyway, I could stick around. Andro'd be wanting somebody else to help him on the van, just a few hours a week like, but it's all in the hand.'

'Aye,' said Billy, 'whereas in the bush . . .' They laughed. Sean had this old proverb he liked to trot out: 'A push in the bush is worth two hand-jobs.'

'Ya fuckin robot,' he said now.

'No, but,' said Billy, 'working for Andro's all right, but it's no the same as a wage, is it, even after paying the tax.'

It wasn't about money for Sean, it was about a lassie. Billy knew this. She was nineteen years old – six years younger than Sean – and he'd been seeing her for three weeks, a record for him. Billy could see that this was the problem, even though Sean wasn't admitting it.

'It's that Susan Donovan, isn't it?'

'Eh? Fuck off!'

'Aye it is. Her with the three big brothers.'

'What's that supposed to mean?'

'Nothing. Just, you fancy a shotgun wedding, do ye?'

'How? She's no up the pole.'

'She might be, with your methods. Or lack of them.'

'Fuck off!'

'Fine. It's your funeral – I mean, wedding.'

Sean and Billy had these arguments, about contraception and that. Sean wouldn't use anything. Said if the woman wanted to, that was up to her, but he wasn't sticking one of thae bloody things on. What about AIDS, Billy would say. Sean said, 'I don't go with junkies and I'm no a poof.' But now Billy could see he'd set him thinking, about the number of times he'd done it with Susan Donovan, who probably didn't use anything either, and after about a minute he said, 'Right, let's go the morn.'

Between them they had enough money for a bit more bevvy and food to get them up the road, maybe enough for a B&B if they couldn't make it in one day. It never occurred to them to do anything other than hitch. That was part of the whole thing, taking off up north. Bugger the bus – full of tourists and drunk teuchters. And then Sean said about wanting to go up the west side, he knew these two women that were spending the summer waitressing in some fishing hotel and he wanted to drop in on them, take them by surprise like, meet them after they got off duty, charm them onto their backs and shag them senseless.

'A fitting start to this new chapter in our lives, Billy,' he said.

'Your brain's in your Y-fronts,' said Billy, but he was stupid enough to go along with it, he was that pleased with himself for getting Sean away from Susan without so much as a goodbye. Which was why they'd spent the previous night getting plastered in a hotel bar miles off the main road – 'This is definitely the place,' Sean kept saying. 'I know this is the place, I'm sure this is the place' – until finally they were so drunk they had to book *into* the place – twenty pound each for a twin room and breakfast . . . It would have been daylight robbery if it hadn't been nearly midnight.

Billy needed the work. They both did, but Billy was determined this was going to be more than just another chapter. If there really was three or four months' work to get out of the job he was going to be disciplined about it. He was going to save money. If that meant staying in the camp or B&B or wherever they were going to be instead of getting bevvied every night, even if it made him unpopular with the rest of the crew, so be it. If they were being put up in a hotel he wouldn't go near the bar. He would read books, listen to his Walkman, write letters, wank (play the free one-armed bandit, as Sean put it), anything to save money. If he could put a few hundred away, a thousand maybe, enough to get the airfare anyway, then he was going to Australia. He knew a guy who'd done it two years ago. Once he was past immigration he'd just disappeared, invented a few names and national insurance numbers and hopped around from job to job for eighteen months. The money he earned was unbelievable. Thousands and thousands of dollars he made. Right enough when he finally left the country he got a black mark against his name, would probably never get back in, and right enough too he'd spent all the money when he got home again and wasn't working now, but Billy wasn't going to make the same mistake. He was going to work himself into the ground out there, pocket the money, then come back and buy himself a nice wee flat somewhere. Nowhere he was known. Glasgow or some place big enough to get lost in. Well, it would have to be Glasgow then, if he was going to get lost in Scotland. Or Dundee, he'd never been there in his life, nobody knew him in Dundee. Buy a place, cash down, no mortgage shite or nothing, and then never work again. Or just enough to pay the bills. Work at will. No more wage-slavery. If you had a paid-for roof over your head and nobody depending on you, you wouldn't need much in the way of an income. And he had enough skills to pick up work and drop it again as it suited him. Things were bad but they weren't so bad that Billy couldn't find himself something if he needed it enough.

But all that was hanging on him getting this job, and right at the moment the possibility of failure had to be admitted, the possibility of not getting there in time. No, wrong attitude. That was the mind-set of the Seans of the world. Wouldn't do at all.

'It's going to need a fucking miracle for somebody to stop for us here,' said Sean.

'It's going to need a miracle for anybody to be on this road. So if there is, they'll stop for us.'

'Christ,' said Sean, 'that's some logic. See if you were driving along here and you saw the pair of us tramps standing about with our thumbs out, would you stop for us?'

'Aye, I would,' said Billy. He meant it.

'Well, you'd be fucking daft,' said Sean.

'Well, who would you stop for, if you were driving along?'

'Michelle Pfeiffer,' said Sean without hesitation. 'I'd stop for her.'

'Aye, well your logic's as shite as mine. What's Michelle Pfeiffer doing hitching lifts in Scotland in the pouring rain?'

'How do I fucking ken? It might be in a picture or something. She does real things in the fucking pictures.'

After a pause, Sean started up again.

'All right, no Michelle Pfeiffer. Any bird. I'd stop for any bird.'

'Supposing she had a bloke with her?'

'Well, of course I fucking wouldna. I'm only picking her up to fucking shag her, amn't I?'

Sean tried to roll a fag. As fast as he worked the paper got soaked and torn. On the third attempt he dropped the tobacco pack on the road and then the rest of the papers. He saved the tobacco but the papers were ruined. 'Bastartin fuckin rain!' he shouted, kicking the papers across the road.

Billy thought, how do I know about Jonahs? We must have done it at Sunday School or something. Christ, *that* was a long time ago! Funny to think his folks had been quite religious in those days, wanted him to know his Bible and that. A Jonah was someone who slept soundly on the lower deck while the storm raged and worried sailors jettisoned cargo. He looked at Sean and then he looked at himself. Maybe I've got this wrong, he thought.

'Maybe we should split up,' he heard himself say.

'What?' said Sean.

'I'm just thinking, if we split up there's mair chance of us getting lifts out of here if anybody does stop. Further up the road too. I mean, if we're going to get to Kenny in time.'

Sean looked at him. 'You want us to split up?' he said.

'I'm just thinking there'd be more chance, maybe . . .'

Sean gobbed on the road again, then he said, 'It's me, isn't it? You don't think we're going to get there the pair of us, do you?'

'Well, we shouldn't have ever come this way in the first place.'

'Aye, you wouldn't be blaming me if you'd got your fucking hole, would ye?'

'Aye, but I didn't, did I? In fact, we never even found the women, Sean. All I'm saying is, it's taken us all day to get from that hotel to this wee village, one lift, and we're probably cutting our chances in half sticking thegither.'

'There's only been three cars in the last hour and they were all full. The road's no exactly been teeming with cars going, sorry lads, only room for one of yous, has it?'

'It's just with the rucksacks and everything. If we'd gone up the A9 on our own we'd be there by now.'

'You should have thought about that when we set out. It's no my fucking fault there's no traffic on the road. Think I'm bad for you or something?'

'Naw. But we've no been having much luck the last day or two, have we?'

'Oh, that's my fault, is it? Think I'm bad luck, ya bastard? Well, I'll tell you, you're no Mr Opportunity fucking Knocks yourself.'

'All right,' said Billy. 'All right, all right, all right! I'm just getting depressed, that's all.'

'Join the club,' said Sean. They stood listening to the rain falling and the total absence of traffic.

'I mean,' said Billy, 'I'm no even sure about this job either.'

Sean came over to him and stood with his face at an angle an inch or two away from Billy's. 'Say that again?' he said.

Billy shrugged. The movement caused more rain to trickle down his back. This bothered him more than Sean's aggression, which was all thunder and no lightning anyway.

'Are you saying the job's no definite?' Sean wanted to know.

'Naw,' said Billy, 'course it is. If we get there in time. That's no what I mean. I mean, the ethics of it.'

'Aw, no that again,' said Sean. 'I thought we'd been through all that.'

'Aye, we have,' said Billy, 'but I'm still turning it over. It's no that simple.'

'It's this bloody simple,' said Sean. 'If we don't do the work some other cunt will. That's all there is to it.'

He stamped his feet up and down the road to get the circulation going. After a couple of minutes he stopped.

'Bugger this,' he said. 'I'm freezing to death here. I'm away back for another pot of tea off that nice wee lassie.'

'May as well stick it out now we're soaked,' said Billy. 'Somebody's got to come by sooner or later.'

'Aye, probably later. Come on, let's go back and get warmed up.'

'Aye, maybe.' Billy pulled back his jacket sleeve to check his watch. 'Look, it's just gone quarter past four. Give it till half-past and if we're still here we'll go back.'

'Christ, the café'll probably close at half-four. Nothing's coming, Billy. Let's go for the tea.'

'We've got to get out of here, Sean. There's a guy coming up the road this minute that's destined to stop for us. No, I'm wrong, it's no a guy, it's this gorgeous oversexed American divorcee on her holidays, looking for some local talent. And her pal. I don't want to miss the only lift going just for another cup of tea.'

'Well, I'm chancing it. We'll take it in shifts. Heads I go first, tails you stay, ha ha. Then when I come back you can go. Come and get us if anyone stops, eh?'

'Come on, Sean, you can't get folk to stop and then say, oh, eh, by the way, could you just back up the road to that wee tea-shop there, my mate's just finishing his scones. I mean, can you?'

'Well, I'm fucking away. You coming or staying?'

'I'm staying. I'll wait till half-past.'

Neither of them would give way. Sean walked off a few yards. Billy tried to put some action into standing his ground. This was the deal, if it was one: Billy would make his point of principle for fifteen minutes, then join Sean in the café. He would make his stand and hope a car wouldn't come along to put it to the test. Sean slouched off through the rain towards the café.

★ ★ ★

The ethics of it. The night before, waiting for the women, they'd had this long discussion about the tree felling. It was a programme Billy had seen on the telly that started him off, about this massive Forestry Commission plantation that had been sold off to some pop group or Terry Wogan or someone. It had been planted in the 1950s, according to a plan. The plan was that the trees would be regenerative, if that was the word. You'd harvest them over a period of thirty years or so, so that the next lot would have grown up by the time you'd finished. The crofters in the area could get part-time work every single year for decades, taking out the mature trees in partnership with the Commission. The whole thing was about community involvement.

'Then the Forestry Commission's forced to sell it off when the trees are about to mature and some rich bastard buys it who never comes near the place and one day his accountant tells him to realise his assets and take the whole fucking lot out. That doesna seem right at all to me.'

'Aw, come on,' said Sean, 'don't get so pious. You're in it just the same as everyone. You need the work and I need the work, and what's more, we can do the work. If it wasn't us it would be someone else.'

'That's the point, though. It shouldn't be us. It should be about sustaining the local population, not bringing in the flying squads.'

'The world's fucking changed, Billy,' said Sean. 'You might not like it much, and I might not like it, but it's changed and you have to change with it. See when they sold off British Telecom and British Gas and that? Did you buy the shares and make a few hundred quid selling them on?'

'No,' said Billy. 'That wasna right either. How, did you?'

'No, but no out of principle. I didna have any cash or I would have done. And there was plenty of folk I ken that did.'

'Aye, and what have they got to show for it now? They might have made a few bob but look at how much profit BT makes these days. Hundreds of pounds every bloody second. And how much of that are you and me and anybody else in Hicksville Scotland ever going to see? Not a fucking penny.'

'Well, moaning about the rights and wrongs of it isn't going to make it better. You had your chance for a slice of the action and you missed it.'

'We both did,' said Billy. This forestry thing, it was like American mining companies ripping off Indian land for uranium or something. The same idea.

Sean shrugged. 'Grab it when you see it,' he said. 'Work, women, money. That's the only way to live these days.'

Billy and Sean. It sounded like a sectarian stand-up comedy act, and in a way that was exactly what they were. They got on all right, they played off against each other, but Billy wouldn't have said they'd ever got close. He wouldn't say that about him and anybody though. Especially not his male friends. You just didn't do it. The closest you got was kicking a ball about, or on the terracing watching Scotland (at club level it was different teams for him and Sean), or drunk together in the pub. You needed something external like that to be able to show your affection, any warmth. So probably the closeness wasn't even there if you took away the circumstances. It was all artificially induced. Men were like herds of rutting stags, or tigers wandering about in the jungle. They didn't much like each other's company so they invented sport and pubs to make it bearable. What they really wanted to do was roam around on their own, occasionally home in on unsuspecting women and engage in an elaborate mating ceremony, then fuck off into the jungle again. Or up on the moors or wherever.

Women now, that was different. Women friends were close to each other. Christ, they wore each other's clothes and shared their beds and their most intimate secrets and suchlike. He couldn't imagine what that must be like. It must be great but frightening too. Making yourself so vulnerable. But warm too, when it was working right. And of course a man and a woman could be like that. The man could get a real friend out of his female lover. What did the woman get? She might get a lover out of a male friend but could she get a friend out of her lover? Not according to the accepted wisdom, it seemed.

Women friends. He had a few. There was Marian that worked behind the bar at his local, but she was every man's friend. You could talk to Marian about whatever you wanted and she'd listen but that was her job, somehow even though you could have a great crack with her you felt she wouldn't let you get close to her, she had another life when she came round the bar. Good for her too, you didn't grudge her that. He was still friendly with a couple of old girlfriends. They were married now, to mates of his, and that was fine, there was no aggro about it, and he could chat to them and dance with them at parties and nobody cared. But there was a line there, a line beyond which the conversation could not go. Partly the line was drawn by himself, but mostly it was there because of conventions. You do not discuss your sexual frustrations with your mate's wife who happens to be an old flame, for example. Just not the done thing, open to mis-interpretation *et cetera* by all parties concerned. Sometimes – at nights out or weddings, say, especially weddings – he saw the women in wee groups, talking nineteen to the dozen, and even though physically there was no barrier in fact, he knew they were on the far side of the line. He'd look across the dance floor and all he'd see was drunk men standing at the bar together, and single men circling the dancers.

He was sick of the male thing. If he could do it for another couple of years maybe he could stop, get into his secure place, and start being human. That's what he felt like, that most of his life he spent not being human, not being himself, but trying to play a role. He looked at a guy like Sean and he thought maybe he should just give in, but it wasn't good enough. That was his trouble. Nothing was good enough for him. He couldn't help thinking beyond where he was.

Jonah in the Bible. Some folk called him Jonas, was that right? He seemed to remember that from somewhere. Anyway, whatever his name was, the thing about him was if he hadn't run away from God he'd have been all right. It was because he was running away from God that he was jinxed. When the storm blew up the crew knew that meant someone was bad luck, so they drew lots to find out who, and it was Jonah. So they threw him overboard and he got swallowed by the whale. But suppose it hadn't been him? Suppose it was someone else that was jinxed? He drew the short straw but that wasn't exactly conclusive evidence. Then he came up with this shite about having displeased

God, so they took that as proof and chucked him in the sea. He was Jewish and they weren't, that was another thing. This business of upsetting his God wouldn't mean much to them, it wouldn't be a proper reason for pinning the blame on him, and anyway he'd told them about it before the storm. What if they'd got rid of him and the storm hadn't died down, would they have drawn lots again, thrown each other in until it stopped? No, that would have made the whole story pointless. The point was, the only thing that made Jonah the Jonah was the story. It had to be him for the story to work.

There was a swishing sound and a car came into view out of the village, its headlights taking Billy by surprise. However his thumb was experienced, it went out instantly, and as if it exerted some magical influence the car slowed to a halt beside him. Great moments, thought Billy. He still got a thrill when it happened. He stepped over just as the driver was leaning across to open the passenger door.

'How far you going, pal?'

'Inverness,' said the driver. A man in shirt-sleeves and tie. His jacket was hung on a plastic peg behind him. 'That any use to you?'

'Aye, brilliant,' said Billy. 'Eh, I've got a rucksack here, is that all right?'

'Aye,' said the driver. 'Just sling it in the boot, there's plenty room.' He pressed or pulled some control under the dashboard and the boot sprang open.

'Great,' said Billy. He looked back down the road for Sean, then at his watch. It was ten to five. Come on, ya bastard, where are you, stuck in the cludgie or something?

He tried to take his time loading the rucksack into the boot and closing it.

'That you first in the queue, son?' the driver called. Billy went back to the open door. 'What's that?' he said.

'I'm saying, are you in a queue? I see there's another rucksack there.'

'Aye, well, actually,' said Billy, pointing back to the village. 'Eh, it's just like, there's someone else.'

'I can see that. Well, come on, hop in, the seat's getting wet.'

'Aye, I mean, it's my mate like. He's back there at the café.'

The driver leaned right over again, his face staring up into Billy's. He was some kind of sales rep, probably. He looked quite a hardman.

'Right, well, I haven't got all day. I'm doing you a favour, son. Are you coming or not?'

Billy hesitated again, his hand on the passenger door. There was still no sign of Sean. He'd be chatting up that lassie behind the counter, he knew it, he could just about hear him at it.

The driver revved his engine. 'Fuck's sake,' he said. 'You didn't have your thumb out in the fucking rain for nothing, did ye? Make up your mind, pal.'

'Sorry,' said Billy. From Inverness he could go anywhere. It wasn't the kind of statement you ever expected to hear – 'From Inverness you can go anywhere!' – but it was true. Maybe he'd keep going north, find Kenny, get the job. Or maybe he'd tell him, no, I can't do it, Kenny, I can't take part in this massacre, and head off back down the A9. Or just not bother. Aberdeen, maybe. Try to get out on the rigs again. Aberdeen, then Australia. Aye, and maybe it was him after all, he'd get thrown overboard, swallowed by a big fish.

This was all in a moment. A moment like all these moments in his life when he felt he was being tossed like a coin. For a moment the chances hang spinning in the air, and then you call.

'Right,' he said to the driver above the noise of the rain. He almost shouted it.

The Claw

My grandfather's hand is turning into a claw. That's what I'm thinking as I watch it raise the coffee cup. The finger-joints are swollen and the fingers themselves permanently curled, and the tone of the flesh is distorted by bruise-like browns and blues. Liver spots, I think the term is. They come with old age. The grip on my arm when he pulled up out of his chair to greet me was so fierce that it felt like he would never let go. Looking at the hand now, hard and unyielding on the fussy handle of the cup, it seems independent of the rest of him. Evidently the brain is still sending out orders, but between it and the claw everything else is crumbling.

His upper arms are thin as ropes, his whole structure like some skeletal macramé. He can barely walk across the room even with his sticks or a zimmer. He needs help to get to the bathroom or to the dining room. The latter journey is painfully slow, involving him being loaded into the chairlift at the top of the staircase and helped out of it at the bottom. When the staff are too busy they bring the meals to his room instead. This is happening more and more, I know, because he tells me. 'They're keeping me a prisoner here,' he says loudly, before the woman who brought the tray has closed the door behind her. I laugh in a way that is supposed to sound to her like an apology.

In addition to the infirmity of his legs, other faults have developed in the last year. He likens himself to a motor car – that's what he calls it – and says that with 98,000 miles on the clock it's not surprising that the bodywork is a bit rusty and some things don't work very well anymore. He's already had two hip replacement operations and now he says they're not making the parts for his model, so he won't be going up on the ramp again, thank you very much.

Or to put it another way: he says he's on borrowed time, each year he chalks up beyond the biblical span a debt that God might call in at any moment. He can no longer go to church, of course. The minister comes every so often, and twice a year he receives his own private communion. His faith is unquestionable, but what exactly it is has never been discussed. He would resent even the minister – especially the minister – interfering in that matter.

His bladder is weak, his bowel easily upset. He can no longer take a bath – he is given one. He is almost totally blind and even with his hearing aid turned up full he is pretty deaf – although everybody says he sees and hears more than he lets on. I find this idea disconcerting, as his knowledge of me is constructed on a set of evasions and unrevealed truths and I wonder if he can hear them in my voice or see them in my smile. When someone has lost the full use of their senses you become careless and drop your guard. But if my grandfather has his suspicions he does not display them. That is not the done thing with him.

He'll wait to be told, and if he's told nothing he'll assume there's a conspiracy and come up with his own theory to fit it.

He has a very ordered mind, which has always extended to his own presentation. He shaves every morning with an electric shaver and takes a pride in always wearing a collar and tie, and having clean shoes. Not that the shoes can get dirty as he never leaves the home now, not for birthdays or weddings or Christmas or any other family occasion. 'There's only one event I can think of that I'll get out of here for,' he says. 'I hope you'll all attend!' He has three children, eight grandchildren and twelve great-grandchildren and on each of their birthdays a card drops through the letterbox, the envelope addressed in an anonymous hand, his signature scrawled under the greeting. This year he sent mine to my mother as I was in America again, and she forwarded it to me. Various multi-coloured cats in acrobatic poses spelt out the words HAPPY BIRTHDAY. It was months ago but one of the first things he said to me when I got back was, 'Did you get my card? I sent it to your mother. One of the people here chose it for me. They said it had a lot of cats on it. I hope you don't dislike cats very much.' It takes someone born in another century to come out with a sentence like that.

The woman who brought the coffee – 'one of the people here' – her name is Meg. She called him 'Mr Stewart', and smiled at me one of those understanding smiles that go with the job. Most of the residents get called by their first names, but not my grandfather. It is not so much that he is too formidable, rather that there is a sense of propriety about him which defies over-familiarity. Probably this becomes more important as, bit by bit, his physical dignity is stripped away. A decade separates him from nearly all the other residents, a generation or two from the staff, and from me.

I watch the claw move over the table between us, locating the saucer, then the plate with the biscuits, then one of the pink wafers. Even at such a late stage the brain can still learn new tricks: in this case, how to be blind. Three times I have visited him since I came back, three times in three months, and each time his body is frailer but his face seems stronger, in spite of the sightless eyes. It's as though the mind has finally lost patience with the useless flesh which encumbers it. My grandfather is ninety-eight. He had a turn last year and everybody thought he was on the way out but now his mind has rallied and, although he doesn't mention it, he must be aiming for the hundred and that fabled telegram. There were times when people of his vintage feared the arrival of official telegrams, but now the only one he is going to get is a hope and a challenge, growing nearer with each passing day.

I am only thirty-five but watching him I feel as old as he looks. I am HIV-positive. In the last year I've studied my soul from all sides, and every morning I begin the examination again.

'New York,' he says. He says it as if the novelty has not worn off the name, as if English York should still feel aggrieved at being usurped. 'It must be very exciting. Of course I've never been to any of these places.' I'm not fooled by the self-effacement – we're all well used to the impli-cations by now: I've never lived, I've never done anything except this – this getting to be an old man; you young people today live lives we could never have imagined. This from a man who spent six months being shelled on a beach at Gallipoli, then a year in the mud in France, watching the other young men around him dying, and wondering if the war would be over before his turn came.

I went from extreme youth to some kind of wisdom in less than ten years. Maybe a war does that for you too, I wouldn't know. I have to say that we – I mean our community in New York – reacted very quickly once we realised the horror that was upon us. But the damage was already done: we had been too much of a community and we suffered like one of those companies wiped out on the Somme, when all the men came from one town or district. God dispensing justice, some say.

'I've never really known any Americans,' he tells me. 'Never had much dealings with them. Of course a lot of our people ended up there.' By this he means the emigrants: our people became their people. 'A big country,' he says, 'with great cities. I should like to have seen some of those cities. A lot of opportunity there, I should imagine.'

I have known many Americans, and I have taken opportunities and had experiences in their greatest city which if I were to tell him would appal my grandfather, assuming that he believed his own flesh and blood capable of such things. If I were to tell him, but naturally I will not. My years over there, as far as he knows, have been about study and travel and more study, and a little bar and restaurant work on the side to help finance me, and that famous American hospitality. But in reality it was the friends who kept me there, kept me going back. Yes, I have known many Americans, and they have known me. This was in the days of manifest destiny, when we still believed opportunity was there for the taking. Of course we were hated and feared for it. We always have been.

I don't know if I will be going back. I'm not even sure if they would let me through immigration.

'A lot of Irish there too,' says my grandfather. 'The Scots and the Irish have plenty in common in their history.' He says this with wonder in his voice, as though it has just occurred to him, although it's a familiar preamble. It is one of the things that amazes me about him: his constant ability to re-energise old facts and thoughts that have been his companions longer now than any living thing on earth. He never tires of them. Now that I have lost so many, my lovers and other friends, I understand this honing of memory. What was once tedious to me I see has a kind of comfort. I find myself welcoming what comes next: his recital of the league table of national prejudice.

'Always liked the Irish – friendly, open people. Take life as they find it. Tragic as well, of course, their history – like ours – more so. Don't like the Welsh – never trusted them. The English, well, we all have to get on with the English, don't we? Spent most of my working life among them. London. Hm, yes, they were always very civil, I have to say. They liked us, you know, when we went to London. We were thorough, exact. What's the word? Conscientious. Yes, we were conscientious.'

He pauses. He has dealt with these islands. His mind drifts across the sea.

'I like the French.' He decides in their favour, as he always does. In the twenties it was a little risqué to like the French, and now it always will be. 'Delightful people. And the Italians – charming. Never could run anything though, not even under Mussolini.' The Italians are forgiven their little mistake; it wasn't really anything they could *help*. As usual, the fun dries up here. Naturally no one of his generation need even consider the possibility of liking the Germans. And the Germans are about as far as one seriously needs to go in such a line of thought. All those conflicts in the Middle East, all those shades of nation and race – Asia, Africa, the Americas – too distant, too *different*. And yet once he said to me, shaking his head at some new conflagration, 'We must, we must try to understand. Otherwise it'll just go on and on as it always has.'

There it is. My grandfather is like the rest of us, caught between history and hope, but history weighs heavy in his scales now, and every year it feeds faster and faster, gobbling up hope. He looks back on his life and it isn't just that he's had the best years of it, it's that it's over, actually over, and all he can do is sit in his armchair which faces the spot where the portable TV used to be and wait for a royal telegram and whatever it is his faith has promised him.

Anyway, it's nonsense to say he has not lived! Quite apart from the war. He worked in London for nearly four decades as an accountant, maybe not the most glamorous of professions but – what decades! The twenties, thirties, forties and fifties! In the twenties, when the civil war was on, he went to Dublin every year to oversee an audit for a client company there. He used to play golf with the company chairman. 'You'll be fine with me, don't you worry,' the chairman would assure him – a Brit in the new, bloodily born Free State. On the ninth tee the chairman pointed to a dyke running alongside the course and said to him, 'Just last week I was playing here, there was a foursome up ahead on the fairway, these three fellows with guns came out of nowhere, took one of the foursome away and shot him against the wall. I tell you, it shakes you up, a thing like that. We didn't know whether we should finish our round or not.' That's the Irish for you, says my grandfather. He chuckles at the memory.

When he had his turn last year his memory went into overdrive. My mother had it partly from himself, partly from the staff. They would find him at night in his pyjamas in the corridor, fuelled by something so powerful that it made him able to walk completely unaided. It was a struggle to persuade him back to bed. Once he was looking for his wife. Once he said he was trying not to step on the faces of the dead men on the floor. Perhaps this is how we prepare for death, by revisiting the people that were dearest to us, or whose being taken from us was the worst to bear. Perhaps we have to apologise for surviving.

I'm not ready to do that yet. My people are not far enough away.

My grandfather grew up in and around Dundee. As the century turned he was five, then six. One day his father, who was a lawyer and well-connected, took him on an expedition with a friend who had just bought a motor car. They drove all the way to Perth and made a telephone call to say they had arrived safely. Then they had tea at the Salutation Hotel before setting out on the return journey. My grandfather reckons he must have been one of the first people to make that trip by car. I consider this to be a miraculous story; so simple, so innocent. I always encourage him to tell it.

'Of course, nowadays people fly all over the world and don't think anything of it!' he says. 'Like you. You've been to all sorts of places, done all sorts of things.'

How can I tell him, how could he believe me, that I long to be that little boy, ecstatic on that dusty road beside the Tay? How can I tell him that I think I know what lies between that happy, excited trust in the transport of the future and the tough old bird who sits opposite me now, his claw neatly placing the wafer biscuit on the saucer? How can I tell him that I would willingly travel back and forth on that road for eternity, and never tire of it? I would like to try to explain, to say that I've been in the trenches too, that I have held the heads of my dying friends and that the wound I have carried home with me has not bought me safety. He's so incredibly old. Nothing should surprise him anymore.

Instead we sit and talk about jobs I might do, places I might go next. I'll say this for him, he has never criticised my lack of career. There is envy in there of course. He never had the chance. But then again, he believes life is for the taking. 'Take it!' he says. 'You've nothing to lose.'

Then something goes wrong. He puts his cup and saucer down too suddenly, and a little spurt of coffee and pink wafer shoots out over his chin and stains his tie. His face seems to collapse and drain of colour. He hunches forward. 'I don't feel well,' he says. The words are small and childlike.

There is a bell which I press for help, and while we're waiting I reach out and take his hard hand in mine. 'It's all right, someone'll be here in a moment.' The trouble is, in spite of everything, I'm still useless in these situations. I don't know what to say or do, except to touch. The door opens and it's Meg who enters. 'Now, Mr Stewart, are you not feeling well?'

'He seemed fine,' I tell her, 'and then everything suddenly seemed to stop.'

'It sometimes happens,' she says, 'He just needs to lie down for a while. He gets terribly tired, you see.'

Between us we help him over to the bed. He keeps saying he is very sorry to cause a fuss. Meg quiets him, gently lays him on the bed. Suddenly I see the fear swirling in his milky eyes. 'Who's that, who's that?'

'It's only me,' she says. 'It's Meg.' I feel helpless and afraid too, and draw back a little. Too many things are flooding in. Meg sits beside him on the bed, stroking his hand. This is a country where it still falls to the women to save us. To bear us, to tend us, to take our hands, to comfort us even to the grave.

'Will he be okay?' I ask. She holds me with a look – there is kindness in it, I think, and maybe scorn too, it's hard to tell – as if she can see me exactly as my grandfather cannot, as if she knows what's going on in my heart. Maybe she'll gossip over her tea downstairs: 'That grandson of his, he's a bit, you know . . . Doesn't look too well himself either.' The kind of things my own mother can't admit. Meg looks about ages with her. She's probably got a son too, in the army or something.

Then she smiles at me and says, 'Don't worry, it's just sleep, he just needs to sleep. It'll be all right.'

'I'd better go,' I say.

'Yes,' she says, 'I think so. And don't worry.' No scorn, then, just kindness. I think I'd rather have the scorn.

'Goodbye,' I say to him, but of course he doesn't hear. I touch his hand, but he probably thinks it's Meg, if he notices at all. Suddenly I wish I was away, and never coming back. I can't stand the thought of invalids. Of being at the mercy of others.

Bastards

Across the way, on the corner, Shandon saw the lights of a bar. The streets around here were deserted. He'd been wandering block after block, trying to get his mind round things, round something. Now there was this bar across from him. He felt like he was standing at the edge of one of those lonely-looking downtown American paintings by Edward Hopper, all streetlight and shadow. It was cold, and the bar offered warmth. He crossed over and pushed in through the door.

The place was almost empty, the lights were up and there was no music playing. Probably the lights had never been dimmed, and there was no evidence of a jukebox or any other sound-system. It was ten to eleven.

The man behind the bar was reading a paper. He didn't look like he was expecting a last-minute rush. Shandon thought, if I was the publican I wouldn't bother applying for a late licence for the place, not midweek anyway.

'Still serving?' he asked.

The barman raised his head. 'Aye,' he said. His tone was mildly indignant, as if he'd been asked to justify his presence.

'A double whisky, then. No, wait a minute, what malts have you got?'

The barman half-turned and pointed to a row of bottles on the gantry. 'That's them.'

There was nothing very unusual up there. Glenmorangie, Glenfiddich, Glenlivet, Glengoyne. Well, Glengoyne. 'A Glengoyne,' Shandon said. 'A double.'

He turned around while the barman measured it out, and took in the other people. A man was sitting further down the bar with a pint, staring into space. In one corner there was a young couple, their glasses empty. They were shrugging on their coats, getting ready to go. In the opposite corner another man and woman, older, maybe in their sixties. What was notable about them was that they were in evening dress. The man had on a black dinner-suit and bowtie, the woman a blue dress with a stole. Pearls were at her neck and ears. They weren't talking to each other; they were looking over towards him.

'Two pound eighty, please,' said the barman. For a moment Shandon was taken aback at the price but then he shrugged and got the money out and pulled the glass towards him. Glengoyne. Lowland. Unpeated. Quite good, he seemed to remember. He made himself wait for it.

If you got twenty-six drams to the bottle and say it cost twenty pound in the shops, but a bar would get it cheaper, say eighteen, that was eighteen divided by twenty-six, which worked out about seventy pence a dram. That was a healthy mark-up, a hundred per cent no less. Jesus. No wonder the place was empty, everybody was drinking at home.

He raised the glass.

Ah, but it was a good one right enough. Glengoyne. He'd forgotten it.

He had to ask himself what he was doing. Had he left her or had he not? And for what, if he had? Physically, of course, he hadn't left her. He'd be going back tonight, of course he would. But had he not left her in every other sense? And how much longer could he not physically leave her, in that case? Jesus.

And what about her, what was she thinking? They never asked each other anymore.

He'd gone out halfway through the news, just stood up and said he was going for a walk, maybe a drink, he'd be back later; thinking as he said it that maybe he wouldn't be. She hardly acknowledged his going. On the screen a small country was breaking up; there were bodies everywhere; women and children were herded and huddled together; houses burned; patriots defended what they were doing. He couldn't stand it. But she watched on. What was she thinking?

'What time do you close up at?' he asked.

'Quarter to twelve,' said the barman. Shandon was surprised – it hardly seemed worth it. But he knew he'd be staying till the end.

'I'll take a half-pint of heavy,' he said. Usually he said please and thank you but not tonight. He wasn't in the mood for it.

'Sixty-five,' said the barman. He wasn't wasting his breath either. That was fair enough.

The young couple had left. Only the empty glasses proved that they'd ever been there. The old couple still weren't talking. The man was staring ahead of himself, the woman

81

was fiddling with her necklace. The man down the bar finished his pint and ordered another. Then there was the barman and himself. Christ, they were a right bundle of laughs, the lot of them.

He took his drink in silence. He couldn't think about her. You came out to think about one thing and you ended up thinking about something else. The future. What the hell he was doing with his life, going to do with it. He was angry at himself for being self-indulgent. All over the world folk were simply surviving, or wishing they were dead, one or the other, and he didn't even know what he was doing. What was the point of his life? And why did it go by so fast? And the life that he was leading with her, that she led with him, why did they go on tolerating it? They would have to stop. If they didn't stop it their lives would never have the chance to restart.

He was aware that the man at the far end of the bar had come up beside him, and was addressing his profile:

'I know you. I know who you are.'

Shandon thought, Christ, here we go, some fucking eejit, I'm not in the mood to humour some other drunk bastard.

'No you don't,' he said, and carried on drinking. Didn't even look at him.

'Aye,' said the other man. 'Aye, I do.' There was something menacing in his voice that made Shandon turn to see if he should recognise him after all. They both eyed each other for a few seconds, and then just as his pinched cheeks and scraggy moustache and slouched shoulders were beginning to look familiar the man said, 'You're the cunt my wife left me for.'

Shandon felt his skin go cold. It was as if someone had come in the door, letting in a gust of icy air as they did so, but nobody had come in. He wasn't sure how he was going to deal with this, but he really only had the one option – to brazen it out, shut the bastard up before he started.

'Who the fuck do you think you're talking to?'

'I know who I'm talking to. I'm talking to you.'

So there was going to be a fight, was that it? Shandon was in no mood for a fight. He wasn't feeling charitable, but he felt too slow, too tired. He wanted the barman to intervene, throw the bastard out, but the barman had disappeared through the back a minute or two before and was on the phone. Probably the guy had seen his chance then, to sneak up on him.

'It's all right,' the man said, 'relax. I'm not going to batter you. Here, shake on it.'

Shandon wasn't daft. He did not extend his hand.

'No,' said the guy, 'I mean it. No violence.' He held one hand up, palm towards him. 'My name's Jack Mathieson. Not that you need me to tell you that.'

'I don't know you from Adam,' said Shandon. 'You're making a mistake, and if you don't fuck off you'll be making an even bigger one.'

'Nasty,' said Mathieson. 'That's a nasty streak in you. But I don't want to fight. I want to talk.'

'Listen,' said Shandon. 'Let's get this clear. I don't know you and you don't know me. And I don't want to talk to you. All right?'

'We don't know each other,' said Mathieson. 'Is that what you're saying?'

'You got it in one, pal,' said Shandon.

'Fine,' said Mathieson. 'If you say so.'

'It's not that I say so. It's that it is.'

'Fine,' said Mathieson. He didn't move.

'Funny,' he said. 'You look just like the cunt.'

By rights Shandon should have let him have it right then and there, but the barman came out again, and not being a witness to the first part of the conversation he would have seen Shandon laying into the smaller, frailer-looking man for no apparent reason. So Shandon moved away slightly, saying to the barman, 'Tell this wee shite to get off my back, will you?'

The barman didn't even hesitate. He pointed a finger at Mathieson and nodded down the bar. 'On your way, Jack.'

Most likely he tried it on with any stranger, any face that might fit. He'd had a disaster of a marriage and never got over it. But it was a bit close for comfort. Maybe Shandon would be like that one day. Aye, maybe he would, if he didn't get his act together and decide what to do with himself. He ordered another whisky – a single – and a pint this time. But coming out to drink on your own was as bad as staying in in front of the wars on the telly. It didn't solve anything. What you needed was something to inspire you.

'I mind, Tom, I mind how I got in with her in the first place. Mind it clear as if it was yesterday.'

'Aye.' The barman sounded bored, but maybe he thought this way he'd keep the guy down at the end of the bar, away from Shandon.

'Clear as yesterday,' said Mathieson.

'How was that then?'

Then Mathieson was talking, as if he had reached a stage of the night or a state of mind which triggered something in him. His voice was calmer than when he'd spoken to Shandon. Shandon stared ahead, not looking; listening.

'She'd just split up with her previous man. I didn't know this at the time but she had. And he was a personal friend, a good friend of mine. Except he ceased to be, after what happened between her and me, I mean. We never spoke to each other again. Probably just as well or he'd have killed me. I met her in this pub somewhere, God, I can mind what it looked like, the interior and that, but I'm buggered if I know where it was now. Down in London it was, but where exactly . . . We were all working down there in these days.

'Anyway, there we were, sitting next to each other in the corner of this pub – I can't even remember but I think she'd phoned me, arranged to meet, and I'd not thought anything of it – and I says to her, "Where's Paul the night?" She says, "It's over." Just like that. No tears or nothing. Right in there – it's over.

'And straightaway I'm thinking, you know what I'm thinking, Christ you could be in here, mate. You've always fancied her. Could catch her on the rebound if you play your cards right. I mean, I was sorry for her if she was upset, but to be honest that's exactly what I was thinking.'

'You weren't wasting any time,' said the barman. He was supplying the punctuation, the pauses for drink to be taken.

'Aye, but you know how it is, you caw canny. I waited. I let her do the talking. That was the idea – ease in gently, establish some basic facts. Like, is she angry or distraught or couldn't care less? So I tried it out. "I'm sorry," I says. "I'm not," she says. Okay, so that meant she was angry.

'Then she says he could be an animal. Is this in bed?, I'm wondering. But no, she goes on, "He could be a right bloody animal, farting and belching around my flat like he owned the place."'

'Is that what she said?'

'Aye. Well, that made things a wee bit problematic. I'm partial to a wee bit farting and belching myself. All in good time but. Have to break them in slowly sometimes.' The barman gave a false kind of laugh, as though he didn't really agree with the sentiment but didn't want to make an issue out of it. 'She says, "He's a bastard." Well, what a cue. "Well," I says – it wasn't my place to say anything but – "now you're finished I suppose it's all right to say I never did trust him all together."

'She says, "I thought you were his pal." "Aye," I says, "but if you two are finished like . . ." She says, "Well, he's a fucking bastard." And she tells me why too. Some of the things. The farting and belching, that was just the tip of the iceberg. What it boiled down to was, he didn't respect her. That's what she reckoned. She kept going on about this respect thing. I couldn't see it myself, but I played along with it. Didn't want to blow my chances, you know. I just sat back and let her use me for an audience, till she got it out of her system. It like, sets you up as the opposite of the guy they're slagging off, know what I mean?

'Anyway, she talks for quite a while, me nodding away in time to her, then she's nothing left to say. So we're sitting there the pair of us, not really drinking much, and I suppose she's thinking over all the things she and him did, all the things that were good while it lasted. Or maybe all the bad things, I don't know . . . the things women think about. Me,

I'm wondering, should I put my hand over hers just now, friendly like, comforting, give it a squeeze, or is it too obvious? Too soon? Maybe give it another five minutes and then the arm round her. And then she says, "Can I trust you, Jack?" And I says, "Course you can, Audrey." And she just kind of snuggles in. That's what she was looking for – reassurance or something. Well, it felt great. I hadn't even put her under any pressure or nothing and she'd just melted.

'Audrey. I always fancied her. And you know, these women, they always go for it. I went home with her that very night. Never spoke to him again, either of us. And then we got married. Five years of it. Makes you think, eh?'

'Aye,' said the barman. A sound less like that of someone thinking was hard to imagine.

'She always went for bastards. First him, then me. Then she left me for some other bastard.'

'Oh aye?'

Shandon waited for it. He felt himself tensing up. But it was as if Mathieson had forgotten he existed. He downed the rest of his pint. 'Oh aye, I'm a bastard all right. No question. We all are. Aye well, it was good while it lasted. I'm away. I'll see you the morra.'

'Aye, right you are. Night.'

'Night.'

And he walked out. Just like that. Never even looked at Shandon again.

Shandon said to the barman, 'That guy, does he come in here much?'

'Aye, he's a regular. Was he giving you bother earlier?'

'Aye, nothing serious but. What's his name, do you know?'

'Jack,' said the barman. 'That's all I know – Jack. You can get too close to some of these loners.'

'An occupational hazard, I would think.'

'Aye,' said the barman, glancing at him. 'Not if I can help it.' He went down the bar to get the empty glass. 'Are you wanting anything before I close up?'

'Yes, please.' It was the old fellow in the dinner-suit. He'd come up behind Shandon without making a sound.

'Same again, Gordon?'

'Same again, Tom, thank you very much.' His voice was rich and plummy, not English but what some people would call educated Scots. He had a big chest and thick grey side-whiskers; his silver hair was well combed and oiled. These things seemed to go with the voice: they stood for power, maturity, self-confidence. But when Shandon looked more closely he saw food stains on the white shirt-front, and an unsightly clump of hairs sprouting from his ear.

'All right, my friend?' said the older man. He leaned heavily on the bar, turning sideways to look directly into Shandon's face. 'Doing all right?' He spoke very loudly, and it was clear he was well on.

'Aye, I'm fine,' said Shandon.

'Don't mind that chap that was in earlier. He doesn't mean any harm. Just a poor unfortunate sort of chap.'

'Aye, it's no problem,' said Shandon. The barman had the drinks ready – a gin and tonic and a white wine. The man handed over a fiver. 'Would you like one yourself, Tom?'

'Thanks, I'll have a half-pint of lager,' said Tom. He got the change and poured his own drink. 'At the theatre again the night, Gordon?'

'That's right,' said Gordon. He was poised, holding the drinks, about to walk back with them to the woman at the table. 'Noel Coward, I think. Or was it Terence Rattigan? I can never remember. Mary would know.'

'It was *Private Lives*,' the woman in the blue dress called. Her voice was also loud and rich. 'He knows perfectly well.'

'Good, was it?' asked the barman.

'Marvellous,' she said.

'It was rubbish,' said Gordon. He carried the drinks over and slid in beside her. They said nothing to each other, but started in on the drinks.

'Did you say you wanted something?' the barman asked Shandon.

'Eh, no, I'm just off.' But he nursed the last of his beer for another few minutes. He'd no idea people still got dressed up to go to the theatre. Well, nobody did, except these two.

When the barman was away putting chairs on tables, he walked out.

It was cold. The sky was clear but he couldn't see many stars because of the glow of the city. He crossed over the street and was about to head off when something made him stop. It was the realisation that he was going back. He had resolved nothing. He wished the bar was open till two, or three. He'd stay there all night if he could.

He pulled his coat around him and rested on a wall. It was too cold to be hanging around, but still he waited. After a while he saw the old couple coming out of the bar. They stood for a moment, he looking up at the sky, she adjusting her stole. Then they began to walk, unsteadily, arm in arm along the pavement.

Shandon didn't move until the storm-doors of the bar, as if unassisted by human hand, swung shut. He heard the sound of bolts being shot home. The barman would probably leave by a back entrance. He thought about the man Mathieson, who had left twenty minutes earlier. Mathieson could be waiting for him, somewhere out here. Mathieson could be waiting for Shandon and Shandon could be waiting for Tom, the barman. It was an interesting scenario, all of them waiting in the shadows. But what would he be waiting for Tom for? Only after he had thought about it for a while, how it might have come about, only then did he push himself away from the wall and start to move. He had a fair walk ahead of him.

Facing It

Then one day he looked down between his legs and he knew it could no longer be avoided. He looked down and saw white and then the bowl filled red and dark and nothing solid in it at all and he knew something was very wrong. Just for a moment as he sat there in privacy, his throat constricted, and he thought he was going to cry. But he held that back at least. Everything else had failed him. He went through another quarter-roll of paper but he knew no amount of paper could staunch the flow now, the lemon-scented air-freshener had failed him and the open window, beyond these the attempt to keep an upright posture, the firm handshake and cutting out the whisky, even in the last few weeks a kind of muttered, embarrassed praying – more a plea really against the pain – everything had failed him, he knew it was all coming apart in there, it was breaking up into pieces and flowing out of him. He would have to go to the doctor but he would go without telling *her*. He could hear her busying herself in the kitchen as if she knew what was happening, but she didn't. He didn't want her to worry or be upset but when it came to the bit that was what would happen.

And the doctor would say, he could hear him saying, yes, it's very bad, I'm afraid it's very bad indeed, so maybe he wouldn't go there after all, maybe if he just gave himself a final wipe and flushed away all that stuff that was himself, flushed it twice and got himself on his feet and composed, deep breaths in the mirror, he could just call to her, not have to go into the kitchen at all, just call saying, I'm off out for a paper, and once outside turn left towards the park and then with the back held as straight as possible keep going, keep walking, walking, walking, through the park, through the city, through the suburbs, out towards the hills, as far as he could go until he dropped.

What Love Is

Something in the light changes, and Dan, who is not long home from his work, realises it has started to snow. He goes from the kitchen to the front room of the flat and stands at the bay window, looking down on the traffic and the orange glow of the streetlights. A small thrill shivers through him as he watches the first flakes pass by. It's like being a child again. A gust of wind blows the snow upwards, and the falling flakes mix with the rising. Dan looks into the cloud-laden sky over the grey city. He sees it as a great sagging mattress stuffed with tiny feathers. The mattress has burst and there are feathers everywhere. He looks at his watch. It's half-past five. He thinks about Joan coming back on the bus through the snow, but she won't leave her work until after seven. He has a couple of hours.

Amazing what you can see through windows. Once, through this very one, he saw a woman fly. She lived on the other side of the street, on the other side of the constant stream of cars and taxis and buses, in a fourth-floor flat. She cleaned her windows by climbing out on the ledge and holding on to the frame while she wiped and polished.

Forty feet above the traffic she stood, on a ledge six inches wide, and Dan could hardly bear to look at her. He closed his eyes because she frightened him, balancing there, and he saw the arc of her body falling backwards and being held like a sheet of paper in the air and then suddenly her gift of flight – this being the only way to save her – and when he opened his eyes again the window was closed and the woman gone.

Another time, he was washing his breakfast things in the kitchen sink before leaving for work, and across the back-greens he saw a young woman doing the same, directly opposite but one floor down. As his hands moved in the bowl of soapy water he saw her stop and lower her head. She was wearing a white blouse and he saw her fingers, which must, like his, have been wet, go to touch the front of it. Then she reached for a towel, wiped her hands, and swiftly unbuttoning the blouse she slipped it off. She must have spilt something on it, coffee or marmalade or something. She held a corner of the towel under the tap for a moment, and he watched her dab at the blouse with it. He imagined the tops of her breasts curving out of her bra – it was too far for him to really see this – her hair falling forward, her breasts rising and falling as she worked at the stain – even through two lots of glass she seemed very alive to him. After a minute she held the blouse up to the light, then draped it over one arm and left the room. Tears sprang into Dan's eyes. He was leaning hard up against the sink unit. He took his wet hand away from himself. Sex. That was what he wanted. He couldn't, though. He couldn't go back to bed. He couldn't wake Joan because she was on the late shift and would want another hour's sleep. He felt guilty because in any case he didn't want to have sex with Joan, he wanted it with a woman across the way, in another room in another flat in another life.

Dan isn't frightened of other lives. He imagines them all the time. The only life he is frightened of is his own.

Every morning, whether she is on the early shift or the late one, Joan takes a bus to her work. She works from eight till five or ten till seven, and she does a morning every third Saturday as well. She would drive to work if they owned a car, but they can't afford one. She learned to drive when she was eighteen, in her father's car, and she passed her test first time. She needs this skill for her job. She works on the reservations desk of a car-hire firm. Self-drive, to use the jargon. She has to be able to drive the cars from one area of the forecourt to another, and park them in confined spaces. The self-drive desk is only one part of the place, which is a big Ford dealer's. There is a showroom for new models and a parking lot full of second-hand ones, and there is the self-drive desk. Joan has been there for fifteen years.

Other lives disturb Joan. The bus is full of them, different ones at different times of the day, and when she finds herself thinking about them she does her best to block them out. She doesn't want them to encroach. Her life may not be perfect but it is hers and she has it worked out, the routine of it. The routine is what keeps her going; she will not allow it to oppress her.

'How was your day?' Dan asks her. He is cutting up vegetables for tea. He cooks the tea on the days when she is on the late shift.

'Just the usual,' she says. Once – only once – Dan went to see her at her work. It was a summer afternoon and he decided to walk at least part of the way home. It wasn't much of a detour to go by the Ford dealer's place. Afterwards he wished he hadn't. There were three women on the self-drive desk, Joan and two others. They were dealing with five customers and all the phones were ringing. The women were making bookings, taking money or credit cards, inspecting driving-licences, explaining the insurance, checking that returned cars had full tanks, taking customers to their cars and demonstrating the controls to them. Whenever they got out from behind the desk they seemed to be about to break into a run. Their manner was polite, efficient and subservient. All of the customers were men. Dan stood just inside the door watching this scene for a few minutes, without Joan seeing him. Thirty feet away, a couple of sharp-suited salesmen were standing about in the showroom. They were doing nothing, and seemed oblivious to the frantic activity of the women. Occasionally one of them would run his finger along the roof or bonnet of one of the new cars, as if to demonstrate his expertise, his familiarity with the merchandise. They paid Dan no attention because he did not look like someone with the money to buy a car. This was true. Several of the models on display cost more than his entire year's salary. He quietly left before Joan saw him. He never mentioned to her that he had been there.

'Just the usual,' she says, and Dan is horrified and ashamed that his wife has done that job for fifteen years. He chops the carrots with a vengeance.

★ ★ ★

Yvonne at his work keeps lecturing him, in a friendly, good-intentioned way. 'You're too willing,' she tells him. 'You're too conscientious. Nobody should have to put up with the amount of work they give you.'

Yvonne herself is no slacker. She's the receptionist. Apart from not having to deal with the cars, her job is as frantic as Joan's. She fields the phone calls and the visitors and does some typing and she even finds time to give Dan advice. She is twenty-two – half his age – but she doesn't see any irony in giving advice to a man old enough to be her father. Dan's official job title is Requisitions Manager. The firm – a small but industrious firm of architects – gave him this name and a ten per cent rise after he'd been with them for five years and 'Storeman' had become too much of an under-statement to be ignored. As well as running the stores, Dan is in charge of repairs, equipment, the post room, and health and safety. He is responsible for the maintenance and cleaning contracts and the stationery purchases, and often he acts as a courier, delivering documents to other locations in the city. When he has a spare half-hour he'll sometimes work the switch-board to let Yvonne get on with something else. He is indispensable to the firm, and this gives him enough satisfaction to offset the nagging feeling that he is underpaid and overworked. Yvonne, who is not long out of college and is afraid of no one, fuels his suspicions. 'They take advantage of your good nature,' she says. 'They exploit you, you know they do. You shouldn't let them.'

Dan at home. He has a big record collection. He loves the sound of a woman singing, and it doesn't much matter to him if it's Jessye Norman or Mary Black or Nina Simone.

There's something about any woman's voice which is worth listening to. That's what he thinks. But most of all he listens to Billie Holiday. He could listen to her sing for hours and think only minutes had gone by. He has about twenty different albums of Billie Holiday, many of them with different recordings of the same song, little variations that he has become totally familiar with – so that he can listen to a song and say, 'Yes, with Ray Ellis and his orchestra, 1958 sessions.' Joan likes Billie Holiday too, but she gets irritated by this perfectionism. 'Sometimes I think you don't listen to the songs themselves anymore. You listen for the bits that are missing.' Dan gives her his smile, the one that says, yes, you're right, but you don't know anything. 'You don't know,' Billie sings, 'what love is, until you've learned the meaning of the blues.' What a life, thinks Dan, alone in the front room at two in the morning, what a life she had to have, to sing like that.

Joan sits on the bus and different lives come at her, veering away at the last moment. She tries to be untouched by them, but it's hard. One morning there are three Asian girls going into town. Their hair is thick and black – she can imagine how heavy it must feel just by looking at it – but their loose black silk trousers look lightweight. Although young they seem very dignified, aloof even. She is not a racist, but she is sure of one thing: their lives and hers have nothing in common.

Another time, coming home in the evening, it's three white girls. They are loud but at the same time conspiratorial, trying to impress the bus with their grown-up talk, which is about the different stages of undress they have reached with their boyfriends. Joan, who could be their mother, is embarrassed and intrigued. She can't stop herself listening. Then a woman of her own age stands to get off the bus, and as she passes the girls her rage comes pouring out: 'You're disgusting! Decent people having to listen to your filth! Dog-dirt! You're worse than dog-dirt!'

'Piss off!' the girls chorus as she steps off the bus. Joan finds herself turning to watch the woman disappear on the crowded pavement.

One day there's an old drunk man giving the world-view to everybody on the bus. It's only mid-morning but already he's had a skinful. 'Too many people 'assatrouble. Westafrica'neastafrica'ntha. Six families tae a hoose. The Ashian shituashion. I know, I know.' The other passengers seem to find him funny. He's a Scotch comedian pretending to be a drunk. They nod and smile and shake their heads to one another. Joan is alone.

Then one night, with winter coming on, she gets on the bus to come home and as soon as she sits down at the back she knows she has done the wrong thing. There are three boys just in front of her – all these young lives seem to come in threes – and apart from them the lower deck is empty. They are busy carving up the seats. She should get up and move to the front but she doesn't want to draw attention to herself. She listens to the blades slicing through plastic. The bus stops and an Inspector gets on, a Sikh. 'Oh, here we go,' says one of the boys, 'a fucking towelheid. Eh, lads, feet up on the fucking seats.'

Joan sits mesmerised. The Inspector is a middle-aged man with a full, greying beard. He comes down and checks their tickets, then hers. As he goes back past them he says,

'Take your feet off the seats, please.' He can't help but see the ripped covering. 'Fuck off, ya black cunt ye.' He calmly walks to the front of the bus, where he speaks first to the driver, then into his radio. At the next stop the boys run off the bus.

Joan breathes out. The air is so oppressive. She just sat back, shrank back in her seat and hoped it wouldn't touch her. She has to admit her fear.

It's not just that she is frightened about things like that. She thinks about what she is becoming, has become. She keeps telling herself that she could be a lot worse off, that she and Dan have a roof over their heads and two jobs that are secure and a holiday every year (not that they go away, but the option is there) and all right it would be nice to have children, but she doesn't really know if it would be, she just says that because it's expected of her, not that anyone ever says, 'Wouldn't you like children?', she wouldn't think much of someone who came out and asked as personal a question as that, not after all this time. But she can't avoid the truth. She can cope with her own life now simply because, at some point, she can't remember when, she lost the courage to change. It's not that she doesn't have fear – she has. It's that she doesn't have courage.

And what would her children be? Like those boys, those girls? It's too late, but she can't help wondering.

Yvonne says to Dan, 'You've got to put your foot down. Brian abuses you, Diane exploits you. You're exploited. I mean, we all are, but we get paid enough for it. You do far more than you need to for them. Coming in at the weekend last week. Staying on to change her office around for her.

They don't even thank you for it. You're a really nice man, everybody likes you, we only want to see you getting fairly treated.'

'I'm all right,' he tells her. 'I appreciate your concern, but really I'm all right. I'm quite happy doing that kind of thing.'

Although they don't own a car Dan and Joan have a problem with car ownership. Many of the neighbours who have cars have had them fitted with alarms, and the alarms keep going off, usually at two in the morning. Dan hates them. 'It's just blatant selfishness,' he rants. 'Every time they go off they're saying, I'm looking after Number One, don't touch, I've commandeered the space in and around this tin box and if the wind buffets it or someone knocks it trying to squeeze by to get to the pavement and your sleep's disturbed that's tough, that's not my problem.'

Joan says, 'They have to protect their property. I know what you mean, but they have to do something.'

'They're noise pollutants,' says Dan. 'Those alarms going off is a worse kind of pollution than the exhaust fumes.'

One night Dan's going to sort them. He'll go down into the street in his pyjamas and take a hammer to the windscreen of the screaming car, and for good measure he'll smash in the headlights flashing in time with the alarm. 'Now you've something to make a fucking noise about,' he'll shout. And all the people leaning out of their windows in their nightwear, the non-carred, cheering and applauding.

Joan at work. One of the salesmen is called Maurice. The first thing to notice about Maurice is his hair. It stands upright and waves like a cornfield in the breeze. It does this by design not by nature. He keeps it corn-coloured too and it looks absurd on a fifty-year-old. Margaret, who works with Joan, christened him The Coxcomb, and they all take the piss out of him, but Maurice is immune to anything that might alter his own good opinion of himself. If you're on your knees in front of the filing cabinet Maurice is the guy that always says, 'Say one for me when you're down there, love.' Or if you're not wearing your best smile he'll say, 'Cheer up, it might never happen.' At quiet moments he deigns to lean on their counter, practising his chat-up lines. As soon as a customer appears he skates off again: 'A woman's work is never done, isn't that right, Joan?'

'It's well seen a man's work never gets started in here,' says Margaret. But Maurice can make a sale in twenty minutes and float back with his ego refuelled. An Asian man approaches the desk.

'Oh-oh,' says Maurice under his breath, 'looks like you'll be trading on the black market this afternoon, ladies.'

'What was that, Maurice? I didn't quite catch that,' Margaret calls after him, but Maurice is back among the new cars, on his own territory.

The women are talking about *Thelma and Louise* one day. It's not long out on video. Margaret's saying, 'It's brilliant, the way she lets that bastard have it,' and suddenly Maurice is there, sidling in.

'Is that the film about the two lezzies?'

'No, Maurice, it's not,' says Margaret.

'Only joking,' he says, 'I saw it myself. Liked the music.'

'Oh, just the music?'

102

'Well, some of the rest of it was a bit O.T.T. if you want my opinion.'

'Did you not think he was asking for it, then?'

'Oh, now, I'm not saying he was right, of course I'm not. The guy was out of order, no question.'

'He was raping her, for God's sake,' says Margaret.

'Aye, but he backed off. I mean, she shot him after he'd backed off. A bit strong, surely.'

'Sounds fair enough to me,' says Joan. She's amazed at herself. She hasn't even seen the film.

'Joan, I'm disappointed in you,' says Maurice. 'I didn't think you were into women's lib. All these years we've worked together, Joan, and I never knew you were for burning your bra.'

'You're pathetic,' says Joan, 'if that's what you think women's lib is about. You're pathetic anyway.' She can't believe she said that. Neither can Maurice. He retreats, pink-faced, the coxcomb bouncing ludicrously. Margaret hoots derisively at his back. 'Imagine being married to it,' she says.

And Joan feels good. She suddenly feels alive. She feels sorry about telling Dan to stop moping about with Billie Holiday. She wants to speak to him, to tell him that they do know what love is, they've just let it get buried somewhere along the way. As soon as she gets a quiet moment she's going to phone him, just to see if he's home, just to let him know she's thinking about him. All this distance they've let come between them, a lot of it's her fault, she wants to try and break it down. Maybe they could move away, start again somewhere where no one knows them. Maybe it's not yet too late.

★   ★   ★

Twice, sometimes three times a week, Dan has the flat to himself for a couple of hours. And one Saturday morning in three. These times are good for listening to records, reading the paper, watching something on the telly that Joan doesn't like or approve of. And sometimes they're good for other things.

Sometimes Dan gets out his magazines. The best bit about the magazines is after you buy them but before you start to read them. Even before you get home, walking back with them under your jacket, it's like you've bought an entry into another life. At this point they can contain anything, anything you want them to. The perfect woman might be in there, the woman that's perfect for you. It's only once you read them that the disappointment sets back in. You're always disappointed. The other life never lives up to your expectations. This is the nature of the magazines, their purpose, to leave you dissatisfied and send you back, sooner or later, for more. Dan understands this, but it doesn't stop him doing it.

Lately some of the magazines have started advertising phone-lines. Lately Dan has started reaching for the phone. It's a new thrill, he knows it won't last for ever. But just for now he likes what he hears, the security of the women's voices, the repetition of familiar phrases. He likes the posh voices that say, you can suck my nipples, and the taunting voices that say, get down on your knees and beg for it, but most of all he likes the close, breathy voice that says, I'm glad you're here and we're all alone . . . It's pathetic really, he knows what a con it is. Maybe it's this, and not the loneliness in the woman's voice, that sometimes brings the tears after he has come.

All Dan wants is something else, for life to be something more than what it is. He is a nice man, a decent man. Really he is. But when he looks in the bathroom mirror, cleaning up, he does not much like what he sees.

Joan has a breathing space, a lull. No phones ringing, nobody returning their car. Outside, the air thickens. She dials the number. In the space before the connection is made, she wonders if he'll answer, if he got home before the snow. She hopes so. She hopes he is safe. She wants everything to be all right.

'What's it about? That's the only question in the world worth asking.'

'What do you mean, what's it all about?'

'Not *all*. Just what's it about. What's it all about's a different question and it's too big.'

'All right. What's it about. What do you mean anyway, ya picky bastard?'

'Well, like you're in a museum, or a gallery, say, looking at a painting, and you ask, what's it about? Or you read a book, or you go to the pictures, or you see something on the news, or a fight in the pub. Or a woman crying in the street. Anything. What's it about?'

'Probably it's not any of your business.'

'You can still ask it though. Into yourself like.'

'Then you wouldn't get an answer.'

'You might. You've only got to ask the question and find out. But all right, so maybe you don't get an answer. You still asked the question. You can come back to it another time. If it's important you *will* come back to it.'

'You might think you've got an answer but it's the wrong one.'

'It doesn't matter. You've still got an answer. I'm not saying it has to be right. You just have an explanation. Maybe the next time you come back to the gallery and go to that painting, you'll think, ah, *that's* what it's about. All right, so you were wrong before. It was still the only question worth asking. And anyway the answer can change. The answer is fluid. Only the question is a certainty.'

'I'll tell you what's a certainty. You talking a lot of bollocks, that's what.'

'Thanks, neighbour. You want me to roll another one of these?'

There was a time when Alan was ten, or maybe twelve. And this was what he was thinking, that that time was two-thirds of his life away. Right enough there was a time when he was five that was even worse – six-sevenths of his life away – but you don't remember the very early years at all, not at all. And yet they're the ones that make you. You're made in just a few years, and then the rest is unmaking. Did he really believe that? It was just that sometimes it seemed everything you did was a response to conditions. You didn't make yourself but were made by others, by what happened to you in childhood, and then as an adult it was as if you could only behave the way you'd been designed, buttons were pressed and levers pulled and all you could do was react. Parts of his childhood he remembered with amazing clarity, feelings and smells that immediately transported him back, and yet it was so distant, it was like somebody else's life. A previous existence. The clock was ticking and back then he had been impatient with its slowness but not any longer. Now it went with a speed that was terrifying and there was a simple reason: he wasn't young anymore.

But even then, at twelve years old, he was worrying about the big things. He used to lie awake at night, spinning in his bed, pondering the mysteries of the universe: he was in bed because it was night; it was night because the earth turned on its axis once every twenty-four hours, and during half of these hours the side of the earth with Scotland on it faced away from the sun; here it was dark, on the other side of the earth it was light. And the nights were long now because it was winter, and winter was because it took the earth three hundred and sixty-five and a quarter days to orbit the sun, and in the winter months Scotland was further away from the sun than in the summer, while in New Zealand – the *antipodes*, meaning 'diametrically opposite' although this wasn't really the case – it was summer at Christmas. The further north or south you went from the equator the colder it got because the poles were the points on earth where the angles of the sun's rays were at their weakest. Scotland had a cool climate because it wasn't far from the Arctic Circle, northern Scotland was in fact on the same latitude as bits of southern Alaska. All this was disturbing; it meant, if it was true, that the tiniest shift could completely alter or even destroy the climate. He watched an old film called *The Day the Earth Caught Fire*, in which a series of nuclear test explosions knocked the earth off its axis, and worried about it for weeks afterwards.

The earth orbited the sun because of gravity, and the sun was a huge mass of blazing gases suspended in space, and the moon exercised its influence on the earth also, pulling the waters on the surface of the earth to and fro, creating the tides. And the sun was a star, and at night when Scotland had its back to the sun you could see hundreds of other suns, each of which might have their own system of planets, and the stars you could see in the northern hemisphere were different from the ones you could see in the southern hemisphere, it was like looking out of the front and back windows of a house, and the light from the stars took so long to reach earth that they might no longer be where they had been, they might have burnt out or exploded thousands of years before. And there might be life there too.

There might be life. That was an incredible thought, at once both exciting and frightening. He read *The War of the Worlds* and *The Day of the Triffids* and was invigorated with fear. He couldn't help himself. Only a year or two earlier he'd been reading all the Narnia books and believing in them. He actually believed them and that if he could only find the way in, through a wardrobe or a picture on the wall or whatever, he could get there too, to Narnia. Dangerous books to give to an imaginative child! Aslan, that bloody lion. He'd prayed to a bloody lion, for heaven's sake! Luckily he didn't tell anyone, and within two years just the unspoken memory was embarrassing. But even after he outgrew the lion he still believed that there might be life somewhere else.

And space went on forever, that too was a truly amazing thing, it made your head hurt trying to imagine what it meant, the implications of it. Infinity. At school he and his friends tried to write down infinity: a 1 followed by a pageful of zeros. Or it went like this:

Alan Sangster
31 Wallace Road

Burnside
Wherrieston
Stirlingshire
Scotland
Great Britain
United Kingdom
Europe
Eurasia
The World
The Solar System
The Universe

and some, under this, laid an 8 on its side. Smart-alecks, Alan thought. Their sickly 8 was no measurement of creation at all. Creation was a glass box containing the deep blue of space and all the planets and the sun and the other stars, with God outside holding the glass box, and to think of infinity you had to smash the box and obliterate the white-bearded image of God in an effort to conceive of something that never ever came to an end. It was like living in the fifteenth century and believing the earth was flat, and sailing in a tiny wooden ship to find the roaring cataract that was the edge of the world and never finding it, *proving yourself wrong*, sailing ever onward while your confidence grew and your fear of a quickening current diminished, on and on until you began to doubt your new belief that the world must in fact be round, and then, as the awful truth of infinity grasped you, the fear came again, bigger, bigger than any human could cope with. Then you would believe in God again, because nothing else could explain it. Because, if the universe was constantly expanding, if there was no glass box holding it all together, where was it expanding to? If everything was flowing ever outwards, away, all matter disintegrating in a mad chaotic rush, how long before the earth and Scotland and he in his bed got caught up in the flood and then what? No, no, it was impossible to understand the enormity of it. His head would explode.

He wasn't young anymore. It didn't matter what the old folks said. His grandad and his uncles said he had his whole life ahead of him. If he was unhappy, well – he could always change his job, take up new interests. He was still young enough to start again. But how could you? Starting again was like unmaking, not possible. It was fine for them to talk, the old buggers, going on about their lives. They could justify themselves. Their lives had big things in them. There was a time when he used to scoff and yawn at them when they spoke about the past, especially about the wars, but not any longer. He'd never been in a war so he should just shut up and listen. What was more, he never would be in a war. He was too old for it. He didn't want to be in one, of course, but there was no denying it was something to have lived through – if you did live, that is. It would shape you. Supposing instead of when he was at the university he'd been fighting somewhere. His whole outlook on life would be bound to be different – wouldn't it? He could understand about people not forgetting, he could even understand about them not forgiving. It made his blood freeze over seeing those films of the death camps: what if he'd seen them with his own eyes, smelt them? His grandad had fought in the first war, the one that was supposed to end them all, and he didn't have a good word for the Germans still. You couldn't blame him. And Uncle Jimmy had been a POW in a Japanese camp. He never spoke about it but you knew it was there in him. Maybe his grandad would have got over it but then the second war came along and confirmed all his views on the Germans. Once the name P.G. Wodehouse cropped up – they were doing some of his stories on the telly. That bloody traitor, said his grandad. He had nothing more to add on the subject. He used to like Wodehouse's books but he'd never read one since those Berlin broadcasts. It was like – what? – Alan saying he wasn't going to read Jeffrey Archer because he was a Tory. Well, it was true, he never was going to read Jeffrey Archer though more because he was a wanker than because he was a Tory but there was no comparison really. You had grudges but in these times they tended just to fade away. You didn't nurse them. But his uncle now, being in one of those camps, that wouldn't fade away, it would always be with you, you'd carry something like that around inside you your whole life. Like if you were an American who fought in Vietnam. Or a Vietnamese who fought in Vietnam – funny how they always got forgotten, poor bastards, it was their country, they'd had it a lot bloody tougher than the Yanks. Or if you were sexually abused. Raped. How would you ever get over something like that? You wouldn't. You'd just carry it. It would be part of you, for good or ill.

He made it through school and then he was no longer a child. But neither was he the person he would become, he knew that in retrospect. The mysteries of the universe still interested him. Sometimes he would discuss them with the friends he had in those days. They were all students. There were one or two among them for whom there was no mystery: the same ones that at school had wrapped it all up with a symbol. For them, everything was explicable in terms of relativity, everything was physics and chemistry, maths and matter. Alan had lost touch with these guys – they always were guys – through a lack of mutual interest. It wasn't that he didn't like them at the time, he simply didn't believe them. They were only twenty or so, like the rest, they were just starting out too, and he didn't believe that they knew all the answers. Still, he enjoyed their company, listening to them dismissing God and telling everybody else how simple the universe really was, especially – and this was usually how these conversations got started – if there was a joint or two going round. If you had a head full of hashish then it almost seemed as though you could make sense of it all. And, yes, there might even be another universe on your very own thumbnail.

Gradually he came down to earth. Specifically, he grew more and more concerned with life on earth, those closer-to-home mysteries. He loved the idea of animals and birds and fishes and plants. They were real things but it was the idea of them he loved, the idea that they existed as much as the existence itself. He loved trees and walking among them, touching their bark and trying to reach around their trunks, or just imagining doing so. Because you didn't want people to see you at it. The minds of most people weren't open to the idea of things, only to the things themselves. If they saw you hugging a tree or even just thought you were contemplating doing it they'd have you marked down as a hippy or a loony and that wasn't it. He was profoundly ignorant about nature, but he loved the idea of the hare changing its coat in winter, of the snake shedding its skin, of the salmon's return to the place of its own spawning. He loved the turning of the seasons, of hidden crocus bulbs pushing their flowers up to mark the start of spring, of an entire wood shedding its leaves in autumn, of whole lochs and burns freezing over. When he bought his flat with the small, shared garden he put up a bird-table so that he could watch the blue-tits and sparrows squabbling over the food. One early evening in winter he saw a fox cross the garden, beautiful and glowing in the snow, and in the morning he found that the snow had melted and then frozen again where its paws had left their tracks. It was as if it had walked across Alan's memory, leaving its presence there indelibly. He felt privileged.

He led a quiet life. After university they all went their own ways and his was solitary. He had been a quiet one from the start really. There were worlds going on in his head and that seemed enough. Ten years on, the only fellow student he was still friendly with was Mike, and although Mike had discussed space with the others, he wasn't like them at all. He wasn't one of the know-alls, he was better than that, he was a know-nothing. He believed that the fact of his being alive was utterly insignificant when measured against what he understood of time and space and energy, and that therefore he should adopt a suitably humble attitude to his environment. This caused him to drop out of his engineering course in the third year. He decided there were enough machines around already, and engineers like himself should show some respect for the planet in their profession. It was better to repair than to create, he said. Ever since dropping out that was what he did, repaired things for people – cars, washing machines, lawnmowers, power-tools. He took cash in hand and did enough work to satisfy his needs, which were few: home-brewed beer and an assortment of other more or less harmless drugs, some books, a guitar, jeans, a motorbike. He got semi-seriously into New Age philosophy and he told Alan he was settled for life. His motorbike was only a Honda 125 and when he rode it he wore an old denim jacket because he couldn't afford the leathers but he said he was happy. Alan was envious, although he was earning a lot more than Mike's uncertain income. They used to talk about these things over many beers in the pub or – more often – out at Mike's. They were still serious about the universe but they were getting down to particulars. 'Life's a doughnut,' Mike said one time (he was halfway through a joint admittedly): 'you,' he said, 'are living in the middle of the doughnut because you think that's where the jam is, whereas I am living on the edge.' 'Where the sugar is,' said Alan. 'Where I *know* the sugar is,' said Mike.

One Saturday in April Alan went to the edge, to visit Mike. He hadn't planned to. He drove his compact and efficient second-hand Vauxhall Nova away from the shopping centre, through the town, over the railway tracks and out past the industrial estate (where he worked through the week as a product control manager in a packaging factory), and turned into the straggling scheme where Mike lived with his dad. Theirs was the last house on the scheme, hard up against a dull red wooden fence on the other side of which was a muddy field. There was a big sign up in the field and a bulldozer had been at work there. This is not uncommon, Alan thought. This is what happens. You go to the edge and when you get there you find that Miller Homes are putting up sixteen houses to the acre just beyond it.

He'd phoned up half an hour earlier from a call-box in the shopping centre. His lip was swollen and his jaw was starting to ache.

'Can I come and see you, Mike?'

'Aye, just come out. What are you phoning for? You should just have come anyway.'

'Oh, I wanted to make sure you were in.'

'I'm always in, amn't I? My dad's away to the game. I'll get the kettle on. Mona's here by the way.'

'Oh.'

'That's all right, isn't it?'

'Aye, great. Thing is, Mike, I'm in a bit of a state. I've just been in a fight.'

'Fuck's sake. It's three o'clock in the afternoon. What happened?'

He'd gone into town, just for something to do. The pavements were thick with shoppers, even though it was sunny and dry and you'd think anyone with an ounce of sense would be getting out in the open. He didn't know why he was there himself. He saw the crowds of women and their men, and the bored wee kids, and the roving gangs of bored big kids, and he understood that most of them probably didn't know why they were there either. A nation of shoppers. He wandered around looking at CDs and books and sound-systems, at clothes and labour-saving devices for the home, and even at sporting equipment. What on earth was he expecting to find in it all, some kind of revelation about himself? Maybe if he had a wife, or a girlfriend. But that wasn't it. There was something about everything that alienated him. His work, well, that was fair enough, everybody felt alienated from their work, the nature of the system did that. But he seemed to be cut off from everything society had to offer, and from most of the people as well. He tried asking himself Mike's question – what's it about, what's it about? – but it wasn't working, he was getting no reply. He suspected that this was because he couldn't help slipping an 'all' between the 'it' and the 'about', even though Mike had told him not to. The only things that appealed to him were wild things – animals, nature, the stars – but he couldn't touch them, he couldn't make them a part of himself, or himself a part of them. It wasn't human to do that. Or was it? He hadn't a clue. He hadn't a clue about anything. He was even alienated from his flat, for God's sake. His new flat that was supposed to be home – he didn't want to be in it.

He found himself on a narrow street behind the centre, lingering outside a door through which he could see a long, low-ceilinged room stretching back, all ablaze with lights and loud with bells and buzzers. A sign above the entrance announced 'AMUSEMENTS'. It was years since he'd been in one of these places. He'd played a bit of pinball in the student union, but hardly ever since then. He stepped inside.

It was important not to be caught watching the people at the bandits and other games. Although there were quite a few folk scattered through the rows of machines there was no sense of a crowd, only of individuals grimly entertaining themselves. People became very defensive in here. They wanted to be left alone. They grew protective of the fruit machine they were playing. If they saw you watching them at *their* machine they feared you were waiting till they ran out of cash so that you could move in and clean up with a single coin. They suspected you of an intimate knowledge of their favourite machine and it made them jealous. People snarled and snapped at each other. Sometimes there was a scuffle.

He went to the booth where a fat, balding man changed his five-pound note for coins. He wasn't interested in gambling, he wanted to play pinball, try out his skills, see if he could still rack up a few replays. But the pinball machines were different from when he had last played. They were all electronic, with impossible targets and too much fancy gadgetry. He tried a couple but it seemed the machines controlled your play rather than the other way round. He scored ridiculously low scores.

He wandered down the aisles, dismissing the monster-zapping and the motor-racing and the missile-launching as childish and humiliating. He caught sight of himself in a mirror on a pillar and realised how awkward he looked. Anyone who thought being in this place was humiliating didn't have the right attitude to it, and should just leave. But he didn't. He was looking for something to relate to.

Then, towards the very back of the arcade, he saw a doorway leading to a smaller room. It was quiet and completely empty, and the reason was obvious: it contained six aged pinball machines, the old mechanical kind. They were beautiful, if a bit battered, real pieces of art, but boring compared with the technology out the front. They were exactly what he was wanting. He could deal with them.

He checked each one in turn, familiarising himself with the points systems, the targets, the bonuses, how to trigger replays. He noted the images and the names: 'JOKER POKER', 'GUNSLINGER', 'STARSHOOTER', 'MATA HARI', 'BILLION DOLLAR BASH', 'BABE RUTH'. He settled for 'JOKER POKER' because he recognised it from his student days. He knew he could beat it.

He played two or three games without success, but at first this didn't matter. He was just getting back into it. The same movements, the same holding and releasing of the flippers, the same thrill of shooting a ball back up an alley it had just descended. But no two machines are identical, he should have remembered that, not even when they're the same game. This one was very sensitive. It reacted to the slightest nudge or knock. In the old days he'd been able to move the whole machine without getting a tilt, but not this one. Even if he hit the flipper a little too hard the lights went down and he lost the score for that ball. It began to irritate him.

He moved on to 'GUNSLINGER' to see if that was any better. It was more complicated, though, and he would have to spend a lot of time on it to get a half-decent score. It was 'JOKER POKER' he wanted to master again, but the machine wouldn't let him. The bastards who ran the place had set it wrong. He'd just be holding the ball with the left flipper, and letting it run with a wee jump over to the right flipper, and the machine would go fucking dead on him. He looked under it to make sure it was fully plugged in. It was. He simply wasn't being allowed to play it properly.

He'd paid good money and he wasn't being allowed to play. It was fucking crap. The third ball died on him only 200 points short of a replay and he swore at the machine and gave it a good kicking, stubbing his toe in the process.

A big guy in a T-shirt that said 'AMUSEMENTS' walked through the door from the front and came up to him.

'Who d'you think you are, Roger fucking Daltrey?'

'It's set wrong,' said Alan.

'It's set fine,' said the guy. 'You're supposed to play it with your hands, not your boots.'

'Don't fucking get on at me,' said Alan. 'You just have to touch the machine and it tilts, you should get it fucking sorted.'

'I'll fucking sort you if you don't get the fuck out of here,' said the guy.

'It's your fucking machines, man, they're all fucked,' Alan shouted.

The guy belted him in the mouth. Before he could hit back Alan found himself being bundled out past the fancy machines in the front, another guy coming to help and sticking a couple of punches on his kidneys to prevent any retaliation. Through the mist Alan saw a man half-turning to watch him go, but the rest kept their eyes trained on the screens and dials in front of them. In a moment he was lying on the pavement, gasping for breath and tasting the blood in his mouth.

The guy in the 'AMUSEMENTS' T-shirt stared down at him. 'If you've got a problem, pal,' he said, 'don't bring it in here, okay?'

'Just come over,' said Mike. 'Mona's a nurse, remember? She has to deal with the likes of you every weekend in casualty.' He laughed. 'Well, every weekend she's on. The one weekend she's not you turn up to keep her hand in.'

Mike was out in the garage when he arrived, working on an enormous engine that looked as though it could have come out of the builders' bulldozer over the fence. Alan had a swollen mouth, aching back and sore foot, and as he brought the car to a halt he wondered about himself again. What was he doing, disturbing Mike on a Saturday afternoon just because he'd got a beating he'd asked for? All over the country the other young men were well occupied: Mike was sorting something broken and he probably wasn't the exception Alan thought he was; others were at the football (including Mike's dad, and he wasn't even a young man), watching it or playing it, or waiting for the results to come up on the television; others were climbing mountains, painting houses, washing cars, building boats, looking after the kids, fishing, walking the dog, shopping even. Not Alan. He was keeping Mike from his work and looking for something. Company, answers, a laugh, a plan for the night. He was bored and lonely. He was looking for answers.

Mona was Mike's sister. She didn't live at home anymore, she was just back from Glasgow for the weekend. She cleaned up his face while Mike made the tea. How useful they all were, these people. Here was Mike making things work so they wouldn't be thrown away, and his sister making people work so they wouldn't be thrown away, and their dad used to be a miner till British Coal threw away the pit, and their mum had been a gem, producing and nurturing this really useful family (until she died because she wouldn't stop smoking) – and then there was Alan! Not for the first time he felt inadequate. And it wasn't just the incident in the amusements place. That was nothing. It was everything else – his job, his house, his life, everything. Packaging was a *bad* scene. It was not environmentally a friendly way to behave, not with the packaging his company produced – full of CFCs and other time-bombs. I am not a useful person at this moment, he thought. I am out of kilter with the scheme of things.

Mike went back out to the garage after he'd heard about the fight – he had a good laugh about it – but Alan stayed for another cup with Mona. They'd met once before at somebody's wedding and she'd seemed all right but she was with some guy with sculptured features who didn't like her talking to other guys so they'd not had a chance to speak.

'What are you doing getting into fights?' she said. 'You don't seem like – I mean, from what Mike's told me about you – you don't sound like that at all.'

'I'm not,' he said. 'I don't know what got into me. I think I'm having some kind of crisis.'

'What, about pinball?' she said.

'Aye, I'm hooked on it,' he said. 'I'm selling the furniture in the search for that elusive triple replay.'

'So what's it about?'

'Christ, you sound just like your brother,' he said. But she kept staring at him, expecting an answer.

'I don't know. I suppose I'm getting to that stage of wondering what I'm doing. I mean, I'm comfortably off, my job's pretty secure, but it doesn't seem good enough. I know, I know, that sounds like I've reached my thirties and can afford the luxury of gazing at my navel, but that's how I feel. The trouble is, it's not really anything new. I've been like this all my life. I'm the world's worst worrier, but not about wee things – about muckle great big things. Sometimes I wonder if I'm the next Messiah but somebody's forgotten to tell me. It's a cliché but there's got to be more to life than this.'

'A relationship, maybe?' she said.

He shrugged. 'I suppose it might take my mind off it.' Then he asked her, 'You still seeing that guy?' It might have been a leading question but it wasn't.

'Which guy?' she asked. Then she laughed. She knew fine. 'No, he chucked me. I'm giving it a rest just now. It's hellish trying to have a serious relationship when you do the shifts I do.'

'Well, have a non-serious one,' he said. So maybe it had been a leading question after all. 'With me.'

She laughed again. 'For a guy with a burst lip you're not backward in being forward anyway.'

'Aye, well,' he said, 'don't mind me. But honestly, what do you think? I mean, what do you think it's about?'

'Your crisis, or life in general?' she asked. 'Or can we apply the same question to both?'

'Aye, definitely,' he said. 'I think I'm having a crisis because I feel I should know by now what it's about. I mean, what are we here for, if not to know why? Or to wonder why? If we don't even wonder, what's the point of anything?'

'Oh, dear,' she said. 'What did you study at uni?'

'Business studies and management,' he said. 'Probably a mistake.'

'Probably just as well. Imagine what you'd be like if you'd done metaphysics and moral philosophy.' Mona reached behind where she was sitting on the floor, leaning against the sofa, and pulled a carrier bag towards her. She said, 'I know just the thing for you. I was reading about it earlier. Pelmanism.'

'Eh?'

She pulled out a handful of paperbacks from the bag. 'I collect these,' she said. 'The old green-covered crime books. Penguins mostly, but also the Collins Crime Club ones, Crime Book Society – look.' He flicked through them. 6d or 1/6 a time, they were mostly from the thirties and forties. Some of the earlier ones had the dust-jackets still on them. 'Do you read them all?' he asked.

'Oh, aye,' she said, 'I like a good thriller. But it's the editions really – they seem to be so much of a period. I don't go beyond 1960 – well, you have to draw the line somewhere. Everybody seemed to do them in green until about then. And after that the jacket designs aren't uniform. I've picked up hundreds for virtually nothing. I just got these today – there's a second-hand bookshop up Spittal Street.'

'I know where you are,' he said. He looked again at the books. Rex Stout, Seldon Truss, Hulbert Footner, Erle Stanley Gardner, John Dickson Carr. 'Great names,' he said.

'Anyway,' she said, 'the books are irrelevant to what I was going to say.' She picked up *The Broken Vase* by Rex Stout and turned to the inside front cover. '"The Grasshopper Mind",' she read.

'What's that?'

'"You know the man with a 'Grasshopper Mind' as well as you know yourself. His mind nibbles at everything and masters nothing."' She broke off. 'This is an advert, not the plot. Isn't it great? Do you recognise yourself? I tell you,

I'm convinced and I've not even got to the bit where you send off for further details.

'"At home in the evening he tunes in the wireless – tires of it – then glances through a magazine – can't get interested. Finally, unable to concentrate on anything, he either goes to the pictures or falls asleep in his chair. At his work he always takes up the easiest job first, puts it down when it gets hard, and starts something else. Jumps from one thing to another all the time.

'"There are thousands of these people with 'Grasshopper Minds' in the world. In fact they are the very people who do the world's most tiresome tasks – and get but a pittance for their work. They do the world's clerical work, and the routine drudgery. Day after day, year after year – endlessly – they hang on to the jobs that are smallest-salaried, longest-houred, least interesting, and poorest-futured!"'

'Now you're talking,' he said.

'Me more than you,' she said. 'I'm a nurse, remember?'

He put his hand to his jaw. 'How could I forget?'

'"What Is Holding You Back?"' she said. '"If you have a 'Grasshopper Mind' you know that this is true. And you know why it is true. Even the blazing sun can't burn a hole in a piece of tissue paper unless its rays are focused and concentrated on one spot! A mind that balks at sticking to one thing for more than a few minutes surely cannot be depended on to get you anywhere in your years of life!"'

'This is depressing,' he said.

'It's all right,' she said, 'it gets better. "The tragedy of it all is this: you know that you have within you the intelligence, the earnestness, and the ability that can take you right to the high place you want to reach in life! What is wrong?

What is holding you back? Just one fact – one scientific fact! That is all. Because, as Science says" – that's Science with a capital 'S' by the way – "you are using only one-tenth of your real brain-power!"'

'If that, this afternoon at any rate,' he said.

'"What Can You Do About It?"' she demanded. 'You're not going to believe this.'

'What?'

'"Take up Pelmanism now!"'

'The card game?'

'No,' she said, 'though I think this must be where the name came from. Something called the Pelman Institute, Norfolk Mansions, Wigmore Steet, London. Established over fifty years, callers welcome. "A course of Pelmanism brings out the mind's latent powers and develops them to the highest point of efficiency. It banishes Mind Wandering, Inferiority, and Indecision, and in their place develops Optimism, Concentration, and Reliability, all qualities of the utmost value in any walk of life."' She closed the book. 'Alan, this is for you. God, that was as good as a novel itself.'

'It's uncanny,' he said. 'You hardly know me, nurse, and yet you've described me to the very roots of my being. Are you some kind of witch?'

'That's what my dad thinks. He thinks Mike and me are both witches because we're into things like aromatherapy and yoga and meditation.'

'What about astrology?' Alan asked. 'Or tarot?'

'Naw,' she said, 'that's all shite. I'm a practical down-to-earth kind of witch.'

'Well, that's reassuring,' he said. He picked up the book

and looked at the ad. He turned to the inside back cover. 'Hmm, I think I prefer the other solution to life's problems: "Chocolate, chocolate, chocolate, chocolate, chocolate – I WANT CADBURY'S!"'

'That's just a temporary fix,' she said. 'I think we should try this Pelmanism thing out.'

'Och,' he said, 'even if they're still going they'll not still be at that address.'

'I don't mean that,' she said. 'I think we should have a *game* of Pelmanism. Sharpen your senses up a bit.'

'All right.' She had a very persuasive manner. He was forgetting she was Mike's sister and thinking of her more as a nurse skilled in the ways of the black arts, which was an appealing combination.

Mona stood up and fetched a pack of playing cards from a drawer. She shuffled them, then laid them out on the floor face down in eight rows of six and one row of four.

'I haven't done this for years,' she said. 'Do you know how to play?'

'Aye, it's just memory, isn't it? Collecting the cards in pairs?'

'Well, you start then,' she said. 'Your need's greater than mine.'

'I don't really see how this is going to help,' he said. But he picked up a card from the top row, then one from the bottom. The ten of diamonds and the ten of spades.

'Wow!' he said. 'Do they have to be the same colour?'

'No, not this time,' she said. 'Any pair will do.'

He wasn't so lucky with his second shot. Mona had her turn without success. That meant there were four cards to remember. They both began to concentrate.

The door opened and a grey-haired man in a camouflage jacket came in.

'Hello, Alan. Been in a fight, Mike's telling me.'

'Hello, Mr Aitken. Aye, nothing serious but. How was the football?'

'Ach, terrible! Two-nothing. That's them back down to the Second Division next season. I don't know why I bother going.'

'Because you enjoy it,' said Mona.

'Must be a masochist then,' said Mr Aitken. 'Anyway, looks like I'm interrupting. Anyone wanting a cup of tea?'

'No, thanks,' said Alan. 'I've tea coming out my lugs.'

'Right you are. Mona?'

'Not for me. Right, Alan. On you go.'

'Wait a minute,' he said. 'Can we start this again?'

'How?'

'Well, we ought to be doing it right. Matching the colours, I mean – hearts with diamonds, spades with clubs.'

'If you want,' she said. 'You feeling lucky?'

'I'm feeling something,' he said. It was true. Something was building up in him. Maybe it was the house – Mike and Mona and their dad – it felt very good. He thought of his work, and how he had to get out of it. His heartbeat quickened.

Mona swept up the cards, shuffled them again, and laid them out.

'Right,' she said. 'Strictly by colour.'

Mr Aitken came back in with a cup of tea and sat down in an armchair. 'Is it going to bother you if I put the results on?'

'Course not,' said Mona. 'Alan's staying for his tea, if that's okay.' She smiled across at him.

'Fine,' said Mr Aitken. 'What are you two up to anyway?'

'We're sorting out the universe,' Alan explained.

'We're sorting out Alan,' said Mona.

'You want to watch her,' said Mr Aitken. 'She's a witch.'

The results were being read out on the television. The volume was down low, and there was something very soothing about the rise and fall of the familiar voice, down for a home win, slightly up for an away win, level but up for a no-score draw, up on both sides for a score-draw. Alan felt himself slipping into it, even though he wasn't taking in the actual information. He began to turn up cards to the rhythm of the voice.

After about half a minute he heard Mona say quietly, 'Dad, take a look at this.'

He was turning them up now, one after the other, his hand moving across the spread of cards smoothly and easily. It was as if his hand knew which card to go for. His mind watched his hand doing it with amazement, then with growing confidence. Suddenly he knew he was going to do the whole lot in a oner.

He was aware that Mr Aitken had turned in his chair and was watching what was happening. Mona was resting back on her heels, one hand held to her mouth as if she was frightened to breathe. All that was needed was for Mike to come in and see it. But he couldn't stop now, he couldn't wait for Mike. There were the three of them in the room, all concentrating on the cards on the carpet, all watching his hand glide across them, turning up the two red queens, the two black fours, the two black aces, putting them to one side, going back for the next pair, on and on without hesitation, so that soon there were only a dozen cards left. And he knew it was going to be all right, that nothing could stop him now, that he would go on turning up the pairs and never make a mistake, not one, until he could pause, with only one pair left face downward on the floor, and look at them both, Mona and her dad, and they could all breathe again, knowing that the last two had to match, they had to, and nothing could possibly come between him and their matching, no matter how long he waited.

Republic of the Mind

He was beyond the politicians. Way beyond them. If they couldn't get their act together when it was so obvious, he wasn't wasting his time waiting for them. He was off already – gone. To the republic of the mind. That's where he was.

It wasn't Robert, however, but Kate who threw the bottle through the TV set on election night. The Stirling result was what did it.

'I don't believe it!' she screamed. 'If they can't get it right *there*!' The opinion polls had been like huge signposts pointing at the one opposition candidate who could capture the seat, but the good folk of Stirling appeared not to have taken the hint. Kate launched the empty Frascati bottle at the smiling face of the Government Minister, and his expression – happy or smug, depending on one's political viewpoint – exploded from the tip of the nose outwards into nothing. Everybody else in the room stared in awe at the dead screen. It was the kind of thing they'd always wanted to do – to politicians, princes, weather forecasters, game show hosts, footballers, sitcom characters – but their anger had never quite overcome their reluctance to pay the price.

There were seven or eight of them, and they had come to celebrate. It was understood that, even should the Tories get back in overall, they would be annihilated in Scotland. This would force a constitutional crisis. But only a few hours had passed since the polls had closed and already Scotland was snatching ifs and buts from the jaws of certainty. Kate's act of frustration at least put an end to the agony of watching any more results. After another couple of drinks the TV began to look good – much better than it ever had done – and even the next day, clearing up the cans and plates and the powdered glass of the screen from the carpet, neither Robert nor Kate wanted to disturb the bottle. It was a monument to the moment when they left the politicians behind; a regrettable but glorious moment to be forever relived. Every time they looked at the neck of the bottle sticking out of the hole they were reminded of the Minister's exploding face.

Kate was reading a passage in a history book about the execution of Mary Stewart. She had learned to think of her by that name, it made her more human somehow. Kate wasn't into royalty:

Then her dressing of lawn falling off from her head, it appeared as grey as one of three score and ten years old, polled very short, her face in a moment by so much altered from the form she had when she was alive, as few could remember her by her dead face. Her lips stirred up and down for a quarter of an hour after her head was cut off.

Then Mr Dean said with a loud voice, 'So perish all the Queen's enemies . . .'

It was a different world, of course it was. It was four centuries ago and these people were the most important people in the land. And yet that was all they were, just people. The game they played – treaties, alliances, invasions, marriages, plots, executions – was a game of chess with human beings for the pieces. Queens, castles, clerics and knights, and, somewhere else, in a separate world again, cities full of pawns, a countryside dotted with pawn peasants.

For some days after the election Kate went around the flat muttering, 'Hopeless, hopeless. Guns and bombs, guns and bombs, that's all there is to it.' But she'd already had her act of violence. And Robert, too, simply shook his head and headed off to the republic of the mind. The politicians could follow when they were ready. Robert was there, and Kate a lot of the time, and also many of their friends, although they didn't always know it.

Sometimes, before she got there herself, Kate would realise he was in the room but absent from it. If the telly hadn't had a bottle in its face they would have been watching the news, or some other useless programme. As it was, they'd be sitting – reading, maybe – and his book would fall aside onto the arm of the chair. Then she'd see the change in his face.

'Is that you away again?'

'Aye.' His voice sounded distant.

'Where is it you go to?'

'Och, just away. I just think what a waste of time it is, having to wait to be a normal country, having to waste all this energy identifying ourselves. So I bugger off anyway. To the Scottish republic of the mind.'

She thought about that. It sounded not a bad idea at all.

'Oh, aye, what's it like there? Is it any better than the Scottish province of the body?' So Robert could tell she was probably almost there herself, coming out with a remark like that.

'Brilliant,' he said. 'It's brilliant.'

It might have been a drug, it might have been something you scored in pub toilets, but it wasn't. It was better than that, and it didn't fuck you up either. It didn't make your nose cave in or give you monsters in the shadows or even just a rotten head; in fact it was an antidote to the post-election hangover. One day everybody was going to be there. The last folk off the last bus would be the political parties claiming they'd just wanted to make sure nobody got left behind.

It was more than some utopian fantasy about society. It filled the gap between actuality and possibilities of all kinds. Somebody once said that the art of life lay in recognising the luminous moment. Robert wasn't certain about what that meant, what that moment might be, but he had some ideas. The novelist Neil Gunn had this concept – the atom of delight – a state of contentment and completeness – '*I came upon myself sitting there.*' The republic was something like that, except it was constant, and for everybody. It was a state of being in which all the people understood themselves, and what they were doing, and why they were where they were. The more often you got there, the longer you stayed. And this was the secret of it – it didn't depend on the politicians at all. It didn't need constitutions and laws, but simple self-determination. It was as if every individual made their own Declaration of Arbroath. It was like going up to the mountain, and coming down whole.

Robert could remember with startling clarity the first real moment between him and Kate. This was a different kind, though, a moment shared between two people only. They'd known each other for months but up till then nothing had happened between them. Afterwards they discovered that they had each thought they were unnoticed by the other. They were in a crowd in some bar, surrounded by friends, and finding themselves pushed closer and somehow isolated from everybody else, they both became suddenly aware of their togetherness. It was as if all the people in the bar withdrew some distance, leaving them in a space of their own, although the fact was that the elbows and arms still jostled and squeezed around them. They kissed. Everybody might have been watching but they wouldn't have seen that kiss. It was beyond the din and heat of the bar. The kiss was loaded with possibilities. It was what had carried them forward to where they were now, two years later. They were still unwrapping the possibilities it had contained.

That was just one moment. It meant everything, Robert was certain – it and other moments that stood out of daily life like islands in a loch. How, if they meant less than everything, did they return over and over to him? He knew that in ten or twenty or thirty years they would still be as clear and miraculous as they were now, as they had been when they first took place. He gathered them like the jewels of life.

He understood that he had a religious frame of mind. He was not church-going, he was past that, although he didn't mock it as he once had. He was in his thirties and sometimes he thought he would like to go to church again, but it wasn't for him. On the odd occasions when he did enter a church – at weddings, at funerals – he sat upright and watched, and knew he wasn't a part of it. From his place in the pew he confronted the pulpit, the communion table. He was not being irreverent. It was a throwback, maybe, to his upbringing, to the Presbyterian in him, to a grim determination to meet God halfway, open-eyed, on equal terms.

And yet he was religious. Or, rather, he understood what religion was. He understood that its purpose was to explain. He knew he was a speck of dust, almost nothing, and yet he saw himself in relation to everything. He could be himself and yet be outwith himself. Christ was man and God. That was him too – dust and life, nothing and everything. There was something in that universal relationship that made him sick with excitement. He could see how a man like the ecologist John Muir could take the best from his father's harsh, rigid creed and turn it into a celebration of existence, a hymn of joy. He believed that Muir must have had these moments too. In fact, a man who would climb a tree in a storm, to see what it was like to be a tree in a storm, probably had them all the time.

Kate met him at the door of the flat one Tuesday evening. 'Your mum phoned,' she said. He knew at once that it was his father, that his father was dead. Kate hugged him. 'I'm sorry,' she said. 'It was this afternoon. Your mum's just back from the hospital.'

They'd been waiting for the phone call for days. They'd been waiting for the days of waiting for months. Only two weeks ago they'd seen him, apparently recovering, but Robert knew, from what his dad had said before, that death wasn't far away. Just around the time of the election he'd been found to have cancer. He'd gone out to vote with a vengeance – 'One last push for independence!' he joked, knowing that that wasn't going to happen but sure, like them, that something must give in Scotland. He didn't have the pleasure of seeing that, Robert thought. He went in and out of hospital, had days of slipping down and days of holding fast, then decided not to fight it any longer, that he wanted only to have some peace and to be free of pain. That was what he had told Robert. 'It's time to go,' he said. 'Your mother doesn't think so because I'm only sixty-six, but it is.' And now he was gone.

'Are you okay?' Kate asked him. She let go and stepped back. He nodded. 'Aye, I'm fine. How's my mum?'

'She's all right, I think.' He had sisters. They were with her. He picked up the phone and dialled, and spoke to them each in turn. The funeral was to be on the Friday. Robert would drive up there in the morning.

'Look,' he said to Kate, 'I'm all right, but would you mind holding the fort? Folk'll be phoning and I don't think I can handle it. I want to go out for a bit.'

'Fine,' she said. 'Will you come back, or will I meet you?'

He thought of a quiet bar a couple of streets away. 'Let's meet at the Ruthven. Say, in a couple of hours?'

He'd intended to go for a walk before having a drink – it was May, and the days were long and dry – but his way took him past the Ruthven anyway and he thought, to hell with it, I'll have several drinks. On my own. A wake without the body.

He'd cut back on the beer of late because he was getting a bit of a belly, but he wanted a long drink. A long drink and a short – a half and a half. He was thirty-one ordering an old man's tipple. He heard John Lee Hooker's raucous voice somewhere in his head belting out, 'One Bourbon, one Scotch, one beer.' There were occasions, it seemed, when drinking was the best possible thing you could be doing.

There was an older man sitting next to him at the bar, a folded newspaper in front of him. They were both away with their thoughts. This was good: there was no necessity for small talk. But after about twenty minutes, when he was into the next set of drinks, the man said, 'I'll just say one thing, friend, and then I'll not bother you. Just one thing. See this privatising the water, it makes me boak. It makes me want to join the tartan army or something.'

Robert gave him a grin. 'I know,' he said. 'They'd privatise the air if they could bottle it.'

'That's all I wanted to say,' said the man. 'I'll not bother you anymore.'

'It's all right,' said Robert. 'I don't mind if you want to talk.' It was true. He'd come in thinking he was going to do some thinking, but that wasn't how thinking happened. Not about your father who was dead. You had to come upon it, or it came upon you, more subtly than that.

The man was probably in his fifties. His jacket had seen better days. So had his trainers. His hair was thin and straggly and his face thin and tired-looking. But he had very bright blue eyes. They were what people would remember about him.

'The trouble is,' he said, 'we're powerless because there's too many issues. If water was the only thing on the agenda

138

they wouldn't have a chance. Or if it was just about having our own parliament – if that was the only issue we'd have it by now. But it's not, we keep having to try to get Labour in down there as well, to, like, minimise the damage. Ken what I mean?'

'Aye,' said Robert. He was thinking how nobody ever assumed their neighbour was a Tory in a public house in Scotland. 'But self-government is the one unifying issue. If we had the parliament we could deal with all the other issues the way we wanted.'

'Maybe, maybe,' said the other guy. 'But it's hard, isn't it? I keep thinking I'm going to stop doing it, vote Labour I mean, but then the next election comes along and there's all these other things you want to vote on. Don't get me wrong, I'm all for it – a Scottish parliament – but you can't isolate it like that. Sorry. 'Scuse me if you're SNP or anything.'

'You've put it in a nutshell,' said Robert. 'And you're right. But self-government's the key, it's getting there that's the problem. I'm a tactician myself. I vote for whichever party's got the best chance of beating the Tory. Sooner or later we'll get what we want by default.'

'So you'd not call yourself a nationalist?'

'My dad's a nationalist. That's as close as I get. He's on the thinking wing of the party, though, always has been. Understands what folk like yourself are saying. Me, I'm on the thinking wing of the people.'

'Aye, right enough, most folk don't think much about it at all. And why should they? Seeing the politicians making such an arse of it.'

'You're a man after my own heart,' said Robert. To prove it, he bought the guy a drink. He was aware that his dad

139

had come into the conversation. He should tell the guy he was dead. It didn't matter, but he should. He would, later.

'To be honest,' he said, 'after the last disaster, I've kind of given up on the political parties. I've kind of just gone ahead, myself and a few others. As far as possible I live life as if the republic's here already.'

'That can't be very far,' said the guy. 'Or very possible. Bit of a pipedream that, I would say.'

'Well, it is of course, but I don't see what else to do. I mean, if your mind's already arrived there, if you're psychologically and emotionally and culturally in that other place, it's just tearing yourself apart getting frustrated about the fact that the actuality is different. So, I know what you're saying, but it seems to me, if the attitude is there, the rest will follow.'

The guy nodded. 'I understand. But there's folk out there with fungus on the walls and no job and their benefit getting cut and fuck knows what else – I don't think your wee nirvana's going to help them much.'

'Neither are the politicians. Politics has failed these people. Completely passed them by. They can forget about politics because the political system as presently constituted has forgotten about them. And maybe I am indulging in a bit of fantasy, but we can't all be Tommy Sheridan.'

'He's as bad as the rest of them,' said the guy.

'I'd have voted for him if I stayed in Pollok,' said Robert. 'At least he shakes the complacent bastards up a bit.'

The guy bought them another round. Robert could understand why the auld fellows bought halves and halves. It got you fucking steaming. No doubt he would pay for it the morrow though.

'Well, I'll tell you,' said the guy, 'this water thing, this is the last straw. They may not call it privatisation, but they'll try to sell it somehow, through the back door. I mean, how can you own it, for God's sake? It falls out the fucking sky!'

'"One does not sell the earth on which the people walk." Crazy Horse said that. You know, Crazy Horse, Sioux chief?'

'One does not sell the water in which the fish swim. I said that. That's how poaching's all right by me – and everybody else I ken. You can't own the water so you can't own the fish that swim in it. Would you not say?'

'I would,' said Robert. They drank to the fish that were nobody's, and pulled their stools closer. Robert got another round in.

At some point in the evening he looked at his watch. He had an idea that Kate was coming to meet him. He still hadn't managed to tell the guy about his father.

'One day,' he said, 'we'll get what we want.'

'Aye, will we? I feel, personally, I feel time is passing us by. Suddenly you realise you're getting old and there's a chance you might not see it in your lifetime, ken?'

'See what?' Robert asked.

'Anything,' said the guy. 'See anything you want to see. I'm not talking just politics. I'm not meaning home rule or independence or whatever. I mean, bigger than that. Everybody should see something in their lifetime that they'll never ever forget. That they're a part of. That nobody can take away from them.'

We're a nation of philosophers, Robert thought. That's what we are, at the end of the day. A nation of fucking philosophers.

'The big things in life,' said the guy. 'Life and death and that.' And Robert remembered his father.

'I haven't told you,' he said. 'There's something I haven't told you.'

'Me too,' said the guy. His bright blue eyes were brighter still.

'It's about my dad,' said Robert. 'Mind I said about my dad earlier, about him being a nationalist?'

'You're beautiful,' said the guy.

'Eh?' said Robert. 'No, about my dad.'

'You're beautiful. I'll just say that. The most beautiful bloke I've ever seen.'

'What?'

The guy's blue eyes were full of tears.

'Do you want to come back with me?' he said. 'Do you want to come back home with me?'

'Oh, God,' said Robert. 'Oh, God, I'm sorry, mate. I didn't even know what you were talking about. No, I'm sorry. I'm not that way, you know? I'm sorry.'

The guy looked like he'd heard it before. His face, briefly animated, became tired again.

'That's all right,' he said. 'Sorry to bother you. Don't fucking, don't fucking hate me, eh?'

'Naw,' said Robert. 'Course not. Christ, we've just had this conversation. We agree about everything. I'm just not into it, that's all. You know, with another man. I'm sorry.'

'I'm no a poof,' said the guy. 'Folk always think you're a poof. It's just how I am. I'm a human being.' He made as if to move away.

'It's all right,' Robert said. 'I'm not offended. You don't have to go, for fuck's sake. Please don't feel you have to go.'

He shook his head. He was such a fool sometimes. So blind not to see what the guy was wanting. And yet it wasn't just that. They'd had this long talk. They'd understood each other in other ways.

There was a hand on his shoulder, and he jumped. It was Kate's. 'Sorry,' she said. 'I kept trying to come over but the phone kept ringing. Are you all right?'

'Aye. I'm pretty fou but. What time is it?'

'It's nearly ten. Have you been here all this time?'

'I skipped the walk. Listen, Kate, there's this guy I met. A really nice guy.' But the man was gone. He must have slipped away when Kate appeared.

Robert said, 'I was going to introduce you but I didn't know his name anyway.'

Kate sat on the empty stool and got herself a drink. 'Just one, I think,' she said, 'and then we'd better get you home. Are you all right?'

'Aye. I'm just pissed.'

'You're in a state.'

'No, I'm okay, honest. Kate.' He put his hand to her face for a moment. 'Kate, I really love you, you know that?'

'I know,' she said. 'I love you too. So tell me about this guy.'

They got back into the flat and while the kettle was boiling for coffee he knocked over the milk carton.

'You *are* pissed,' she said.

'Sorry.'

'It's okay. I was late. Anyway, if you can't drink at a time like this . . .'

They went through to the front room and sat down. They

sipped their coffee for a minute. She was going to put a record on but decided it wasn't appropriate. She said, 'I mind one time last summer, you were out with Joe and Mark. I stayed in, went to bed early. When you got back, you were really bevvied, really stinking of it. Do you mind this?'

He nodded. She wasn't sure if he was listening, nor was she sure what she was going to tell him.

'You got into bed beside me and that was all right. But after a minute you touched me. I remember I turned my back on you and got as far away as I could.' She stopped again. When she said it aloud it didn't sound very dramatic, not the big deal she had in her head. There must be something more, at the end of what she was saying, but she didn't know quite what. She thought she might be upsetting him. 'Should I be telling you this now?'

'Aye, tell me.' He smiled at her.

'It's just you'll not remember.' In the morning, was what she meant.

'I think I was just trying my luck,' he said.

'Well, you weren't getting anything that night, that's for sure.' They both laughed.

After a pause he said, 'I don't blame you for turning away. If that's what you're wondering.'

'No,' she said, 'that's not it. I mean, it was just at the time. I was feeling pretty scunnered at you.'

'Sorry.'

'No, it's okay. I shouldn't have got so tensed up about it. I lay awake for ages while you started to snore. I was raging. Like you'd deliberately insulted me or something. Completely stupid.'

'Sorry.'

'Don't keep saying that. I'm more angry with myself than you, when I think about it now. I should have got up and read a book or something. Letting a wee thing like that get to me. It was as if I was some snooty old bag in my fifties.'

'What are you trying to say?' he asked.

'It's just,' she said, 'whenever I think about that, it's very clear in my mind. Just a wee incident. But I always think, wouldn't it be terrible if I'd lost you then? If that had been the moment when I lost you?'

He looked at her, a worried look. 'Have you lost me?'

She touched his hand across the table with hers. 'Never. I know that now.' Then she said, 'I'm really sorry about your dad. He was a lovely man.'

He nodded. 'He was. He was one of the good guys.'

Robert went to bed. Kate sat for a few minutes, letting the day go out of her head. She liked to do this, to think through the day and let it go bit by bit. She went to the bookcase and picked out the book of Scottish history. She kept going back to it, to the famous passages, as if it were a Bible. Nearly always she went to the brief fame of Kate Douglas, who tried to save her king, James Stewart, first of that name, before his assassins had him cornered in the sewer and finished him with sixteen deadly wounds to the breast:

And in the menetyme, quhen thay wer slayand him, ane young maidyn, namit Kathren Douglas, quhilk wes eftir maryit upoun Alexander Lovell of Ballumby, steikit the dure; and because the greit bar was hid away be ane traitor of thair opinioun, scho schott hir arm into the place quhair the bar sould haif passit; and becaus scho was bot young, hir arm was sone brokkin all in sondre, and the dure dongin up by force, throw quhilk thay enterrit, and slew the King with mony terribill woundis.

'Scho schott hir arm into the place ...' Such simple, desperate courage. One moment in a woman's life, and down the centuries all that was left of her life was that moment. But what a moment! What it spoke of, and left unspoken!

She got into bed beside him. They lay side by side. Then they turned and kissed for a while.

'Do I stink of beer?' he asked. 'Or the whisky?'

'It's fine,' she said.

He felt her mouth moving down his chest, across his belly. Then her hot breath was on his balls and penis. She ran her tongue up and down it. He felt himself slipping in and out of her mouth.

It wasn't right, though. It was great but it wasn't right. Maybe because he was drunk and she was sober but he didn't want them to be apart like that. He pulled her gently up towards him. 'Come here.'

They kissed again. It was better, her mouth and his. But in a minute she was off again, and this time he let her go.

He stretched out on his back. He felt he was on fire below the waist. But he couldn't connect with it. Images of his father were there. It was as if he should be guilty about what was happening, as if there should be no pleasure with his father dead. He wondered if she was enjoying herself, if she thought he was. Well, he was but it was remote, like watching a sexy scene at the pictures. He had never felt such a strangeness from her before. And yet he loved her more intensely than ever. What was going on? He lay there with her mouth on his prick, trying to connect.

There was a good turn-out at the funeral. His parents had stayed in the same town for more than thirty years – in fact Robert had been born not long after they settled there – so his father was well known and well liked. He was a joiner to trade, but in later years, when the money was more plentiful, he'd concentrated on his real love and art as a cabinetmaker. The house was full of fine pieces of furniture, all dove-tailed joints and inlays and carved feet, and he'd made a lot of stuff to order as well. The Minister paid special tribute to his skills. A craftsman, he said, one who loved detail and sought perfection in all he did. A good father and loving husband. An honest man. A kind man. A true friend to Scotland. In such phrases the man in the pulpit touched on the aspects of his father's life. Robert felt as though he were hearing these things for the first time. It was like reading his own obituary – or the obituary of the man he would like to be.

And then there was the burial itself, the lowering of his father into the ground. He was at the head of the grave, his mother and his sisters on either side of him. It was a beautiful day – he could tell people kept biting their tongues to stop themselves from saying how lucky they were with the weather. And yet they *were* lucky. A miserable, gloomy occasion it would have been in winter.

The sunshine put him in mind of his childhood here in this town. Holding the cord reminded him of holding the string of a kite. One year, when he was about ten or eleven, there was a craze for kites. All summer long the hill behind the town wore kites in the sky like a garland of bright flowers. There might be ten or fifteen of them up there at any time, traditional diamond-shaped kites, box kites, kites in the shape of birds and planes, and even one like a skull-and-crossbones. It looked so exciting from the bottom of the hill, it looked like the best thing in the world to be doing. So of course he had to have one.

But funnily enough once he got up there, with his red kite with its long tail, once he'd unwound the string to its full extent and was gripping the little tube at the end, everything lost its interest. You could make the kite dip and leap only so often. Then you withdrew from the other kite-fliers each bidding to outdo the tricks of the rest. And a new feeling came. You wanted to let the kite go. You didn't really but then you did. Let the kite fly off like a real thing, like a live thing, that's what you wanted.

He became aware again that he was standing over the grave. The coffin was being lowered and the others had released their cords onto the lid. The gravediggers had paused in letting down the straps and it was a moment before he understood that they were waiting for him. He heard a voice and felt the touch of a hand on his arm. 'You have to let go now,' said the voice. He didn't do it though, not deliberately, but still he felt the cord slip away through his fingers. Something fell from his face and landed on the wood. He found that he was crying.

He turned from the grave for a moment and wiped his eyes. It was daft, but he didn't want his father to see his tears. I don't want to be here anymore, was what he was thinking. Then he waited, head bowed, while the Minister completed the words about the resurrection and the life.

* * *

There were sandwiches and tea and the harder stuff back at the house, for the family and close friends. Robert had heard his mother going among the folk at the service, picking them out: 'You'll come back afterwards, won't you?' She was being very brave, very restrained. He wished he could be closer to her, but it was his dad he wanted.

The Minister was there, of course. It was some years since Robert had last seen him, let alone spoken to him.

'Would you say my father was religious?' he asked him.

The Minister had the grace to ponder this before nodding.

'Yes,' he said. 'But he baulked a little at the organisation. Like many of us these days.' There was a smile playing about his lips, as if he were testing a heretical view. 'He liked the product but not the firm that marketed it.'

'That's because he believed in humanity,' said Robert. 'The Kirk sees humanity as an expression of God, of religion. He saw religion as an expression of humanity.'

'I think you're being a wee bit unfair on the Kirk,' said the Minister.

'Maybe,' said Robert. 'But that's the essence of it, isn't it? That struggle, I mean. Are we God's or is God ours? I don't go to church but I'm still religious. You can't change that. It's in you, it's a state of mind.'

The Minister said that that was good, in his opinion. He excused himself and moved on. Robert looked around for Kate. She was with one of his sisters across the room. She was wearing a neat little dark suit. She looked wonderful.

* * *

Robert's sister was admiring the little dark suit. Kate made the necessary smalltalk without much sense of being there, in that house after the funeral. She was thinking about what she and Robert would do next. She'd like them to go away, the two of them, just for a few days. It would do him good – to be somewhere else.

And she thought of that curious limbo they were in, that place between what they had and what they sought. They were whole people but they were less than whole because of how their country was. Yet she felt a confidence in herself, that she had reached an understanding of the situation. This was only a temporary lull. It might last a long time but it was only temporary. What she recognised in the hopelessness of the politics was her own hope, her complete inability to give up. That's the thing we have, she thought, the unbeatable hand that we may never play but that we always hold, the thing that they just don't understand. All we are doing is waiting.

He saw her across the room from him, and she seemed both very close and far away. Then he found himself thinking about the big things again: the earth spinning, and the pull of the moon on the tides, like the endless shuttle of a loom, the tide endlessly covering and laying bare all the world's beaches, and somewhere in the west a long white empty beach, where the labours of the sea went unwitnessed by humans for generations. He thought about that empty beach, and where it might be, and he wanted to be there, to be away from all this, on a beach on the far side of an empty island, with nothing to look to but the moon-dragged sea. An island, and himself alone on it. And Kate would be there, but later. In such a place he would become small, insignificant, completely aware of the scale of things. He would step barefoot onto that pure white beach and leave his fleeting trail behind him as he walked down to the pure-blue, ice-blue water, and he would watch the horizon rising to meet the sun and feel himself being tipped with the motion, there on the edge of the world. But then, at the moment of believing himself to be utterly alone, out beyond the line where the waves begin their roll, a seal's head would appear, bobbing, watching, as if to say, I am here, I am with you, I am beyond you, and the only answer that could form in his head would be the only one that matters: I love you, I love you, I love you.

Pretending to Sleep

I could stay here all day like this, pretending to sleep, and no one would know. No one would know how awake I really am.

Sometimes I even fool myself into thinking I'm asleep, and sometimes perhaps I do nod off for a minute or two, and sometimes – perhaps – I'm fooled by the dreams I have into thinking they're reality. I could tell a few dreams that I've had. But I don't think I'm going to. I'm just going to lie here, pretending to sleep.

Nobody tries to disturb you if they think you're sleeping. They can hardly believe that someone would stretch out in the middle of all their wakefulness and fall asleep, and it overawes them. They don't want to be the one to wake you, because they don't know what you're like. You might be cuddly or you might be crazy. You might roll over or you might bite. You're a sleeping dog – better to let you lie.

It's not just that they're afraid. They're envious too. If only they could stretch out in the sun or the rain, and not have to keep going, stay alert, be part of it. You're not part of it if you're sleeping, that's for sure. You can be right in the middle of things – in a street or a park – and you're separate, outside. You're something else.

Even the police leave you alone. There was a time when they would shake you awake and move you on, and if you slumped over ten yards further on they would lift you. Then you'd to sleep in the cells. There was no point in pretending there – you either slept or you didn't, and more often you didn't. You didn't care one way or the other but then again there wasn't anybody there to fool. Nobody could see you, except the guy who came every once in a while to check you weren't dead, and the only reason he came was because it would look bad if you died in his charge. Whether you lived or died was of no concern to him, so long as you didn't die on his shift. But it's a long time since I've been lifted. These days the police are more enlightened. They don't see the harm in a wee sleep. Besides, they've plenty to keep them occupied. A sleeper is way down their list of priorities.

Funny how in the cells they come to check you're not dead. Out here, out in the open, nobody checks. Maybe as they pass they see your chest rise and fall – I don't know. But they never stop and touch you, stand over you, ask if you're all right. This is the fear again, the fear and the envy. They don't disturb you, because you disturb them. Just by lying there, pretending to sleep, you get under their skin, like an itch, you get deep into them.

Sunny days are best but rain can be all right too. With enough layers on, it can take all day to soak through. And the effect on the people passing by is greater, it totally upsets them. A man lying asleep in the pouring rain is like a corpse at a table in a café. He shouldn't be there. He should have been tidied away. But he is there, and he can't be ignored.

Some people think they do ignore you, but they don't. You go into them just the same, but more subtly. You lodge yourself like a parasite in their brain, and they don't know why they're getting these terrible headaches. Long after they've forgotten you you're uncurling yourself in there, eating away at their consciousness, bugging them, you're something gnawing at the back of their mind. They don't remember the figure prone in the park, the drizzle, the slight rise and fall of the chest, but the memory's there just the same.

If I dream, the dream is that I'll never wake up. That's why I know the dreams are not real, because I'm not asleep at all. I'm wide awake, pretending. I do it for myself. And I'll say this, I do it for everyone else too. I do it for all the ones who can't sleep, who can't stop, who can't lie down in the street. I pretend on their behalf.

This is the thing. I pretend for them. They look at me and think I'm asleep, but I'm completely aware of myself, of what's going on. I know who's awake and who's not. I may fool them, but they don't fool me.

There's more of us this year than ever before. You'll have noticed. Every month there's more of us, sleeping out in the open, in broad daylight. I'm not talking about homelessness, that's another story, I'm talking about people who've had enough, who are prepared just to lie down and be counted, or not be counted, to fall asleep and make the crowds step round us.

Only we're not asleep. I've told you that. We're just pretending. You're getting so used to us that you keep forgetting that important point.

One day you're in for the fright of your fucking life.

Opportunities

I came across a poem today by Robert Louis Stevenson, about a lighthouse keeper high above the sea, surrounded by 'the chill blind circle of the night': he is reading, oblivious to a gull beating against the pane of light. The poem finishes with something about the keeper being a martyr to his salary, but it was the gull more than the man that affected me. I thought of the bird drawn like a moth to a flame, and of the dull, irresistible impulse that brought it wearily to the signal that was not meant for it. And I disliked the coldness of the man within, aloof as a god, unaffected by the gull's hope and its despair.

I wish I had known this poem when I last saw Ricky. I would have asked him where his sympathies lay. Maybe the next time I see him I will ask him. But I doubt it somehow. The habit we share is one I really don't like discussing with anybody.

Like me – like Stevenson – Ricky writes poetry. This is amazing really. A less poetic man – than Ricky, of course, not Stevenson – is hard to imagine. The fact that he likes to write was a revelation. Even to Sue, his wife, I expect. You can tell whenever the subject comes up that it still takes her by surprise, this knowledge of the man she is with.

We were round at theirs for dinner. Ricky and Sue, Elaine and me. We've been friends maybe seven years. Or rather, Sue and Elaine have been friends that long. They teach at the same school, and Ricky and I have got to know each other through them. His wife, my partner. We say 'partner' because 'girlfriend' and 'boyfriend' are words that jar when you're both well into your thirties. Sometimes I see Ricky looking at Elaine, and then at me, with what is maybe jealousy. I think what he envies is that we're not married. The fact that somehow we don't seem one hundred per cent committed.

Although of course we are. One hundred per cent. No question. We've been together for years. Nearly a decade, in fact. So really he's jealous of nothing.

I write poetry, but not for a living. Does anybody? I've had a couple of books published and they created a bit of a stir in literary circles. At least, the critics liked them. I didn't understand the reviews, or what they claimed to admire. So I went back and read the books again in the light of what the critics had said and then I didn't understand my own poems anymore. But what the hell, if I was getting the reviews, I wasn't complaining.

Not that critical acclaim has led to riches. Far from it. Fortunately my lecturer's salary means that this is not important. I calculate that over four years I've made maybe £1,000 off the two books, and that includes £500 for a prize I didn't even know existed until the second book won it. (These, by the way, are untold riches for most poets.)

My publisher submitted the book without telling me: the first I heard about the prize was this ecstatic phone call from him. My publisher doesn't make money off poetry either, or so he's always saying, but having inherited a large fortune from his father he doesn't need to. For him it's a hobby, although he prefers the term 'labour of love'. 'If you want to be rich,' he once told me, 'do anything but this. But you know as well as I do, Adam, it's not about money, is it? It's about love. We do it for love.' That's the way he talks. He can afford to.

We were staying the night. Ricky and Sue bought a house out of town when their son Stevie was born, so he could grow up with a garden to play in, and we'd driven out for the evening. But then we couldn't decide who'd drive back. Probably it was my turn, but I knocked back a beer as soon as we arrived and that made me want another. So Sue suggested that we just stay.

Elaine, true to form, spilt some red wine on her dress about eight o'clock, not long after Stevie finally went down, just before Ricky served up the food. She went to soak it and Sue lent her something of hers to wear, a black strappy dress that was quite glamorous. It was pre-Stevie, she said, and she couldn't get into it anymore. But the truth is, even before Stevie Sue was on the wrong side of curvy, while Elaine's just a bit more than skinny.

'Hey,' Ricky said, 'I haven't seen that number in a while. That looks good on you, Elaine.'

Sue said, 'It does, doesn't it?' There was an edge to her voice that sounded to me like envy. Well, you didn't have to give her that one, I thought, if it makes you feel fat. I could see Ricky glancing at Elaine, then stopping himself, then having to look again. I caught his eye, grinned at him. Go on yourself, I was thinking, see if I care, you're paying me a compliment. Then I thought, that's what you *think* you're doing; you don't know the half of it.

Later we sat around the table, the plates pushed away from us, all scraped clean. I'll say this for Ricky, he knows how to cook.

We'd been talking about opportunities – knowing when was the right moment to make a change, strike out. 'Life enhancement', 'self-fulfilment', 'quality time', these were the kind of junk phrases that were in the air. We put on earnest voices to show when we were joking. We were getting drunk. And Sue said it wasn't so much recognising the opportunities as recognising yourself for what you were. There was this programme she'd seen the other week, late at night. Long after the watershed, she said knowingly.

Elaine said, 'What do you mean?'

'The watershed,' said Sue. 'You know, that mythical moment after nine o'clock when all bairns are in their beds and the sex and swearie words can start.'

'Oh, right,' said Elaine. She was looking even paler than usual. There was a bottle of port on the table, which spelt trouble as far as Elaine was concerned.

'So what was it?' I asked. 'What's it got to do with . . .'

'It was totally weird,' said Sue. 'It was about people with these weird sexual interests. And I mean really weird.'

'Perverts,' said Ricky.

'Actually I don't think that word was used once in the entire programme,' said Sue. 'The term they were using,

Elaine, Adam, was para-something. I can't remember. It means if you have a deviant sexual desire.'

'Paratroopers?' suggested Elaine, giggling.

'Parallelograms? Paramilitary uniforms? Paracetamol?' Rick added.

She tolerated them with a thin smile. 'Paraphilias,' she said suddenly. 'If you're into something weird it's called a paraphilia. Like there was this woman who was into corpses. I'm not kidding, it was bizarre. She used to sneak into funeral parlours and, you know, do stuff with the bodies.'

'You're joking,' said Elaine. 'Where was this?'

'America of course,' said Sue. 'But anyway, what I was going to say was, it just got me thinking, you know, there but for the grace of God et cetera?'

'What ever do you mean?' said Ricky. He reached out and touched Sue's wrist. It was the only sign of affection, if that's what it was, I saw between them all evening.

'I don't mean that,' said Sue. 'I mean, this woman explained it all, how it started from stuff in her childhood and so on, and it just makes you think, what makes someone be like that? What makes one person normal and another person weird?'

'What's normal?' said Ricky. It was a most un-Rickylike thing to come out with, and I was astonished. For him, normal is what he is, what he understands, and weird is everything he isn't and doesn't. That's why I was surprised to hear him say that. But then again, there was the poetry thing with Ricky too.

'How did we get on to this anyway?' he said.

'We were talking about opportunities,' I said, 'and then Sue started talking about sex.'

We all laughed, except Elaine, who was getting paler by the minute.

'Are you all right?' Ricky asked her.

'I'm fine,' she said. 'Fine.' I stared at her. She wouldn't look me in the eye.

'How's the writing going?' Sue asked. 'Are you having anything else published?'

'No,' I said. 'I mean, I'm still writing, there's stuff in the pipeline, but I haven't got enough for another book.' I don't like talking about it, and that's the truth. You know, some folk go on and on about how private they are, how shy, how afraid of opening out. Some writers do this: they go on and on about writing, on radio, television, in the papers. I wish they would just shut up and write.

'You send stuff off to magazines though, don't you?' said Elaine. This is something else I detest – Elaine prompting me.

'Yeah,' I said. 'I've had the odd thing accepted here and there.'

Sue fell silent. Probably she wasn't really interested. Probably she just asked out of politeness. Which was a shame, because I wouldn't have minded talking to her about it. Her on her own, I mean. But it struck me at the same time that we really didn't have much in common.

Then Ricky said, 'It's funny, isn't it? I mean, there's me writing poems, and you writing poems, and you're the one that gets them published in a book.'

'Two books,' said Elaine. She got up suddenly. 'Must pee,' she said, and lurched out of the room.

'Is she all right?' Ricky asked me.

I shrugged. 'She's just a bit drunk. She'll be fine.'

'You take care of her,' Sue said. I wasn't sure if this was a statement of opinion or an instruction, it wasn't clear from Sue's tone. 'That's a good woman you've got there,' she said.

'I know,' I said. 'Believe me, I know it.'

'Have some more whisky,' Rick said, pushing the bottle towards me. He and I had moved on to the whisky a while back. There'd been beer, then wine, then port, now whisky. It was shaping up to be another bad Sunday.

Elaine was in the bathroom a long time. Sue went to check on her and when she came back she said, 'She's sleeping.'

'What, on the bog?' Ricky asked. Sue clipped him sharply on the head as she went to the fridge and brought out another bottle of wine. 'No, stupid. She's gone to her bed.' She looked at me. 'I think she threw up.'

'Maybe I should go and see her,' I said.

Sue shrugged. 'Not much point,' she said.

'Christ,' said Ricky. He was rubbing the back of his head. 'Are you cracking open another?'

Sue stripped the foil off the bottle with the tip of the corkscrew. 'Is that a problem?'

'You're not going to drink that all by yourself?'

'Maybe,' said Sue. 'Maybe not.'

Ricky gave me a look. 'Oh God, it's going to be one of these nights.'

Sue poured herself a glass and left the bottle sitting in front of her.

'One of these nights,' she said. 'I'll drink to that.'

She raised her glass and I raised mine. It was an automatic

reflex. When someone proposes a toast I drink to it. But Ricky's glass stayed put. 'Stop sulking, darling,' said Sue.

'I'm not sulking,' he said. 'I'm just thinking what a state you're going to be in in the morning. And who's going to deal with Stevie.'

'I'll be fine,' she said. 'Two pints of water and I'll be right as rain.'

'That never works for me,' I said. 'It just makes me want to puke.'

'Me too,' said Ricky.

'I'll deal with Stevie,' said Sue. 'For a change, like,' she said.

'So?' I said, to Ricky. 'What about it?' I wasn't being defensive, just wondering.

'What about what?'

'About me getting published and that. You started to say something a while back.'

'Oh,' he said. 'Doesn't matter.'

'Aye it does,' I said.

'All right,' said Ricky. 'All right. Supposing it was the other way round. I mean, I've sent stuff off to the magazines. I've tried to get publishers to read my collection. But you're the one they thought whose poems were any good.'

'Eh?' said Sue.

'What?' said Ricky back at her.

'Is that grammatical, what you just said? It sounded wrong.'

'For Christ's sake,' he said, shaking his head. 'You're not marking fucking jotters now. You know what I'm saying, Adam. Supposing my poems were the good ones?'

'Maybe your poems are good,' I said. 'But you never show them to me so how can I tell?'

'Yeah, maybe your poems are good,' said Sue.

Rick looked at her. 'That's nice,' he said. 'She's read them,' he told me. 'She's like this supportive wife person, she's read them, and she says maybe, maybe they're good.'

'Who's she, the cat's mother?' said Sue.

'Well, are they?' I asked Ricky.

'I happen to think so,' he said. 'Aye, I do. I happen to think they are good. You have to be your own judge, at the end of the day.' He swilled his whisky around in the glass. 'As a matter of fact, I happen to think my poems are better than yours.'

'Fair enough,' I said. 'I couldn't say.'

At this point if Elaine had still been conscious she'd have said something pacifying: 'You're not comparing like with like, I'm sure both your poems are good in different ways.' And then Sue might have said, 'Is that grammatical?' or 'Isn't that ambiguous?' – something along those lines. But Elaine wasn't at the feast anymore, and Sue, draining her glass, said, 'Oh God, Ricky, let's not have a competition about it.'

'Maybe you should go to bed,' Ricky said. 'I mean, if you haven't got anything constructive to contribute.'

'Oh, maybe I should.' She poured herself another glass of wine and drank from it. 'To bed.'

Ricky shook his head and drank some whisky himself.

'That was a toast, by the way,' said Sue.

'We heard,' he said.

I didn't raise my glass this time. I wasn't enjoying whatever was going on between them, although it was better than the poetry conversation, which seemed more dangerous. As I said, I don't like talking about my writing. Let the poems do the talking, has always been my philosophy. And the one thing I never write about is writing. None of my poems is about poetry. I make a point of that.

Disappearing up your own arsehole is not my idea of entertainment, for me or anyone watching.

Ricky headed off to the bog. While he was away, Sue knocked back the rest of her glass and refilled it, spilling some wine on the table in the process. I reached over and mopped it up with the paper napkin she'd provided way back at the start of the evening, and I said:

'I don't think I've ever seen you this pissed before, Sue.'

'No?' she said. She smiled. 'Well, Alan, there's a first time for everything.'

'Right,' I said. Then I added, 'Adam.'

'What?'

'Adam. You said Alan.'

'Sorry,' she said. 'I meant Adam. Did I really say Alan?'

'You did,' I said.

'You can't prove it,' she said. 'You have no witnesses.' There was a pause. 'Adam. Loaded with significance, that name, isn't it?'

'Yeah,' I said. I was trying to remember exactly how long she'd known me. To call me by the wrong name, I mean. It seemed she just didn't care enough. But then again . . . I don't know, I was looking at her, wee dumpy Sue I had nothing in common with, and wondering about her and Ricky together.

Something entered my head that I didn't really want in there. What if I got off with her? What would that do to us?

To each one of the four of us. To Ricky. Who appeared at the door briefly, waved at us and said, 'See yous in the morning. Don't drink all my whisky.' As if he was talking about whisky.

It was ridiculous of course. Why should I think there was a chance of getting off with her? Why should he? I didn't even fancy her that much. To be honest, I wouldn't really like her if it wasn't that she was Elaine's pal. So what was that all about, that thought? Getting off with someone you don't like. Okay, we were drunk, we were all drunk, and you do things when you're drunk that wouldn't even be on the agenda in the cold light of day. That's what stops this kind of thing, normally. The cold light of day. Something triggers a warning about how guilty you'll feel in that cold light. So you go to bed drunk and wake up with a hangover.

It was about two o'clock. I said, 'Are you and Ricky, you know, are you all right?'

'Why wouldn't we be?'

'Oh, I don't know. I just wondered. I mean, you seemed a bit short with each other back there.'

'Oh. Did we?' She considered this for a moment. Her face was in profile to me.

Suddenly I felt horribly lonely. I felt alone in the world. And I didn't know what the fuck I was doing in it. It was a sick, nasty, cold feeling. I didn't like it, and I didn't like myself for what it made me do next.

I kind of reached out. Or maybe it was more of a lean. Anyway, it was in her direction. 'Sue,' I said.

But just as she was on the point of turning to look at me, of maybe reaching or leaning back, if that was what she was

165

going to do, there was a movement at the doorway. Everything froze.

There was a figure standing in the door in pyjamas. A small figure, with a dark tousle of hair and a thumb in its mouth.

'Oh,' said Sue. Somehow in a moment she was over there gathering her child up, wrapping him into her. 'Stevie, sweetie, what's wrong? Did you have a bad dream?'

Stevie was crying quietly. He looked very sleepy but his eyes were wide open, startled by the brightness. 'My ears hurt,' he said.

'Oh, baby, it's okay, it's okay.' She was stroking her child's hair, holding his head against her body, gently cupping her hand over one ear. 'It's okay.'

She started to walk up and down the room, between the window and the door, hushing her child, whispering to him. It was as if I had disappeared. It was as if all the furniture in the room had shifted slightly. I wanted to get up and go to bed, because everything had suddenly changed back to the way it was. I wanted to go through to the spare bedroom where Elaine was because that was the only place for me to go, but then again I didn't want to go there. And I didn't want to disturb Sue and her wee boy, remind them that I was there. So I sank back into the sofa cushions and closed my eyes. That way I wouldn't see them and it would be as though they couldn't see me anymore, and I could wait there for as long as it took for the child's sobbing and his mother's soothing to come to an end.

The Shelf

They needed a wardrobe. All the second-hand ones they saw were either too big, too small or too dear. In the end they went to the DIY superstore and got a kit in a flatpack that you fitted together yourself. It was a lot cheaper but not well made like the old ones. Louise said, 'Well, you get what you pay for.'

They had to bring it home in a taxi because they had no car and it was too heavy to carry all the way. At the entrance to their close they did a short balancing act while Ken dug the keys out of his pocket and got the door open. As he backed in he happened to look up over Louise's head. There was a flat across the street that fascinated him. Day or night, weekday or weekend, its curtains were always closed. He imagined all kinds of things going on behind those curtains: it was a brothel, a safe house, a bomb factory. A glance this time was all he needed to reassure himself that it was still shut tight against the world.

Ken's energy came in waves, ebbed like a tide. For the best part of a week the flatpack lay unopened behind the sofa in the front room. After the first day Louise did not mention it at all, until finally her silence shamed him into doing something about it. He had to admit, to himself, that it was far from convenient with most of their clothes still in suitcases, hung on the backs of doors, or laid out in layers on the sofa. There wasn't space to swing a cat in the front room, or anywhere else in the flat for that matter. Not that they had a cat.

Nearly a month had passed since they'd moved in. They'd lived together for a year, then decided to buy somewhere, because financially it made much more sense. The mortgage was less than the rent in the old place, but the flat was much smaller. They would sit in the kitchen in the evenings, after they'd eaten, trying to work out where to put things. He knew Louise wanted to tell him to get on with the wardrobe, that only then could they start getting the place in order, but she said nothing. Maybe, he thought, she was frightened that in banishing the chaos their lives would become petrified in some other way.

As for Ken himself, well, he was already overwhelmed by lethargy. He wasted the evenings fixing other things instead, less important things like the towel rail in the bathroom or the washers on the kitchen taps. Some nights he made out he was just too tired and sat gazing at the crossword. Maybe he was testing her patience. But that wasn't it really. What was bothering him wasn't Louise, it wasn't even the prospect of constructing the wardrobe. It was the shelf on the bedroom wall: he knew he was going to have to deal with the shelf first.

It was useless, that shelf. It was stuck right in the middle of one wall of the bedroom, a strip of wood about four inches deep and eighteen inches long. It was only good for a few ornaments or maybe some paperbacks, although since it had no uprights at the ends even books would have to be laid flat to stay on. Because of its position it was impossible to put any large piece of furniture against that wall. And as the bedroom was tiny, and they needed all the space they could get, that was where the wardrobe had to go.

He'd noticed the shelf when they first saw the flat, and, when their offer was accepted, it at once occurred to him, with a kind of sick feeling, that he'd have to remove it. He must have had a sixth sense about it, otherwise why the sick feeling? After all, it surely couldn't be a big job, it was only a scrap of wood, painted, for some reason, post-box red. But something about it disturbed him, even before they'd settled an entry date.

When he came to inspect it more closely, he realised that the shelf wasn't held up by screws or brackets of any kind. It seemed to be embedded right into the wall. The previous owners had even papered round it as though it were a permanent fixture. It *was* a permanent fixture. He couldn't understand why anyone would put such a stupid thing up. It was perverse, malicious. But then those people left a lot of other undesirable stuff behind them: toenails in the carpet; toothpaste stains all over the basin in the bathroom; a cupboard full of junk that he'd had to arrange for the council to take away to the cowp. All that was bad enough, but at least you could get rid of it. The shelf was a different proposition altogether.

Finally one evening he surfaced from the lethargy and got started, digging around the edges of it, levering at the plaster, and every few minutes he would try to work the shelf loose. It refused to budge. He applied more force and it gave slightly, dislodging plaster with each sideways, upwards or downwards shift. It sounded like a pack of rats scurrying down the inside of the wall. Louise came in once with a cup of tea for him, and when he turned round he saw her mouth open in horror at the wound he was making in the wall. She was about to say something but then she didn't.

'I've started so I'll finish,' said Ken. That was a catch phrase from an old television programme, but he couldn't think which one. He was sweating and his arms were sore from trying to prise the piece of wood out of the wall. She nodded, closed her mouth and went back to the kitchen.

He wondered if he should have left well alone. But with the shelf still in place they could never put the wardrobe up. So he kept going, gouging and tearing away at it. That shelf was like an iceberg: the four inches sticking out of the wall was just what you could see.

I've started so I'll finish. He remembered now. Magnus Magnusson, the presenter on *Mastermind*.

He made jokes to himself, in his head, because he needed to relieve the feeling that he'd made a terrible mistake. Supposing it wasn't a shelf at all, but the projecting end of a beam, one of the principal timbers in the structure of the building? Pull away the shelf and he'd find himself dragging foot after foot of wood out from the wall. Then the wall would collapse, the ceiling fall in and all the flats tumble down in a huge roaring cloud of dust. Maybe the whole tenement and all the lives it contained were held up by this apparently insignificant useless bit of wood. He knew that was ridiculous, he was just getting hysterical. But the hole in the wall as he levered and dug around it was getting larger and larger, like a mouth stretched in an enormous yawn. In the middle the red shelf, coated now with a layer of pinkish dust, waggled insolently when he tugged at it.

He looked at his watch and was amazed to see that an hour and a half had gone by. He couldn't believe it. In frustration he picked up the hammer and lashed out at the underside of the shelf. Bits of stone and plaster clattered away down the building; any minute now the downstairs neighbour would be up to complain. But he could tell the blow had loosened something. He hit the shelf again. And again. After a minute he put the hammer down, grasped the shelf in both hands and pulled, and it came straight out, a good eight inches all told, with a huge lump of plaster firmly attached to its inner edge.

He inspected the gaping hole and it made him panicky. He went to make up a batch of filler. Louise was still in the kitchen so he got water from the bathroom. He didn't want her seeing the state of things. He had to brush out still more rubble and dust before he could slap in the filler. The hole seemed to suck it in and the filler made no impression upon it. He realised he'd have to use cement. Among the junk left by the previous occupants was a half-used bag of cement which by chance he'd not thrown out. He found an old bucket and mixed some cement up in it. Then he set to work to patch the hole.

He had to build the wall back up in layers, allowing each layer to set a little before he pushed more cement into the cavity. He knew he wasn't doing it properly, that it needed more time to dry, but he didn't like the hole and he didn't want Louise to see it so big. When he'd half-filled it he made himself stop to let the cement dry overnight.

After all his efforts, when Louise came through to go to her bed she hardly noticed it, she was that tired. He sat up in the kitchen for a while, thinking things over.

The next night he finished patching the wall. He filled the rest of the hole up and put a new strip of paper over where the shelf had been. He thought about getting some paint to match the colour in the room but then he thought – the wardrobe will hide it, what's the point?

Louise always left for work half an hour before he did, she had further to travel. He would hear her in the bathroom, and then in the front room where she went to dry her hair, put on her make-up and get dressed. He heard the hair-dryer every morning. When she left was when he got up. He would take a shower, have his breakfast, then walk the ten minutes to the shop. He was never late.

The next morning was a Thursday. Friday would be his day off because he was working at the weekend, but he wanted his day off right then. He lay awake for ten minutes after he heard the door close behind her. Then he turned over and went back to sleep.

When he woke again it was ten o'clock. He got dressed and phoned the shop. He said he was sick and wouldn't be in till Saturday. Then he went out for a paper.

He made some coffee and read the paper, and thought about what he would do with the rest of the day. He went back into the bedroom to look at the wall. He'd overfilled the hole; there was a lump beneath the paper where the shelf had been. He'd made a lousy job of it, but once the wardrobe was in place no one would know.

That was when he decided to build it. To cover the lump. Plus, it would be a surprise for Louise when she came home. He broke open the flatpack and read the instructions. He realised that if he built it in the front room, where there was a little space if he pushed everything back against the walls, he wouldn't be able to move it into the bedroom. The doors of the two rooms were only a few inches apart, on the same side of the narrow passage. The wardrobe just wouldn't go round. He was pleased with himself for spotting this before he started.

The bed took up half the bedroom. He considered his options. Either he'd have to dismantle the bed and move it and the mattress and all the bedding out while he built the wardrobe, or he'd have to build it on its side, adapting the instructions, then turn it over onto its base into the space along the wall.

The instructions were in Korean and bad English so it didn't make a lot of difference where he started. He pulled out one of the sides and laid it on the carpet.

Some time later, he was sweating and his arms ached but there was also a surge of satisfaction from having defied the manufacturers' instructions. They'd said to build it one way and he'd built it another. It just showed you. All that was left was to hang the doors. These were surprisingly heavy for a piece of kit furniture. He decided to have a cup of tea before he fitted them.

He was sitting on the bed sipping the tea, and as he allowed his spine to sag he felt a twinge. He had to sit back

173

upright, which was difficult as the mattress on the bed was too soft. So he stood up, carefully, and went to the narrow window overlooking the street.

The curtains of the flat opposite were closed as always. Below, in a gap between the buildings, was a little rockery and a bench set back on the pavement. Sometimes a man would sit there and smoke a cigarette; sometimes a woman with a pushchair; sometimes a couple would huddle together of an evening, watching the city darken against the sun. There was a couple there when he looked down, holding hands, not talking. It was about two in the afternoon.

They were young, maybe eighteen or nineteen. There was something about them. They wore clothes that looked poor and out of fashion. The man's hair was a straggled mess. The woman's was covered by a headscarf. He thought this odd because he associated headscarves with much older women. The two of them reminded him of people you might see on the news, in the wake of an earthquake or walking out of a war zone. They hardly exchanged a word, but they seemed to be communicating some shared need to each other.

As he watched from his window, he became aware with a kind of slow disbelief that they were preparing to have sex. The man was fiddling with the buttons of his trousers, while the woman was adjusting her clothing under her skirt. Suddenly the woman slipped across the man's lap. There were a few seconds of clumsy jolts and shiftings and then the man stood up from the bench with the woman clinging to him, her legs wrapped around his waist. They were having sex in broad daylight in the middle of a quiet residential street. Were they not right in the head or something? Ken watched in amazement as the pumping movements of the couple gathered pace. They seemed to have melted together, like a tasteless ornament, and he thought he could hear through the glass a few grunts and moans. But it was over as suddenly as it had started, in just a few seconds. They separated like a pair of animals, without any kind of tenderness, and, re-covering themselves matter-of-factly, they stood up and walked away together down the street.

He found that he had shrunk back from the glass, as if he was the one who should be concealing himself. He had the idea that if they'd looked up and seen him, they'd have shouted abuse at him: 'Pervert!' He imagined the echo of their shouts as they disappeared at the end of the street. He had to ask himself if it was true, if he had really seen what he had seen. But he knew it was true. And suddenly all the energy he had gathered while building the wardrobe rushed out of him.

When Louise came home he was in the kitchen, making the tea. She stood in the doorway unbuttoning her coat. 'Hi,' she said.

'Hi, there,' he said over his shoulder.

'Listen,' she said, 'you're off tomorrow, aren't you? Well, I took a holiday too. I thought we could put that wardrobe together, and then maybe I would go and look for new curtains.' (The previous people had left some thin, dirty curtains along with the rest of their rubbish.)

She seemed very decisive. He turned smiling from the sink where he was washing vegetables and said, 'Go and look in the bedroom.'

'Why?' she asked.

'Go on,' he said. 'Just go and look.'

He heard her little squeal of pleasure through there. When she came back she walked over and kissed him on the cheek. She tried to put her arms around him but he shrugged her off. 'My hands are wet,' he said.

'When did you do it?' she asked.

'I came home early,' he told her. 'I said I had a headache. I just wanted to get it done.'

'That's brilliant,' she said. 'Now we can get everything put away.'

'What about your day off?' he said. 'You'll not need it now.'

'Well, then,' said Louise, 'we can get a long lie. We can still go looking for curtains.'

Later they stood together at the front window of the tiny flat. Louise had spent the previous hour loading the wardrobe with her clothes. She seemed animated, happy, for the first time since they'd moved in.

'There's just one thing,' she said. 'One of the doors isn't hanging right. You have to kind of give it a wee lift to get it to close properly.'

He knew all about that. A wave of frustration went over him. He'd spent ages adjusting the hinges. He'd done his best but when you got the top hinge right the bottom one went out of line. And she'd had to point it out.

'It's these kits,' he said. 'They're badly finished. I'll have to get new hinges.'

In the flats in the building opposite, the corner rooms had windows to the front and side. Louise envied them, because, she said, they must get so much light. But in the flat on the same level as theirs the curtains were closed, although it was only eight o'clock, and still not dark.

'Have you ever noticed about that flat?' she said.

'What?' he said, but he knew what she was going to say.

'The curtains are always closed,' she said.

'Aye,' he said. 'I kept meaning to mention it.' But that wasn't true. He hadn't said anything to her about the couple in the street either. 'It doesn't matter what time of the day or night it is, they're always closed tight. It's weird, isn't it?'

'Always,' she said. 'When I'm drying my hair in here in the morning, before you get up, it's become a kind of habit of mine to check, and I've never yet seen them open. I thought maybe whoever stays there works nightshifts, but they're closed all the time.'

'Even on my days off I've never seen them open,' he said. 'And at weekends too. No sign of life at all.'

They stood watching together. And just as he finished speaking, something happened across the street. For a moment, the briefest of moments, a hand appeared, clutching a fold of one of the curtains and pulling it back slightly. All that could be seen was that hand, fisted against the shoddy brown of the curtain. Then it was gone.

'Did you see that?' he said. 'Jesus! Did you see that?'

'Oh God,' she said, 'that *is* weird. Just when we were talking about it. That is *weird*.'

'Did you see it?' he shouted. His heart was pumping. 'Oh God! A hand!'

She laughed, the kind of laugh you give to reassure yourself and whoever you're with. He joined in, and he made a ghostly quavering sound through his lips.

'Oo-oo-oo-ooh!'

'The ha-a-a-nd!' she said tremulously.

They clutched at each other with witches' fingers, laughing and shrieking. 'We're doomed!' he said. Now he was doing his Private Frazer impersonation from *Dad's Army*. 'We're doomed, Captain Mainwaring!'

She laughed and laughed. And just for a moment it was all clear. An unseen stranger across the street had sparked it off, but he believed if he could keep her laughing things might work out. But he saw also that anything was possible, that they might laugh or cry, they might feel safe or frightened, it just depended. It was up to them but then again it wasn't. It just depended.

After a while the laughter died down and Louise was catching her breath. Ken's heart was still going though. He turned away from the window, back to the tiny, cramped rooms of their new home, and began to manoeuvre between the bits of furniture, away from Louise and the strange things that were going on outside.

The Dictionary

I went to look up a word in the dictionary this morning, as one does. Some people think that writers shouldn't have to, that we should know all the meanings of words, and certainly how they are spelt, already. This is like expecting a motor mechanic to work without tools, or a surgeon without instruments. Arthur Scargill once said his father read the dictionary every day. 'Your life,' Mr Scargill senior observed, 'depends on your power to master words.' This is especially true for writers, who make a living from the words they use.

So you can imagine my surprise at finding that the word I was looking for was not there. Or, at least, it was not where it should have been. I can't now remember what the word was, but that is the least of my troubles. I know it began with a D. I opened the dictionary at roughly the place where the Ds should have been – as a regular user over many years, I have become quite good at judging where the letters fall – and they were not there! I flicked back and forward a bit, but still the Ds did not reveal themselves. The Cs, which would have been a useful benchmark at this point, did not appear either. In fact, the more I flicked, the more I noticed that the letters were completely jumbled up, not in the correct alphabetical order at all. Every time I thought I was getting close to where a letter ought to have been, on the basis of its usually preceding or following another letter, it turned out not to be there.

This is a pretty fatal flaw in a dictionary. It destroys its utility. But how could this be? It was my own, my old and trusty dictionary. I had had it for several years. I felt that we knew each other intimately. And now, here it was, apparently playing tricks on me. I tried again: the order remained in . . . complete disorder. I checked the binding of the book, turned it around and upside down and opened it back to front, I even shook it as one might a carton of soup or orange juice – 'Shake well before opening' – but nothing would restore it to its original condition, organised on the fundamental, time-honoured and generally accepted principle of a proper alphabetical sequence. How had the dictionary reconstituted itself into this hopeless confusion? And when? I had no idea, but it put me in an intolerable situation.

I took a bus into town and visited a large bookshop. I went to the reference section, selected a new copy of the dictionary, which was wrapped in cellophane, and carried it to the till. Before the sales assistant took it from me I asked if he would remove the cellophane so that I could check that the contents were in the right order. The man looked at me rather coldly.

'I'm sure they will be,' he said. 'If you discover there are pages missing, or wrongly bound, please bring it back. Or if you are dissatisfied with it for any other reason, you can of course return it for a full refund, so long as it is in mint condition.'

'It may be in mint condition,' I said, 'but still unusable.'

'Well,' he said, 'we sell dozens of these every year and we very seldom have them returned as unusable.'

'Nevertheless,' I said, 'I would prefer to check it now.'

'Of course,' he said. He removed the cellophane and handed the dictionary to me, observing me closely. I opened the dictionary.

A mass of overlapping and unrelated letters seemed to leap at me from the page. It was swimming with illegible text. I felt as though I were suddenly back in front of the old manual typewriter on which I first began to write, when still a child. Sometimes, out of frustration or boredom, I would press down on the keyboard with the spread palms of both hands, so that a clump of keys jammed together half an inch from the point where they would normally strike the paper. Looking at that page of the dictionary reminded me of that tangle of metal and ink-black characters. But this was only a momentary sensation. At once the letters moved before my eyes, their confusion dissolving and reforming with astonishing speed. I turned the page: the same thing happened. I closed the book, and handed it back to the sales assistant.

'It is defective,' I said. 'Like the one I have at home.'

He opened the dictionary and appeared – I suspected him of deceit – to read an entry or two. 'In what way do you find it defective?' he asked.

'The letters are in the wrong order,' I said. 'In fact, they don't seem to be in any order. I can't use a dictionary if I don't know the order of the letters.'

He stepped out from behind the till. 'Excuse me for a moment,' he said. 'I think I may be able to help.' He went over to the reference section and selected another dictionary. He brought it over to me.

'This,' he said, 'is exactly the same dictionary.' This was obviously untrue. 'Except,' he went on, 'that it is thumb-indexed.' He removed its cellophane wrap. 'To locate a letter of the alphabet, you simply insert your thumb at the appropriate cutaway mark, and open the book there. It is slightly dearer, but many of our customers who have difficulty remembering the alphabet find it most convenient.'

'I don't have difficulty remembering the alphabet!' I shouted. 'Good God, man, do you think I'm an idiot? A-B-C-D . . .'

I stopped in midstream. My mouth gaped in horror. The assistant stared at me with great equanimity. After a little while I closed my mouth.

'I'll take it,' I said. He put it in a carrier bag, I handed over the cash, and bolted from the shop.

On the bus home, I struggled against the temptation to look up the word that had caused all this trouble in the first place. I did not have to struggle too hard, because the truth is, I had forgotten what the word was. I still have not remembered it. But, as I said, that is now the least of my problems.

When I got home, I placed the dictionary on my desk, flexed my fingers, and prepared to open it. As I was doing this, I noticed that the index finger on my right hand seemed to have altered somewhat. It had become fatter, shorter, and had only one joint. It had, in fact, become more like a thumb than an index finger. I looked at my left hand. The pinkie and the ring finger seemed remarkably thumblike too. I did not like the look of this.

THE DICTIONARY

I went to pick up my new thumb-indexed dictionary. I could not grip it properly. It fell to the floor. Letters spilled out of it in all directions across the carpet. I let out a cry and, falling to my knees, attempted to gather them up. My hands were by now too clumsy for such intricate work. I was wrist-deep in letters. I began to howl.

The Dayshift

He was a fat, ungainly man, who never said hello or goodbye to his wife. After twenty-five years there didn't seem any point. He left his house every morning at the same time without saying goodbye, and he arrived home every evening without feeling it necessary to say hello. Why would he bother? It wasn't as if he was ever going to find a note on the table saying she'd run off with another man; a miner, a schoolteacher, a car mechanic. He would never find her murdered or imprisoned or the house burnt down. Why else would you say goodbye to someone you knew would still be there when you got back? Why would you say hello when you found things exactly as you had left them? And his wife must have felt the same way, for she never said these words to him either. There were no surprises in their lives.

He would have been a big man – physically, at least – in any line of work, but over the years his sedentary job had turned the gradual spread of his gut into an overhang of belt-bursting proportions. In summer his office – if you could call the tiny box of glass and breeze-blocks an office – became stifling. Sweat bloomed in great crescents on his shirt, and blotched his neck where the collar rubbed. In winter he seemed unaffected by the cold, and could sit without a coat even on the bitterest of days, immunised by blubber, while shivering soldiers took turns to come in and heat themselves at the miserable paraffin heater in the corner. The season of his discontent was summer, but he endured it without comment, as he did almost everything that occurred in his unremarkable life.

It was spring now, and not yet too hot, but something was different. Extraordinary events were occurring, and although he still said nothing he could not help observing them.

His job was to check and stamp the papers of those crossing the border. This had always been his job. In the past the numbers had been small – a mere trickle: businessmen (such as they were), an industrial or cultural delegation, and very occasionally a tourist. Now, with the government in disarray, the trickle had become a steady stream. The entire population seemed to want to see what it was like to step outside their country and back in again. They could hardly believe that to put a foot across a line would no longer be an irrevocable act, a decision that would have the most far-reaching, perhaps devastating consequences for them or their families, or even for the country itself. They seemed almost to be sleepwalking. Or perhaps it was that they weren't sure they were awake, and took each cautious step as if the ground might vanish beneath them.

He didn't understand this need to test the ordinariness of leaving and returning. He was accustomed to ponderously reading the documentation of movement word by word, line by line, and it did not excite him: the passports, visas, permits, exemptions, all the paraphernalia required to authorise foreign travel. He would use one of his stubby, tobacco-stained fingers to follow the text, a deliberate display of his power to keep people waiting. But even as he did this he knew that they were inured to queues, that they found his behaviour tiresome rather than frustrating. They were used to the slow, compelling hand of bureaucracy, indeed their lives could not go on without it, and at this moment of crossing the border they could not proceed without his approval.

Until now. Now, the people moved in spite of him. They couldn't care less whether his fat finger traced a set of justifications across an irrelevant piece of paper. They were going anyway. The government had ceased to govern and he was part of that new situation, although at the same time nothing to do with it. Nobody attacked him for the past but on the other hand nobody any longer recognised him in the present. They just kept pushing by in their endless stream, pushing but patient too. They had waited so long, shuffling behind one another; another half-hour before that step across the border was nothing in the scale of things. What was thirty minutes after more than forty years?

It was becoming embarrassing, him sitting there in his cabin, the people pouring past the grimy little window. He thought about going home but he didn't want to abandon his post. For one thing, he couldn't help thinking that his pay might be affected, although it was true the supervisor was not there to check on him. In any case, he had been doing his job for twenty-five years and he had never left early yet. He had never been sick, never been absent except when on holiday. He was utterly reliable. The soldiers used to joke that they could throw away their watches as long as he worked there. That was how he was. Even some of the soldiers had gone, and the rest were keeping a low profile, but he wouldn't cut short his shift, even though he knew it to be a truly extraordinary day.

He did think, however, about getting home at the end of it. All these people were pressing through to the other side where there was nothing but wasteland for a mile or two before the first grey town, but he was thinking about heading in the opposite direction. Just wasteland – and yet that was enough for them, to walk on wasteland and turn and see their own country behind them, and walk a little further, and turn again, and come back in. No questions asked. Nobody for whom you had to have your reasons prepared. It would be as if you had done nothing except walk in an empty space.

He had no desire to go there, none at all. For twenty-five years he'd been able to see into that other country – he could even stroll a few paces and put his feet on its soil if he wanted to, but he didn't want to. He'd never felt a need to go any further than where he was. He was a true patriot. That was why he had stayed in the job – why he'd got the job in the first place. He was trusted to stay put, not to run away. He was responsible. He was rooted in reality, and the idea that he might be seduced by imagination was laughable.

But now he felt awkward. At first, when he began his shift, he'd tried to inspect the people's papers, but the man he'd replaced had just laughed at his efforts as he put on his coat to leave.

'What's the point of that? Do you think they're going to stop if you tell them their papers aren't in order?'

And then – he could hardly believe it – the man had left the cabin and walked straight into the other country himself.

Of course what he'd said was true: it was impossible to carry out a proper inspection. There were too many people and in their present mood they were not likely to submit graciously to his powers of delay (such as they were). He knew he was only a pawn. It had never, in truth, been the likes of him who had controlled the border, but the soldiers and the police, armed and disciplined. He was there simply to represent the civil authority. These people passing in front of his window did not hold him to account for his part in hindering their movements because they had all been a part of the system, they had all acquiesced, so they could hardly blame him.

He remembered his first day at the border post, being given instructions by the supervisor. There were files for the different forms, there were sheets to be completed in triplicate, there were different stamps for different permits. He listened and watched diligently until the supervisor – not the same man as the current one, who was twenty years younger than himself – paused and asked him if he understood everything. He thought hard for a moment and then said, 'What will I do if somebody's forms are incomplete?'

The supervisor looked at him as if he were mad.

'You don't need to worry about that. It'll not happen.'

'But if it does? If there's ever a problem?'

'It'll not happen. But if it ever did, well, you would contact me of course. But I'm telling you, that situation is never going to arise.'

'So there'll be no problems like that at all?'

'No.' The supervisor's face was like a stone.

He nodded. Then he said, 'It's just that, if there are never any problems, what's the point of me checking everything?'

As soon as he said it he knew it was the wrong thing. The supervisor glared at him.

'Look,' he said, 'who do you think you are? You're nobody. It's a great honour, getting trained for this post. It's not just anybody that gets a chance at it, overseeing who comes and goes at the border. Don't start off on the wrong foot, asking what the point of it is. I can have you replaced just like that.' He clicked his fingers.

'I just thought—'

But the supervisor interrupted him. 'What do you mean, you just *thought*? All you need to do is your job, the way I've explained it to you. You don't have to *think*. You don't have to *worry* about what happens if somebody's papers are wrong. That's not *your* problem. You check the papers and if they're in order you stamp them just like I've told you.'

The room seemed full of anger. The supervisor clicked his fingers again, right in his fat face. That should have shut him up, but he could not help himself. Some dull obstinacy made him speak again.

'And if they're not?'

The supervisor's fist crashed down on the table. 'They will be! People don't arrive at the border by accident, you know. They don't just turn up. All kinds of channels have to be gone through. You're here to carry out a final check. *That's* your job.'

And so it had turned out. The supervisor (who had moved on to greater things, he supposed – at any rate, one day he was transferred to the capital, and was replaced by the younger man) was absolutely right. In twenty-five years he had never had a problem. The paperwork had always been in order. Other people, in other places, had been doing their jobs as efficiently and reliably as he. That was the system. It had its drawbacks, of course. But it seemed to him that, basically, it worked.

There was a lot of talk in the papers and on television nowadays about freedom of speech. Countries that had been enemies were now friendly, ideas that had been alien were becoming domesticated. Words developed new implications, or changed their meanings completely. Some of it was obvious, but much was subtle. People took a delight in splitting hairs. One word, they said, could carry a whole range of values. None of these values should have absolute precedence. That way led to tyranny. *Back* to tyranny, they said.

Well, it seemed to him that these same people had been silent long enough before. They hadn't spoken until it was safe to do so. Which implied that what they were saying was dangerous, or had been, to themselves or to society. Surely someone had to decide which values of which words were the true ones? Because it couldn't be the case that all meanings were of equal value. It suited some people to speak now, but it had suited them to be silent before. Supposing there were things that weren't right in the future, when they were in charge? Would they speak out or be silent? Somehow he felt their behaviour to be immature, selfish. He mistrusted their mistrust of – well, of certainty. He'd had his doubts as a young man, of course, but he'd grown up. They disliked certainty, whereas for him it was what made things work. The last twenty-five years proved it.

Most of the people at the border did not even have their papers with them. Their *identity* papers. They had deliberately left them behind, or decided not to reveal them. That was what they wanted to be – anonymous. He found that hard to fathom. Why would anyone want to be anonymous? They claimed they wanted to be individuals but how could you be without your identity?

For a while he kept up a pretence of checking the cards and documents that a few people, out of habit he supposed, hesitatingly pushed under the glass at him. But it *was* pointless – even he could see that. He nodded at these people as if to thank them for their trouble, but also to tell them it wasn't necessary, that they could go past anyway, that for the moment at least their pictures and names were completely worthless. Then, because it seemed illogical to nod only at those who bothered to acknowledge his presence, he nodded as each person passed through the barrier that was no longer a barrier. Each figure received a curt nod. It was as much of his official duty as he could bring to bear on the proceedings. It seemed to justify his being there. But only a handful of people nodded back. Most didn't even notice him, or if they did they studiously ignored him. So his nods became shorter, more into his chest. And his eyes lowered so that he would not have to meet the bright eyes of anyone who happened to glance his way, would not meet scorn or laughter or amazement with his own – his own what? Embarrassment? Stupidity? Anger? Fear? He didn't know what he was feeling, or when a feeling stopped being itself and became something else. And pretty soon the crowd was streaming past, paying him no attention whatever.

And he, his head nodding almost imperceptibly onto his chest, averted his eyes and would not look at them. As the people passed to and fro, exercising their new imaginations, he began to feel drowsy. He found himself longing for the end of his shift so that he could go home, walk to the station and travel the three stops to his village and go into the house where his fat middle-aged wife would be making soup.

The shadows lengthened, but still the crowds came, ignoring him as he now ignored them. And a new thought came to him, but he considered it without panic, almost with resignation, as if it were only natural to consider such a possibility on a day like this. Something that would once have been an impossibility was now a distinct likelihood but it didn't bother him particularly. He had done his duty. He was entitled to go home.

What he was wondering was what he would do if no one came to relieve him.

But he remembered the supervisor, all those years ago, telling him that if something went wrong it was not his problem. And he had been right. For twenty-five years the supervisor's words had held true.

He thought of the slow, swaying train that he would catch, that left at exactly eleven minutes past five and arrived at his village at exactly ten minutes to six. And the ten-minute walk that he would make to his house where his wife would be in the kitchen. The smell of soup. Always the same smell, always the same soup. And he thought of staring out of the window of the train as it clattered through each tiny station, and how at the stations the stationmasters would be standing at attention, like toys in their sky blue shirts and red peaked caps, with their green and red batons under their arms, as if unwilling or unable to relax; as if they thought the train had eyes and might report them if they slouched; as if they did not know how else to stand in a world that was no longer real.

Don't Start Me Talkin' (I'll Tell Everything I Know)

The woman looked to be in her fifties. On her head was a grey helmet of tight curls. She had the face of a smoker who has been giving up for decades. It seemed to take her an age to shuffle up to the sales counter.

The shop was quiet; in fact, apart from the two of them it was completely empty.

George Johnstone had heard her shoes on the steps outside, and had come out from behind the counter and moved over to the jazz section. He sorted a few CD cases into alphabetical order with a practised air and walked over to her.

'Can I help you?' he asked.

She looked at him hopelessly.

'I'll tell you what it is, son. I've been having a terrible time lately and I just thought if I could get some new music into my life it would help. I want something . . . well, I just want something with feeling.'

'With feeling,' said George.

'Aye. Somehow all my old records aren't having the right effect. And I thought I'd come in and spend a few bob on something with a bit of feeling.'

'A few bob.'

'Aye, in a manner of speaking.'

George considered her face. On the one hand, he really did not have time for this. On the other, he had all the time in the world. He saw such despair in the lines around her eyes that he feared she might burst into tears.

'What kind of music do you like?' he asked.

She shrugged. 'That's what I want to know. That's where I thought someone like you could help me.'

'You want me to tell you what kind of music you like?'

She looked more optimistic. 'Aye, could you?' She looked at him directly for the first time and he half-turned away. 'Are you all right, son?'

'Aye,' he said, managing a smile.

'You're shaking,' she said.

'Touch of the flu,' he muttered. He held out his right hand, palm outwards, fingers extended, and looked at its trembling. He remembered learning that men and women inspected their fingernails differently. He'd read it in some detective novel when he was about thirteen and going through puberty. He'd learnt then that he did it the female way. He still did, although he'd tried to change. Now he turned the hand round, closed the fingers into the palm and the trembling stopped.

'That's better,' he said.

'You should be in your bed,' said the woman.

'Aye, well.' He shrugged. 'Tell me, then, what *don't* you like?'

The woman thought about it.

'This weather,' she said. 'It gets you down. And Christmas – that did my head in. I don't like Christmas.'

'I meant musically,' said George. 'Anyway, Christmas was weeks ago. It'll be spring any day.'

'Aye, but what difference does that make? You've still to pay for it, don't you? From before. I've not finished yet and now there's all the birthdays. It's never-ending, just one thing after another.'

'Look,' said George, 'forget about all that. It's only money. Tell me about music. Musically, what do you want? Something to make you feel happy?'

'Not necessarily. I wouldn't want to buy a record just to make myself happy, it might not work, and then where would I be? I don't care what kind of mood it puts me in, I just want something with feeling.'

'What about the blues? That's mostly what's here.'

She looked at him uncomprehendingly.

'The blues. Blues music.'

'What's that then? Has it got feeling?'

He decided to play some blues for her. There was still nobody else in the shop and although he knew he should get her out and get going, he felt like listening to some blues himself. The shop keys were on a ring in his pocket. He went and locked the door. 'We're closed,' he said to her with a smile. 'I'll take you on a wee guided tour of the blues.'

He was a bit concerned that she'd used the word 'record' when there was nothing but compact discs on the racks, but he didn't want to worry her about that straightaway. He felt it would humiliate her.

He selected some CD cases and went to the shelves behind the counter to find the discs. It was a good cataloguing system, it didn't take him long. Then he started putting music through the speakers – some harp, some guitar, some

Delta, some Chicago, some folk blues, some electric. He played some Muddy Waters and some Lightnin' Hopkins, some Freddie King and some Sonny Boy Williamson. He played 'Black Cadillac' and 'Don't Start Me Talkin'' and 'Sad Letter Blues'. He pulled up a moulded plastic chair for the woman, and gave her a blast of Howlin' Wolf and a sample of Willie Dixon, some Blind Lemon Jefferson and Son House, some Bessie Smith, Big Mama Thornton and Etta James. Hell, after a while he hardly needed to play the songs, he just said the names, while the woman sat and nodded, rocking against the give in the chairback, and blew long streams of smoke from her nostrils. John Lee Hooker, Robert Johnson, Big Bill Broonzy, Leadbelly. The names crowded into the atmosphere and hung there. George and the woman talked a little, and he gently explained that it was very difficult to buy records anymore, most of the music companies had simply stopped making them. He thought about trying to tell her that CDs were themselves becoming outdated, but decided against it. While he talked and they listened to the music, her cigarette filters gathered in an old polystyrene cup he'd found under the counter. Outside, the world grew dark.

Then it was time to go.

'Oh God,' she said. 'I'll need to get back and put their tea on. I'm sorry I can't buy anything, after all that. I'm so out of touch. I feel like I've wasted your afternoon.'

'No,' he said, 'it was important to do this. It's good to slow down sometimes. And I'm sorry they don't make records anymore. There's something about vinyl you just can't beat.' He was putting all the CDs away carefully and returning the empty cases to the racks.

'Aye, you're right there,' she said. 'These new things are all right, I suppose, they're unbreakable and that, but they sound just as scratchy to me.'

'That's the recordings,' he said. 'Some of these are sixty years old, maybe more.'

'Tell me about it,' she said. She began her painful shuffle towards the door. By the time she got there he'd tidied everything away, put the keys back in the till drawer. 'I'm coming out with you,' he said. He held the door for her. 'Mind on your way up, there's a loose step.'

'Thanks for being so patient,' she said, buttoning her shapeless coat against the chill wind. 'It must be nice, having your own record shop.'

'Aye,' he said, 'I suppose so.' He pulled the door behind him, made sure it was properly shut, the way it had been when he came in. Only then did he realise he'd forgotten to take the CD he'd put aside. But it was too late. The spell was broken. He wouldn't go back in there alone.

The woman was halfway to the pavement. He waited till she'd got there, then went briskly up the steps and hurried off in the opposite direction.

He'd never noticed the shop before, although he must have walked along the street dozens of times. The sign, BASEMENT BEAT, was obscure and dirty. He'd only spotted it because it was a day when he was looking at everything. Details. This was a way of asking himself what he was doing there, if not being there would make any difference. One of the stone steps shoogled when he descended. He turned the handle of the door.

It was after three o'clock now, the day was starting to

fade. For a place that didn't appear to be doing much business it was surprisingly well stocked. Maybe that was why. He wondered how much money you'd need to take in a day just to stay afloat. Two, three hundred, if you ran it single-handed? Maybe more.

George quickly understood that it was a specialist shop. Jazz, blues, R&B, soul. He didn't know much about jazz, but blues, that was his thing, and there were stacks of it. Nothing much from the 'Hit Parade'. He almost said it out loud. The place had a gloomy, old-fashioned atmosphere that made a phrase like that seem appropriate. And the oddest thing, for a music shop – it was in absolute silence. He looked around. No customers. No staff either. It was as if everybody had gone out for a tea break and forgotten to lock the door.

He flicked through a few CDs. They made a slapping sound against one another, advertising his presence. But no one came through the doorway behind the counter. He began to feel the need for something on the sound-system. The speakers stared down at him like security cameras.

He saw a Johnny Shines album he'd been wanting for years. The sticker said £12.99. He couldn't really afford it but he'd probably never see it again. He carried the empty CD case up to the counter and coughed.

After a minute he said, 'Hello? Anybody in?' His voice was startling in the silence. He felt like he shouldn't be there. He stepped around the counter and leaned through the doorway into the back room.

There was a man in there. He was maybe in his sixties. He had thick black-framed spectacles and strands of sandy hair plastered over his bald head. One strand had come loose and hung like a bell-pull over his right eye, brushing the lens of his glasses. He wore an open-necked shirt and the waistcoat from a pinstripe suit. He was slumped in a chair behind a desk and the desk prevented George from seeing if he wore pinstripe trousers as well.

'Hello?' said George. But he realised that the man was not sleeping but dead.

His arms hung at his sides, his chin was resting on his chest, framed by the V of his shirt. In front of him was an opened can of cola and a half-eaten sandwich resting on a baker's paper poke.

George felt a curious calm wash through him. He crossed the floor of the room knowing that there was no urgency, no need to panic. He touched the man's cheek with the back of his hand. The skin had a cool clammy feel. He picked up the can and felt from its weight that it was about half-full. When he held it to his ear he could hear the faint ping of almost expired fizz.

Heart attack, he thought. Maybe. He wasn't a doctor. There was no sign of violence or disturbance. It looked like the shop owner – if that's who he was – had just died sitting there eating his piece. George glanced at the sandwich. He could see the ragged curve of the man's toothmarks where he had bitten through grated cheese and pickle.

He went back into the shop. From behind the counter it seemed even emptier. He himself had been the sole customer, now he was gone. He realised that he was still clutching the Johnny Shines case. He laid it down on the counter.

The cash register was switched on, the green display reading 0.00. George pressed the no sale button but the machine started whining. He pressed the cancel button. He tapped in 12.99, rang it up as a sale, then tapped in the same figures as cash tendered and pressed the sale button. The till drawer sprang open and a receipt was printed.

There wasn't much money in there. Two ten-pound notes, a fiver, nine pound coins and some other change. George lifted the tray out and looked in the drawer. There was a little pile of notes and cheques at the back. He counted five twenties and seven tens and put them in his pocket. He put the cheques back and replaced the tray. He took the thirty-four pounds from the plastic compartments, then put back the fiver and eight pounds. He took a penny in change and put it with the other money in his pocket. In one of the compartments was a bunch of keys. He took it out and closed the till. He tore off the receipt and dropped it on the floor.

He thought about walking home. But he didn't want to go home. He shared a flat with two other people. Whether he went back there or not he would be neither missed nor noticed. Sometimes several days would pass when he wouldn't see one or the other of his flatmates. Sometimes he wouldn't see either of them. He never wondered where they were, if they were safe or in trouble. He knew that, for them, the same applied to himself. If he closed the door of his room and stayed in there for a week they wouldn't know or care. This was supposed to make him feel free.

He was ten minutes' brisk walk to the train station. And the bus station. He thought of cities in England he could go to. Places he'd never been before. Manchester, Birmingham, Leeds, Bristol. Beautifully anonymous-sounding places. He wanted to walk through a crowd on an unfamiliar street.

He went back through to the office. The body hadn't moved. He remembered reading a Western when he was a boy, in which a corpse had suddenly sat up and groaned, terrifying everybody except the hero, who knew that this was what corpses sometimes did.

He tried to imagine what it was like to be alone in a room with a dead man. He tried to see himself in a book or a movie. Outside there were the sounds of cars and buses rolling by, the tapping of women's brisk heels and, in the distance, the cry of a siren. Inside there was the desk, some shelves loaded with files and catalogues, a stack of mail-order forms. There was another table on which sat an electric kettle, a couple of mugs, a spoon with a brown tide-mark, an assortment of tea bags, sugar, milk. George lifted the can of cola and drank from it, feeling its warm flat sweetness against his throat.

He felt as if he and the shop owner were special, as if they shared something denied to everybody else. He wondered what the man's last thoughts had been.

He wondered what was the last ever piece of music the man had heard. He went to check the sound-system, but there wasn't a CD in it. He thought again how strange that was, for a music shop. Just then he heard someone coming down the steps.

The woman trailed her way back across the city. She had been out all day. She didn't want to go home but she knew she would. Somebody had to feed them. She would need to stop in the Co-op on the way for some messages: beans, tatties, chops. She could hear the grill spitting and hissing at her as she cooked them.

She crossed the river by the pedestrian bridge. If you were on it and somebody else was coming from the other side it bounced you, made you feel like you had new energy in your soles. She liked the feel of it. Sometimes she'd stop halfway across and let the energy of other folk throb into her.

It was almost night. The lights of the city gleamed like amber fish in the black water. The clouds overhead threatened more rain, more cold. She hated this time of year. It clenched you up, turned you grey inside. There was no mercy in it.

The river was full, it rushed beneath her towards the sea. She watched a ripple in it that caught the reflection of the lamp behind her. The ripple was constantly turning like a rope; always new water, always the same shape. She could feel people passing behind her, the bridge going up and down.

She felt utterly alone.

The music had been unlike anything she'd ever heard, and yet she felt she recognised it. She'd not understood the rhythms of some of it, hadn't been able to pick out all the words that were moaned, wailed, screamed, muttered. Some of it had sounded like ghosts coming from a long time ago. But one thing she knew: it had feeling. Oh aye, the young fellow had been right about that. Songs like that made you want to start walking and never stop. They made you want to lie down and sleep. They made you want a drink, a greet, a laugh. The people who made those songs, she thought, they didn't wake up in the morning and wonder what to sing about. The stuff was in them, *was* them. It just came pouring out.

She was going back there, definitely. Tomorrow, or if not tomorrow the next day. She wanted to get a CD player so she could take some of the music home with her. Or one with headphones, so you could sit on a bus and travel with it in your ears. She wanted to ask the guy in the shop where to start, who to listen to first.

She looked down into the black swirling water and felt she was on the edge of discovering something.

Willie Masson's Miracle

Mrs Bovie appeared in the doorway, and Willie Masson made the noise that was his laugh now. He couldn't help himself.

'That's him angry,' said Mrs Bovie. She was his neighbour. 'The one that always keeps you right,' was how Kathleen used to describe her. 'There's one on every stair.' Willie ran through the names Kathleen had had for her: Mrs Bovine, Madam Ovary, Mrs Hoovery, The Rovin' Stovie. (Mr Bovie was long gone – dead or run away to sea or vacuumed into oblivion.) Ach, she wasn't all bad, she just liked to dip her spoon in other folk's broth. And she was wrong about everything. Apart from that she was fine. But he still didn't like her.

The woman from the chemist's shop jumped when Mrs Bovie spoke. It had taken Willie and Kathleen twenty years to get used to her and the woman from the chemist's shop had only been in the house a couple of times. Willie had decided she must be from the chemist's up the road because it was the only place nearby where the girls wore those slidey uniforms like the one she had on. He had no idea how she'd got into his house but he assumed it was on account of her job: apparently you could get prescriptions home-delivered these days if you couldn't get out much. Inside his head he could hear Kathleen: *Aye, and you're not ever going far again, are you?* Anyway the woman seemed very efficient and so far she hadn't nicked anything that he could see. Not that he'd be able to stop her if she did. He wouldn't even be able to yell at her, he'd be lucky if it came out as a whimper.

He watched the uniform slide over her backside as she bent for something from her case. He quite enjoyed that aspect of her visits. She must have gone on a training course because she could do everything unsupervised. She gave him tablets, shaved his face, changed his pyjamas and washed his private regions with a sponge. In the old days the girls couldn't even sell you paracetamol if the pharmacist was out on his dinner.

'Oh, did I give you a start?' said Mrs Bovie. She advanced across the room to the window, and pulled back the curtain a little so that the sun shone straight into Willie's eyes. Willie made his protest noise.

'That's better, isn't it?' said Mrs Bovie. 'He likes to see the sun, don't you, Mr Masson?'

They had lived next door to each other for decades but she'd always persisted with this Mr and Mrs business. Kathleen had said to her once, 'Just call me Kathleen,' but she wouldn't. They didn't know her first name but it began with an E and they reckoned it must be so awful that she'd rather keep things formal. Esmerelda, Ermintrude, Euphemia, something like that. They used to stick the possibilities in front of the other names they had for her and then feel ashamed of themselves.

Kathleen, before she'd gone funny, had had such a wicked sense of humour. Not quite cruel, but mischievous certainly. Once – it must have been after a wee Bovie session (that was Willie's phrase, but he kept it to himself) – they were talking about names, and Willie recalled a family he'd known when he was a boy, they were Congregationalists and had three daughters, Faith, Hope and Charity. 'Can you imagine the complexes those poor lassies would grow up with?' he said. 'I mean, you might as well have driven them straight to the door of the nearest brothel.'

'Were they triplets?' Kathleen asked.

'No,' he said, 'a year apart, like a row of Russian dolls.'

'But for heaven's sake, that was a terrible risk to take,' Kathleen said. 'Supposing the third one had been a boy? They'd have looked pretty silly trooping off to church as Faith, Hope and Eric.'

'Eric,' said Willie, 'why Eric?'

'I don't know,' she said, 'I just like the sound of it. It takes the wind out of the other two's sails.'

Mrs Bovie had a key, ever since Kathleen had started to forget things. Willie hadn't wanted to give it to her, it felt like an admission of guilt, but once he'd come home from the pub and found Kathleen shivering on the stair because she'd locked herself out, and another time Mrs Bovie had had to take her in for the evening until Willie got back. Poor Kathleen. She'd been quite distressed in Mrs Bovie's front room, she thought she'd been kidnapped. When Willie came for her she'd stared at him accusingly. 'What are you doing here? That's not my television. How much money do they want?'

'I'm sorry,' he'd said to Mrs Bovie – who was backing

away from the smell of drink on him, even though he'd not really had that much – 'I'll give you a key and you can let her in if it happens again. She's all right on her own once she's home.' Mrs Bovie nodded, thin-lipped, disappointed, perhaps, that things might not be so dramatic in future.

It made things difficult for Willie, though. He liked his drink but he couldn't bring it into the house. It was the one thing Kathleen and he differed on, the drink. Her own father had been a heavy drinker, had been violent to her and her mother. She didn't trust men and alcohol together and you couldn't blame her. But Willie wasn't like that, he wouldn't hurt a flea. He would certainly never lift a hand against Kathleen, whom he loved as much in her seventies as he had when they'd first met fifty years before. So they respected each other's opinion as far as the drink was concerned. Once or twice in a week Willie'd trauchle down to the pub and play a few games of doms with the boys, drink a few drams. When he came back Kathleen would be in bed, face to the wall, already asleep. He wasn't to wake her or kiss her goodnight with his whisky breath. Their backs bowed away from each other like a pair of brackets the wrong way round. But in the morning it was fine again, they had breakfast together and shared the papers and read out to each other the mad, stupid, incredible things that were going on in the world that day.

Once Kathleen got wandered, though, he couldn't get out to the pub so much. He decided he'd buy a half-bottle at a time and stash it away somewhere. She was getting so confused she'd never notice if he had a dram. The trouble was, she was into everything. She kept mislaying her purse, or the book that she carried even though she couldn't concentrate on it anymore, or her teeth. When she went searching for one of these items, she sometimes came perilously close to unearthing the half-bottle. Willie used to watch her, he used to say, 'Warm, warm, colder, brrr,' just to get her away from wherever he'd put it. He felt rotten because sometimes the purse or the book or the teeth would be nearby and she'd head off into the lobby while he put the missing object somewhere really prominent for her to find when she returned. He could have just given the things to her but he didn't want to take away her independence. Somehow he believed if she kept on finding them herself it meant she might get better. It meant he might still be able to reach her again.

But she didn't get better. One day there was a crash in the kitchen, the sound of breaking glass. Willie rushed through. Kathleen was backed up against the sink, holding by the neck the jagged remnants of the half-bottle he'd put behind the wastepipe in the cupboard below. Whisky and blood were running together down her arm, and she was crying. When he came through the door she lifted the broken bottle at him as if he had threatened her. 'Kathleen, Kathleen,' he said, trying to soothe her, 'it's all right.'

She narrowed her eyes at him. 'You liar,' she said. 'You drunkard, you liar. Get out of this house or I'll call the police.'

'Kathleen,' he said, 'darling, it's me.' But she only stared at him with hatred, and when he moved towards her she made as if to lunge at him with the bottle.

'Stay away from me, you animal,' she said. And Willie realised she was speaking to her father again, who had been dead twenty years and whom she hadn't spoken to for forty.

So they took Kathleen away because they said he couldn't be expected to cope and they put her to live in a big old house full of fire doors and handrails and a locked front door, a place that was hard for him to get to with the buses not being so frequent. It wasn't another place that began with an H because Willie wouldn't have gone near one of those places, he had a mortal fear of them. It was a Home. He used to visit but there were only brief moments when she seemed to recognise him and they were the worst, they made him feel like he had betrayed her. So he visited less and less. Mrs Bovie, he knew, thought he was callous. She'd meet him on the landing with her dripping mop like Britannia on the old pennies and she'd say, 'I pray for her, I pray for her because no one else will.' She was washing the stair and had put the mats upright against the wall. The water in her bucket had a scent of fake roses. He nodded and shut the door on her because he was free to do so. He'd never bothered to ask for the key back: he didn't want to negotiate with her about anything. The key symbolised something that lay between them and what he hoped was that they'd both forget about its existence, it would lie undisturbed in a drawer or wherever she'd put it. He thought *gathering dust* but he doubted anything was allowed to do that in Mrs Bovie's house.

Holy Bovie, that was another one. She'd been born again just after the menopause, Kathleen used to say. Willie tried to think of other nicknames for her in her religiously fervent state but he couldn't, there was no fun in it anymore. And now too there was no one to stop him drinking in the house or going out to the pub if he wanted to, but he didn't feel like doing either.

He thought about Kathleen up there in that other house that was a Home and wondered what she was thinking. Maybe she was wondering what she was thinking too. Maybe she thought she'd been kidnapped again. Maybe she thought Willie was her father beating up her mother while she was away. Maybe Willie was Willie in her head but not when he came to visit her, and she was having a grand time going on day trips with him in the 1950s. He could feel the sun beating down through the window of the railway carriage as they set off. He could see her skipping along the harbour wall at Aberdour. He couldn't understand why it all had to go wrong like this.

Then the thing happened. He was lying on the floor with the television on. He didn't remember getting there. The cord of the carpet made wee inverted carpet marks on his skin but he couldn't feel it. His arm lay out away from him as if he was stretching for something, but there was nothing there. A terrible silence was in the room and he realised that it wasn't the television, which he could hear quite clearly, it was his own voice. He was trying to make it heard and nothing was coming out.

He was there a long time. He'd never watched night-time TV before but he saw it all now, the bloody lot, a load of garbage, it made you despair for the folk that watched it regularly. Willie knew he was in trouble. The garbage came out of the set into his front room and there wasn't a damn thing he could do about it.

Later he heard someone banging at the front door and ringing the bell. And later still he heard Kathleen's key in the lock. She came in and Willie thought *it's good to see you home, darling, give us a hand up, will you?* but it was Mrs

Bovie, who yelped and went to the phone and then came back and stood beside him saying, 'I don't want to touch you, Mr Masson, I don't want to do any damage.' After that a lot of other folk arrived and got him off the carpet while Mrs Bovie hovered about telling them all, 'I knew there was something wrong after I washed the stair and he didn't put his mat back down. You don't like to interfere but you have to keep a watch out for your neighbours, don't you?'

Eventually he was taken away but not to the place where Kathleen was. He was in a bed but you could tell when all the chemists came to look at him that they really didn't want him in it, you could tell they wanted that bed for somebody else. And Willie only wanted his own bed anyway, his own bed and his own chair in his own house. Somehow the chemists and he managed to straighten it out between them and they brought him back, and sent the woman in the slidey uniform to see him every day.

And Mrs Bovie, who still had the key, popped in and out like a wifie in a weatherhouse. The chemist wifie got a fright from her but you couldn't stay frightened for long, she was harmless really. She *was* a good neighbour, he supposed, he felt sorry for her. She talked about Willie to Willie now, whatever came into her head. 'I pray for him, don't I, Mr Masson?' she said. 'I pray for him because you just think, it could be you, and you should be grateful, shouldn't we? Isn't that right, Mr Masson?'

The other woman nodded and said something Willie couldn't hear. How could he not hear her when he could hear every bloody word the Bovine one uttered? If he had to have a woman in the house and it wasn't Kathleen he wanted it to be the one from the chemist's. She was all right.

She didn't stand for any nonsense. God, in the slidey uniform she even looked a bit like Kathleen had in her WRAF uniform. But could she not speak up a bit? Could she not get the Bovie out of the house, so they could be alone together again?

Willie felt the frustration boiling inside the shell of his body. He made skeletal fists inside his hollow hands and thumped the arms of his chair with them. He could see his hands not moving as he did this, they just lay there like fish on a slab. He didn't know why he thought of that, the cold corpses in the fishmonger's window, all dead-eyed and flat-faced, but pictures like this kept rushing in front of him, pictures from his childhood, from the war, from his young days with Kathleen. He raged away at himself and the chemist wifie leaned over and wiped the slavers from his mouth. He tried to turn his head but his neck hardly moved and he could feel the dim sensation of her hand moving the towel across his jaw, deep away from him on the outside. It was like a dentist's injection beginning to wear off and then not wearing off. It was like being at the mercy of your mother's hanky-tented dabbing finger years after she was dead and buried. Willie hated it. He knew perfectly well she wasn't from the chemist's and that the chemists round the other bed he had been in hadn't been chemists either, he knew fine where he'd been but he was damned if he was going to admit it.

The first day she was in the wifie had said, 'Oh, there's been some mistake here, you can't be left on your own like this, I understood your wife would be able to look after you.' Mrs Bovie had come in and made her jump that day too and explained that she wasn't his wife and the woman had said, '*I see*' in a meaningful tone and Mrs Bovie had gone pink and explained in more detail and the woman had said she would have to get it all sorted out but it might take a couple of days and would Mrs Bovie keep an eye on things till they could get a place for him? Willie had made every protest noise he could think of but they'd just ignored him or simply not heard. And that was how it was going to be from now on, he reckoned, being ignored or not heard, one or the other.

He summoned all his thoughts together and channelled them down his left arm and imagined it getting a jolt of power like the time when he was a boy in the greenhouses where his father worked and he'd touched an old live wire with his fingers wet from the watering can and got flung in among the cucumbers, and suddenly he was amazed to see his hand flip up and catch the wifie a neat wee skelp with the knuckles right on the end of her nose. A gush of blood started from one nostril, and to his delight, before she could step back and stick the towel on her own face, three bright drops fell through the sunlit air and landed in his freshly pyjama'd lap. His left hand lay once again, wooden and innocent, on the chair.

'You old bugger,' said the woman. Her voice was muffled through the towel but she was right in front of him, he could hear her no problem at all. 'How the hell did you manage that? *How did you do that?*'

Mrs Bovie was jumping elatedly in the background. 'A miracle, it's a miracle! O Lord, it's a miracle!'

It was the best thing in ages. If only Kathleen could have been there to see it. Willie made the noise that was his laugh now. Tears were streaming down his face.

The Rock Cake Incident

Gregor Meiklejohn arrived at the dentist's in good time. It was his intention to have ten minutes looking at the magazines before his check-up.

'It's Mr Cruikshank, isn't it?' the receptionist smiled.

'No, no, Meiklejohn.' He didn't recognise her either.

'Of course, silly of me. It's just they have a lot of the same letters in them.'

In the waiting room he sat next to the fish tank, trying to work out how true her remark was. It was a while since his last visit – he couldn't remember exactly when that had been – but there was a comforting familiarity about the surroundings: he remembered being in that very seat. Or had it been the one over by the door? No, it was the one he was in, he was sure, right by the fish tank. The two fish, a big gold one and a wee blue one with feathery gills, came in turn and inspected him, darted off again, then returned to make another check, having forgotten who he was. That was the truth about fish in tanks, they only had a memory span of a few seconds, which was why they never got bored. The fish were there for a reason: to calm people's nerves. Like the piles of old magazines – *Reader's Digest, Country*

Living, Good Housekeeping, The Scots Magazine – their role was to reassure waiting patients that some things never changed, that there was life after dentistry, bliss in ignorance. Something like that. He began to exchange glances with the fish on each of their circuits – if circuit was the right word for their probing, startled tank tours. Hello, little fishies. Do you ever get confused by life? Do you ever forget who you are? Do you ever remember who you are? Life must be one constant round of shocks and surprises for you. *Boo!* (Although he was alone, he did not say this out loud.) Imagine: a surprise you fall for every time, day in, day out.

He had barely reached for the top copy of *Hello!* when the receptionist appeared at the door. 'The dentist will see you now.'

The dentist, a brute of a man, welcomed him in and with a dramatic gesture invited him to stretch out on the reclining chair. Gregor made himself comfortable while the dentist washed his hands and passed aimless comments about the weather. There was a squeaking, snapping noise as he pulled on a pair of surgical gloves. When he came over to the chair, Gregor noticed how the gloves pinched the black hairs at his wrists, and that he smelt of perfumed soap. These were features of the dentist he had not noted on his last visit. In fact, he didn't recognise him at all.

'Now, what are you here for?'

'Well, I've come to see you, of course. A check-up.'

'I think not,' said the dentist, the final 't' making a noise like a dart landing in a bull's-eye. He consulted his records. 'Ah, yes, as I thought. They're all coming out today, aren't they?'

'No, no!' Gregor protested, attempting to rise.

The dentist was powerfully built. He placed a restraining hand on Gregor's chest. 'Relax,' he said. 'It's futile to struggle, Mr Cruikshank.'

'But my name's not Cruikshank!' cried Gregor. 'It's Meiklejohn. You've got the wrong man.'

The dentist began to laugh. 'So sorry,' he said. 'My little joke. I overheard Maureen earlier. You're quite right, you're just in for a check-up.'

Although Gregor felt that the dentist had been somewhat less than professional, he allowed himself to subside in the chair again. He stared hard, trying to locate the dentist's face in the filing cabinet of his memory.

'Still,' said the dentist, 'you never know what we might find. It might just be my lucky day, eh?'

Gregor's jaw swung open automatically at the approach of the dentist's hand, which held a sharp and shining implement. The hand began to poke and scrape around his mouth with it.

'Hmm,' said the dentist. It was an indeterminate noise. It might mean good news. Or bad.

'It would be terrible, wouldn't it,' said the dentist, 'if I really had thought you were Mr Cruikshank and taken all your teeth out. A case of mistaken dentistry, that would be. Ha ha! Mistaken dentistry, I like that!'

'Uh ihuh hui'hang,' Gregor began. The dentist obligingly removed the implement. 'But Mr Cruikshank,' Gregor repeated, 'would presumably object to *not* having all his teeth out.' It was a weak argument. They both knew it.

'Wash your mouth out, please,' said the dentist. 'He might, but by then it would be too late for you, wouldn't it?

But you're right, he might object – if he existed. He doesn't. Ha ha! No, not at all. Just a figment of my imagination. And of Maureen's, of course. Open.'

It was another five minutes before the dentist declared himself satisfied with the state of Gregor's incisors, grinders and molars. During that time they discussed, with the dentist for obvious reasons having the better part of the conversation, the nature of power and control in human relationships.

'I was reading something the other day,' the dentist said, 'in one of our professional journals, about a series of psychological experiments that were conducted in America back in the 1960s. People were persuaded to subject other people to progressively louder and longer bursts of, what's that stuff you hear on the television? Canned laughter, that's the stuff. Always makes me think of Popeye and spinach. Anyway, this canned laughter was delivered through a specially designed television monitor on which these people were watching a totally inane sitcom. Situation comedy,' the dentist explained helpfully. 'They'd been told that the experiment was about measuring the effects of peer group pressure on stupid viewers, but in fact, according to this article I was reading, the idea was to see how far people would go in inflicting mindless television on others if they were told that they would not be held responsible if anything went wrong. Hold still now. Do you wish to spit?'

'Hhn,' Gregor said.

'Well, anyway, first, an individual, who was designated the "teacher", helped to settle the "learner" into an armchair in front of the television monitor. Then the "teacher" went into an adjoining room, separated from the "learner" by a screen, and a pre-recorded sitcom was played on the monitor. Nothing much wrong here,' the dentist said, moving on to Gregor's lower teeth. 'Each supposedly funny line or piece of slapstick was accompanied by canned laughter. Regardless of the reaction of the "learner", the "teacher" would increase the level of canned laughter by some electronic gadget. And here's the fascinating bit. Invariably, the "learner", even if not amused by the show to begin with, "learned" to join in the laughter issuing from the television. With each successively less funny joke the laughter became more prolonged and riotous, and the "learner" too laughed harder, though without, apparently, knowing why. What do you make of that, eh?'

'Uh-ay-ing,' Gregor said.

'Yes, isn't it? Although the "learner" couldn't be seen by the "teacher", he or she could be heard all right, oh yes, giving first a grunt or perhaps a momentary giggle, then chortling, chuckling and eventually howling with desperate shrieks of hilarity. Yes, howling! Oh, I forgot, there was a "controller" present, who assured the "teacher" that they took total responsibility for the experiment. Most of those taken on as "teachers" carried out their instructions fully, although not without considerable stress. Mental anguish, even. The "controller", of course, remained completely calm and dispassionate. That's what controllers do. Sometimes, the "controller" would insist that the canned laughter level be increased, even though no joke had been made. In fact, there was no obvious relation between the funniness of the sitcom and the application of the canned laughter. Personally I don't find much of what's on television at all funny, but this was a long time ago. Anyway, the only real connection, because the whole thing was a set-up, was between the "teacher" operating the laughter mechanism and the "controller" – the one following the instructions of the other. Some people were so obedient that they administered enough canned laughter to cause their "learner" to collapse on the floor. Sometimes the "learner" had a, you know, accident. There were one or two heart attacks, even some temporary brain damage. So the article said. Not that one should believe everything one reads in dental journals. The "teachers" would continue to operate the lever even while clutching their heads and saying, "Oh God, please, let's stop it, can't we stop it?"'

The dentist had become quite animated, in fact he was almost shouting, and Gregor was relieved when he finally removed his instruments and stood back.

'It's amazing,' the dentist said, 'what some people will allow themselves to be put through. They'll trust some smiling person in authority before their own instincts. How do they know this person has any qualifications or expertise? Of course they weren't really administering canned laughter, it was all faked, and the "learners" were acting. At least, that's what we're told. Do you floss?'

'No,' said Gregor. 'It hurts.'

'Of course it hurts. It's a virtuous activity. But it stops all those little bits of meat and things getting stuck between your teeth.'

'I'm a vegetarian,' said Gregor, even though this wasn't true.

'Little bits of broccoli, then,' the dentist said testily. 'Or lettuce or bean sprouts or whatever it is you people eat. Canned spinach.' He pushed a button. The chair jerked upright and Gregor got to his feet. 'Off you go then,' the dentist said.

Maureen the receptionist charged Gregor ten pounds for having healthy teeth, and asked if he would like a card sent to him in six months, to remind him to make another appointment. Gregor said he would think about it. As he staggered out onto the street he could hear her cheerful voice addressing another man in the waiting room. 'Mr Hitchcock?' He covered his ears with his hands and hurried away.

In a café across the street he ran his tongue carefully round his teeth, checking for anything unusual. He didn't altogether trust the dentist, who he feared might have left some equipment in his mouth.

He had not seen the waitress before. She was lovely. The tables were full of women discussing *Coronation Street* and a new game show on BBC Nine called *Whose Genitals?*, which Gregor made a mental note to watch the following week. He observed the lovely waitress moving among the women, serving them cups of coffee, scones, sandwiches and pots of tea. From the feet up, which was the order in which he inspected her, she had on clumpy-heeled shoes, black tights, a short black skirt and a red shirt. A wee black apron too. Her skin was pale and unblemished but she had a stud in her nose. Glittering silver fish were attached by hooks to her ears. Her brown hair was cut in a bob and when she moved the overhead light was reflected in its sheen.

She came over to his table, and he asked for a coffee and a rock cake. She wrote this down on her pad. At least, she wrote *something* down on her pad, he couldn't see what. *I hate my job*, or *check out the guy at table 5*, or a witty little haiku about bungee-jumping, it might be anything.

'I see you've caught a couple of nice salmon,' he said. 'Or are they trout?'

She looked at him blankly until he flicked his own ear lobes. Then she laughed for about half a second.

'Do you ever,' he asked, 'do you ever get the feeling that you're not really in the real world, you're in a kind of bubble, and everybody else is just play-acting around you? Do you ever feel like that?'

She did not reply, but gave him a nervous smile and hurried off, scribbling on her pad. Probably *lunatic at table 5, phone police*. No, she wouldn't do that. She would recognise his loneliness, his feelings of inadequacy, his sense that life was not quite what it seemed. Not at all what it seemed, in fact. She looked like the understanding type. Mind you, you couldn't tell these days. He'd heard of women – lovely, kind women just like her – who took off their wedding rings and went to Ibiza for a week to get as much sex with total strangers as they possibly could while their husbands were away on the oil rigs. That's what they did, the little minxes. Oh, he hoped so, he hoped so. He was going straight to the travel agent as soon as he'd had his coffee.

She brought him what he'd ordered and a piece of paper folded over, smiled uncertainly again and went back to the kitchen. He carefully unfolded the paper. On it was written, *1c, 1ck*.

He scalded his mouth drinking the coffee too fast and when he bit into the cake there was an unpleasant crunching sensation. He removed a small stone chip from his mouth, and a splinter of tooth. He decided not to eat the rest of the cake.

He waited till the coffee had cooled down, took a large mouthful and swilled it round his teeth, then spat it back into the cup. Two ladies at the next table stopped talking, then quickly started again.

He went up to the cash register and the waitress came and took the paper from him. 'Liclick,' he said. It sounded obscene. The waitress looked at him in horror. 'Liclick,' he repeated. 'It's what it says on the bill, look. Table 5.'

'Those are ones,' she said, 'not Ls. One coffee, one cake.'

'I didn't eat much of the cake,' he said. 'And I put most of the coffee back. But don't worry, I'm not going to make a fuss.'

She grabbed the ten-pound note he proffered and gave him his change.

'Do you know if there's a good dentist near here?' he asked.

She looked as if she was about to scream for help, then she half-turned and pointed across the street.

'There's a dentist over there,' she said. 'But I don't know if he's any good.'

'Neither do I,' he said. 'But thanks anyway.'

When he got home he looked in the bathroom mirror for a long time, trying to watch himself age. He wondered if women found him as frightening as he found them. He had not, of course, gone to the travel agent. Nor had he gone for a haircut, which he sometimes did when he felt a need to have his head massaged by a nice young woman. They usually asked if he was on holiday, just because he was a man getting his hair cut on a weekday afternoon. He usually said yes, he was, he worked on the oil rigs and was on shore leave. It was easier than telling the truth, which was that he hated his place of employment and often invented reasons not to be there. He worked in a department of local government which processed small but vital bits of information about road and footpath repairs, and this, he had noticed over the years, seemed to happen whether he was at his desk or not.

He and his wife Jane watched five hours of television that night, which was about average for them. Exactly average, in fact. Six till eleven, oven-ready meals on laps, then Jane went for her bath. Among the programmes they watched were two soap operas, a wildlife documentary, a repeat of a 1970s sitcom, a game show and a fly-on-the-wall programme about some people who were locked up in a house for nine weeks while the rest of the country observed them on television and through their computers. You could see them picking their noses, having baths, lying in the garden, cooking their tea, reading comics and arguing. Every week somebody got voted out of the house by the viewers. The last person left would win enough money to get plastic surgery so they wouldn't be recognised by anyone ever again.

Gregor Meiklejohn quite fancied getting plastic surgery. He would quite like to change his name, occupation, appearance, maybe even his sex, and start all over again. He would like to be a virtual news presenter or a game show contestant, or just a person in a game show audience. Anybody but Gregor Meiklejohn. That was why he did the lottery every week. So did Jane. They did their own numbers and if either of them won the jackpot they would share the winnings, split down the middle, half and half. After that they'd be on their own. First stop Ibiza for him. They'd agreed this verbally but Gregor wondered if they ought to write it down as a binding contract. He didn't altogether trust Jane, especially when she went away on holiday with her sister, as she sometimes did.

He thought, when did life stop being real? Was it when he and Jane stopped going to the pub? Or having conversations? Or sex? Was it at the last general election, and if so would there be a chance to vote for something different at the next one? Not that he knew anything about politics. Or economics, for that matter, or science, or art, or culture, any of that highbrow stuff. Or religion. When did everybody stop believing in God and start believing in the six balls with numbers on them? And when did they stop believing in the six balls? Plus the bonus ball. And what about humanity and trust – when did that all come to an end? And people not knowing who they were? And, Gregor thought, have I always been this lonely?

Oh dear. Now he was feeling sorry for himself. Jane had gone to bed and he would wait till she was asleep before he crept in beside her. He'd have no one to talk to. Not that he talked to Jane anymore. He went into the bathroom and brushed his teeth. He did not floss. He stood in front of the mirror, trying to watch himself age. He couldn't remember if he looked the same as he had earlier. He tried to fix the image of himself in his head so that he could compare it with what he would see in the mirror in the morning. Hopeless. He ran his tongue round his teeth and found a rough bit which hadn't been there when he got up. The rock cake incident. He would have to make a dental appointment. Great. If he phoned early and said it was an emergency they might fit him in the same day. Then he could take the afternoon off work. If he did that he could get his hair cut too.

Old Mortality

'Are you cold?' Alec asked. 'You mustn't get a chill.'

'I'm all right,' Liz said. 'It was just a shiver. You know, one of those shivers? Just standing here in front of this . . . this bloody great stone. Your family.'

'They're not as bad as all that,' he said.

'It scares me, though,' she said, 'and that's the truth. I mean, when I think about everything. What we're going to do. And then here's this thing that represents generations of your family and there's nothing on it. Absolutely nothing.'

'Well, I hope you weren't expecting some big message,' he said. 'You're right, there is nothing. It's a lovely place, that's all. No mystery, no revelation. I just wanted to show it to you.'

'But there are people here,' she said. 'Can't you feel them?'

'No,' he said. 'It's just a graveyard, sweetheart.'

'There's more to it than that,' she said. She reached for his hand. 'There has to be.'

'No,' he said, 'this is it. A field full of bones. This is where everybody ends up.'

She shivered again, although there was still warmth in the air. 'I think we're being watched,' she said.

'What?' He glanced round. 'Who by?'

'I don't know. I just feel it.'

He tried not to laugh. When Liz came out with things like this, which she'd been doing a lot lately, it made him uneasy. It was amusing, but he felt it could get out of hand and then it wouldn't be funny at all. But also it made him feel manly, sensible, down-to-earth. It sent a wave of love rushing through him. He would have been embarrassed, though, if anyone else had heard her.

They had been visiting his parents for the weekend. They didn't go very often: work and other commitments left them with little time or energy to make the journey north, and there was also the fact that Liz felt intimidated by Alec's mother. But there'd been a particular reason for making this trip: to tell them about the baby they were expecting. They weren't married, and Liz had anticipated a fuss, an argument about 'doing the right thing'. In fact, all had gone well. Alec's mother had seemed genuinely pleased about becoming a grandmother. Liz felt that perhaps a turning point in the relationship had been reached.

Then on the way back south Alec had turned off the main road in order to introduce Liz to his ancestors. He'd never taken her there before. The place was a ruined church with an ancient burial ground, right on the edge of the firth. To get to it you left the dual carriageway and followed a single-track road down to the water. There were fine old trees, beech and ash, and a big house, with three cars in the drive, that had presumably once been the manse. Through an iron kissing-gate was the roofless church, surrounded by old gravestones and tablets set at odd angles like wreckage bobbing in a green sea. The kirk's west gable-end rose to a small belfry which would once have housed a single monotonous summoning bell. A sign at the boarded up door warned of the danger of falling masonry.

The gravestones were thick with moss, their inscriptions faded and often indecipherable. There was the usual assortment of symbols found in old Scottish kirkyards: urns, skulls, bones, shrouds. Towards the water was a section filled with more recent stones, polished ones from the fifties and sixties that seemed out of place, as if they had been transferred from another cemetery. Between the boundary dyke and the sea a few sheep were grazing a strip of rough pasture. It was early evening in October. The grass was thick and springy, and there was birdsong among the stones and in the great trees shading the parking area. It was, Alec thought, all very peaceful.

'I wish we hadn't come,' Liz said. 'I'm frightened.'

'What's the matter?' he said. He tried not to sound impatient. 'What are you frightened of?'

'Nothing.'

He thought she was avoiding the question, but then she said it again. 'Nothing. That's exactly what.'

His ancestors had once been big shots in the area. Landed gentry. They had been rich at a time when almost nobody else was. Each generation had followed the pattern of the previous one. The eldest son inherited the big house and the younger ones went off to die in far-flung bits of the Empire, while the daughters were married to the sons of other rich families. The wives – all the wives – produced eight, or ten, or twelve children, or died in the attempt. Even the good breeders expired long before their husbands. Their annual pregnancies and early deaths were what perpetuated the system. Nothing lasts, though. One laird died unexpectedly young. There were debts and death duties. Limbs started to break off the family tree: the stout trunk began to crack and crumble. The big house was now long gone, and Alec's parents lived miles away in a new housing development. Alec felt, when he was being cynical, that he was a twig at the end of a fallen branch rotting on the ground.

The ancestral plot was a patch enclosed by a foot-high cast-iron fretted fender. Various centuries-old tablets lay half-submerged in the soft turf. The main feature was an upright sandstone slab, eight feet high and ten feet wide, at the base of which, presumably, the family lay packed one on top of another. The sandstone had weathered so much that only a few words were still legible: BELOVED ... DIED ... TAKETH ... TRUST. Alec ran his fingers over the face of the stone, but the names that had once been there could no longer be felt any more than they could be read. He knew it was the right spot because his grandfather had brought him to it twenty-five years before. 'Pay attention,' his grandfather had said. 'This will be standing long after you and I are both gone. This is where we come from.'

He could read a few of the names back then. There had been an ALEXANDER, which had made him feel sure that his grandfather must be right. *This is where we come from*: he'd imagined troll-like people who looked a bit like him crawling from a hole under the slab. Twenty-five years and nothing much had changed. And yet everything had changed: his grandfather was dead – cremated – Alec was grown up, and the names on the stone were all gone. And he didn't feel the connection anymore.

Something else was different. Beyond the kirkyard, beyond the sheep, beyond the splash of the shoreline, a group of oil rigs rested in the water like great metallic birds. They brought them in from the North Sea fields for refitting or when demand for oil fell and some distant accounting procedure drove them into the firth like birds sheltering from a storm. Alec thought them majestic. The vast structures, all intestinal pipes and rust-coloured legs and craning steel beaks and claws, seemed to be in sympathy with the gravestones, as if they themselves were already becoming monuments to aching toil and hard-earned rest.

'I love it here,' Alec said. He moved behind her, put his arms around her waist and gently turned her to face the water. He felt the bump beneath her shirt and rubbed it with the palm of one hand. 'Beautiful, isn't it?'

Liz said, 'Yes, in a way. But ugly too. Those things out there, they're like monsters.' She turned again to the family monument. 'You know what really scares me?'

'No.'

'The finality of it. This great blank . . . nothing.'

'The End,' he said, and gave a little laugh.

'You don't believe in anything, do you?' she said. 'Not God, not something else after this, nothing at all.'

'Nope,' he said.

'I just can't imagine it,' she said. 'Not feeling, not existing. It doesn't make sense.'

'I believe in you and I believe in me,' he said. 'I can feel us both. That makes sense.'

'What about love?' she said. 'Don't you believe in love?'

'Well, I suppose so, but . . . it's not really something you *believe* in, is it? It's just there.'

'But it has a power. It can make things happen. We know that.'

'Are you going to burst into song, Liz?'

'No I fucking am not.' She kicked him lightly on the shin with her heel. 'I'm just . . . everything just feels . . .'

'What?'

'Empty,' she said.

He let her go and she walked down towards the sea. He wondered if she was trying to tell him something about the baby. If there was something wrong. If she didn't want to go through with it.

Down below, where his forebears had been, it *was* empty. He felt that all right. Their minds and bones long since crumbled away. Ideas and work and knowledge and endurance, all mince for the worms. But there was a comfort in that. One day, there'd be nothing more to face, to deal with. He thought of the morning, Monday, and how tired, almost immediately, he would be.

He was about to call to Liz, ask her if she was feeling sick, if she was warm enough, if everything was going to be all right, when she gave a little yelp of surprise. She was twenty yards away, at the entrance to a stone enclosure – some other family's plot. 'Alec?' she said – quite quietly, but a light breeze had got up off the firth and her voice carried to him as if she were speaking in his ear – 'Alec, come here.'

The body of an old man was stretched on top of one of

the tablets inside the enclosure. He was wearing a heavy black coat with mud splatters around the hem, and trousers with mud encrusted round the ankles. He had old working boots on his feet. On the ground beside him was a Tesco carrier bag with the wooden shaft of some implement protruding from it. His mouth was open and his right arm was flung to the side so that the hand trailed over the edge of the tablet. His skin looked blue beneath the white bristles of his beard.

'Oh, Jesus,' Alec said.

Liz had her hand to her mouth. 'I knew it,' she said. 'I knew someone was watching us.'

'I don't think so, sweetheart,' Alec said. 'I think he's dead.'

He stepped forward and listened. His own heart was pounding so hard he couldn't hear if the old man was breathing. He reached out and gingerly touched the coat at the shoulder. It felt damp and cold. He smelt something unpleasant, mouldy. He shook the shoulder.

The man jerked upright, and Alec jumped away. 'What? What?' the old man said, and went into a fit of coughing. Alec came back and started slapping his back. 'I'm sorry,' he said. 'Don't worry, it's all right. God, I'm sorry. We thought you were dead.'

'Dead?' the old man said. 'I'm not dead. Stop hitting me. What makes you think I'm dead?'

'You don't look very well,' Liz said.

'I was working. I just needed a kip. Who are you?'

'We're visitors,' Alec said. 'We're looking at the graves. Do you look after them then?'

'Look after what?'

'The graves.'

'Oh.' He paused. 'Aye, I do. After a fashion.' Another pause, as if he was weighing the information he had just given them. 'Not just these ones. I look after lots of grave-yards, all over the country. I do repairs.'

Alec and Liz exchanged glances. The old man appeared confused, disorientated. He swung his feet to the ground, cleared his throat and spat.

'Sorry, lass,' he said, less roughly. 'Always have to do that when I've had a kip.'

'I'm sorry we disturbed you,' Liz said.

'Well, it's done now. Need to get on anyway. Finish up for the day.'

The three of them came out of the enclosure together. The old man looked at the sky as if assessing the chances of rain. He spat again.

'What is it you repair?' Alec asked. 'The gravestones?'

'Aye, of course,' the old man said. 'Do you think I'm going to manage the kirk single-handed?' He was more impatient with Alec than he was with Liz. 'The stones, man, the stones. Plenty of them. Somebody's got to do it, get them back to how they were. See?' He opened the Tesco bag and took out a mallet and a stone chisel. 'Tools of the trade, man. That's all I need. Anybody could do it, really.'

'Oh, right,' Alec said. He glanced at Liz again.

'Once the names are gone, you see,' the old man said, 'that's it. Oblivion.' He looked directly at Liz, as if he suddenly recognised her. 'What are *you* doing here? You're too bonnie to hang about a place like this.'

Liz shrugged. She was about to speak when Alec butted in. The old man was beginning to irritate him.

'My ancestors are here.' Alec pointed to the sandstone slab. 'I wanted to show her our stone.'

The old man peered over at the slab. 'Oh aye,' he said, 'I mind that one. How do you ken it's yours?'

'What do you mean?'

'How do you ken it's your stone. There's no names on it.'

'My grandfather told me,' Alec said. 'He brought me here years ago. I remember.'

'You remember, do you?' Something like a sneer slid into the old man's voice. 'Your grandfather? Ach well. If you remember.'

'Yes, he does,' Liz said. She moved closer to Alec. 'He does.'

'Ach well,' the old man said again. 'That's all right then.'

'There were names on it then,' Alec said. 'But they're all gone now.'

'That's right,' the old man said. 'All gone. Nothing more I can do about *them*.'

Liz shivered against Alec. He could tell she was still frightened. There was something about the old man that even he found unsettling.

'Well, I'd better get on.' The man put his tools back in the plastic bag and set off towards the shore, where the newer graves were. They saw him spit on the grass again. After a minute his head bobbed down behind a shiny black stone and they heard the *chink, chink* of his chisel.

Alec screwed up his face at Liz. 'What was that all about?'

'I don't know,' Liz said. 'He seems . . .'

'He's nuts,' Alec said. 'Probably harmless, but nuts. Nobody goes around repairing gravestones. Not like that.

With their tools in a carrier bag? And where's his car? He can't have walked here.'

'Maybe he lives nearby,' Liz said. She pointed at the former manse in the trees. 'Like there.'

'I don't think so. Did you get a whiff of him? He's a tramp. A tramp who's lost the place, thinks he's a stonemason.'

'That's sad,' she said. 'Maybe we ought to tell someone.'

'What would we say? That we met an old tramp in a graveyard and we think he's a bit sad? Forget it. Who'd give a fuck about that?'

They stood together, holding hands, looking out at the rigs. Alec tried to count them, but some were hidden behind others, and he kept having to start again. A dozen at least. Liz was doing the same, or maybe just staring, he couldn't tell. Why was that, if he loved her? And if she was going to have his baby? How could he be so close to her and yet not tell?

The breeze blowing off the water was cool now. The day was starting to fade, and out on the rigs amber and yellow lights were coming on.

'Time to go,' Alec said.

'Do you think we should offer him a lift?' Liz asked, as they started back to the car.

'Who? The old fellow? No chance,' Alec said.

Liz said, 'Wait a minute. Listen.'

They heard a sheep bleating, and gulls crying, but the *chink, chink* noise had stopped.

'Go and see if he's all right,' she said. 'He might have keeled over again.'

'He'll be fine,' Alec said.

'No, go and check,' she insisted. 'I couldn't bear it if we left him here and he'd collapsed. We'll both go.'

But there was no sign of him. They separated, searching through the newer gravestones, calling out, 'Hello, hello,' but he had gone. They came together again by the stone he had been working on.

'He must have had a bike,' Alec said. 'He said he was finishing up for the day. He'll stay up the road somewhere.'

'He didn't have a bike,' Liz said. Then she said, 'Oh, look!'

All the lettering on the shiny black stone had been chiselled away. They could tell where it had been because there were six deep gouges across the face of the stone. On the ground was a heap of chips. The breeze was already dispersing dust across the grass.

'Bloody hell!' Alec said.

Liz stood shaking her head. 'Do you think he did that? He can't have, can he?'

'He must have. There's been nobody else here.'

'But that's terrible. That's sacrilege.'

'Vandalism. The old bastard.'

'Maybe it's some family thing,' Liz said. 'That must be what it is. An old feud. Maybe somebody did something awful to him, something he could never forgive, and this is his way of repaying them.'

'Doesn't matter,' Alec said. 'It still doesn't give him the right. And anyway, this isn't the only one. Look, here. And here.'

They separated and moved among the stones again, finding more and more of them defaced, the names and dates of people obliterated. Every time they found one they shouted out in amazement. They only stopped, and came back together, when it grew so gloomy that it was easier to hear than to see each other.

'He said he did repairs,' Alec said.

'Yes,' Liz said. 'But that's not what he meant. He said . . .'

'What?' Alec said when she didn't finish.

'Something else,' Liz said. 'What was it?'

'We should report him,' Alec said. 'Nobody has the right to do that.' He heard the anger in his voice and wondered at it. He felt Liz clutch at his arm. 'That's what the weather does,' he said. 'The wind and the rain. That's what *they* do. Not some old tramp with a hammer and chisel.'

'I'd like to go now,' Liz said. 'Can we go?'

'Yes, yes, of course.' She looked so pale and weary that he needed to say something, to reassure her.

'I'll look after you,' he said. 'You don't need to be afraid.'

'I know,' she said. But they hurried to the car, and Alec started the engine at once, as if something were pursuing them. He switched on the headlights. The night had swallowed up the day and he felt as if it might swallow them. He wondered where the old man had gone. He thought, maybe he's hiding in the back of the car with his chisel, just waiting till we drive off before he attacks. He ridiculed the thought as soon as it arrived, but he kept it to himself.

He took a last look at the firth before swinging the car round. The lights on the oil rigs stretched towards them across the water in wavy amber lines. The rigs could have been giant floating houses, each one with giant children running up and down stairs, and a man and a woman of ordinary size, coming home from work, exhausted, dividing the labours, one tidying rooms and drawing curtains while the other prepared dinner for their giant children. But it was an illusion, a childish fancy. They were just oil rigs, waiting for the signal from someone hundreds or maybe thousands of miles away that would send them back out to sea.

MacTaggart's Shed

That morning, before it was fully light, before he had drunk a cup of coffee, even before the first whisky of the day, Christie saw ghosts crawling through the field opposite his house. He had come to in the armchair in the living room. He wasn't sure what had woken him. Probably a tractor or car going by. His head ached and his mouth felt like it was stuffed with newspaper. The room was still half-dark and he stumbled over an empty bottle lying on the carpet as he went to the window and pulled back the shabby brown curtain.

Across the narrow road was the big field, and beyond it another road, and beyond that trees and more fields rising up into the hills. There were houses dotted along the distant road and also on the hillside. He could see lights in some of the windows, but it was not yet bright enough to make out smoke coming from the lums. He remembered the smoke that had poured from those houses when they'd been set on fire. He remembered their neat red roofs before the fighting started and later, when the fires were out, the charred rafters through which could be seen the raging green of abandoned gardens. A few of the houses had been repaired since then, by men who had brought their families from other villages and settled into them as if they owned them. Those were the ones with lights showing. But most remained broken and empty, reminders of what had happened. It was as he was thinking this that something caught his eye in the big field and he saw the ghosts.

They were moving with painful slowness through the shaws of MacTaggart's winter crop, from which strips of mist were hanging like tattered flags. Christie watched as the ghosts crept across his vision, from right to left, away from the end of the field where MacTaggart's old shed had been. He should have been filled with horror but he was not, he felt only a dull stirring of the old fear that had been with him for months. It was as if he had been expecting them. He'd not known he was expecting them, but as soon as he recognised what they were it made sense that they were there, and that they were on their hands and knees trying to get away from the shed.

The crop was Brussels sprouts, a vegetable he hated, and the shaws were like miniature versions of those stark, blasted trees that appeared in photographs of the trenches in the Great War. The ghosts might have been the ghosts of soldiers crawling in No Man's Land, but they weren't. There seemed to be a lot of them, far more than there should have been. Christie tried to count them but they were indistinct, and low on the ground. He could hardly make them out at all. He wondered if the dog would have a ghost and tried to pick it out among the shapes, but then they all started to look like dogs. After a few minutes he could not concentrate anymore, and went to the back of the house, to the kitchen.

The kitchen window looked out on his scrap of back yard which ended at a listing wooden fence. Beyond the fence was a dirty wee burn. A couple of starlings were pecking at the hard soil of the yard where he sometimes flung out the crumbs of an old loaf. Christie preferred the wee, bonnie birds – chaffinches and robins and blue-tits: starlings were too ragged and sly and oily-looking to be bonnie, but at least they were real. His hand shook as he filled the kettle and put a spoonful of coffee grains into a mug. When the water had boiled he poured it into the mug. He liked his coffee black and strong. He added a shot of whisky from the bottle that was standing on the worktop next to the cooker. The bottle was almost empty. He wondered when Malky would come.

The kitchen was cold. The whole house was cold. The fire in the living room had died in the night and he would have to reset it later. The television was also dead but it had been dead a long time. He did not remember falling asleep but there was a book crushed between the cushion and one arm of the chair and he guessed he had gone under while reading it. He took his coffee through to the bedroom, slopping some of it on the floor as he went. He did not have any shoes on, and there were holes in his socks. He did not take off his socks nor indeed any of his clothes as he got beneath the covers. None of these things was surprising or unusual to him. The ghosts were unusual, he had never seen ghosts before, but even they were not surprising.

By the time he had drunk the coffee, his hand had stopped trembling. He did not know, nor did he care, whether this was due to the whisky or because he had warmed up under the bedclothes. He thought vaguely about going back to the kitchen for the rest of the bottle but he felt a vague, distant comfort from being in bed. It reminded him of being ill as a child, of the security of being in a sickbed. He snuggled down and pulled the blankets over his head. In a minute he fell asleep.

He had redd out the cold ashes from the hearth and was just putting a match to the re-laid fire when he heard Malky's motor pull up. Christie recognised the sound of its exhaust, the way it coughed and hacked like a smoker. Malky got out and slammed the door shut, leaving the engine running as he always did. Christie heard the front door bang. Malky came into the room with a large carrier bag in his hand, which Christie tried not to look at.

'Aye, Christie. How are ye the day?'

'I'm fine,' Christie said.

'Just up, are ye?'

'Aye.'

They stood together and watched the flames lick up the paper and the kindling begin to crackle.

'Ye'll need tae pit some coal on that,' Malky said. 'Dae ye hae plenty coal, Christie?'

'The bunker's still hauf-full,' Christie said. 'Ye ken that.'

'I just wouldna want ye tae be short. I can get ye mair when ye need it. Here, I've brocht ye a few things tae keep the wolf fae the door.'

He put the carrier bag on the carpet in front of the fire. It was a plain blue bag, its handles stretched by the weight of its contents. Malky began to empty it.

'Some breid,' he said. 'Bacon. A dozen eggs. Four cans o beans. Ye can mak a few meals oot o thon. And here's

243

somethin tae wet yer whistle wi.' He took out two bottles of Whyte & Mackay.

'Ye shouldna hae done that,' Christie said.

Malky said, 'Ach well. They were on special offer for twa. Keep ye oot o danger, eh?'

'Keep *you* oot o danger, mair like,' Christie said, trembling at his own boldness.

'Now, now, Christie,' Malky said. His black moustache seemed to thicken and bristle up. 'Dinna start. I'm just tryin tae help.'

'Aye, I appreciate it.'

'Gillian's askin for ye.'

'She awright?'

'Right as rain. She's no gaun oot muckle these days, though. Like yersel. It's no the season for it.'

'Naebody gaes oot ony mair,' Christie said. He knew this to be the case, but it wasn't because of the time of year. The road outside went to the village and yet there were never more than a dozen vehicles on it all day. As for walkers, there were none at all. Auld Sammy used to take his dog along to MacTaggart's farm and back every afternoon. But he wouldn't be seeing Auld Sammy again.

'She's feart,' Christie said. 'Like me, right enough. She's feart.'

Malky snorted. 'Naw she's no. She just hates this time o the year. Cauld, dreich, dark. *I* wouldna gae oot if I didna hae tae. She keeps hersel busy but. She's aye cleanin and cookin, cleanin and cookin. A right wee domestic goddess.'

Malky moved to the window and stood with his back to Christie. *I could lift the poker and crush his heid wi a single blow*, Christie thought. But he couldn't. The poker was a feeble thin thing, not like the old heavy-duty ones. And he wasn't strong enough. Malky was built like a house-end, he wouldn't even dent.

'MacTaggart's pit his sheep intae the field, I see,' Malky said. 'It's a shame tae see aw thae sprouts away for sheep feed. Still, canna be helped. Naebody tae lift them.' He turned. 'I never really liked sprouts onywey. Do you, Christie?'

'Naw,' said Christie. He wanted Malky to fuck off, but he didn't tell him. Malky was his brother-in-law. And he had brought the food and drink, after all. He was always bringing things. Just about every single day. And he never asked for money. It wasn't about money.

Malky didn't seem to know where to put himself. His bulk took up half the room. He picked up a cushion from the second armchair, turned it over, patted it and put it back. He shook his head.

'Christ, ye're a manky bastard. This place is a cowp.'

'That's how I like it.'

'And what aboot that television? It's years since that worked. I can get ye a new ane. Or a good quality second-hand ane at least.'

'Aye, so ye keep tellin me. But I dinna want a new ane. That ane suits me fine.'

'But it disna work!' Malky sounded exasperated, but Christie knew what he was playing at. If he got him a new television, that would be another distraction. Another way of controlling him, like the whisky. But he'd finished with the television – had left it on day and night till the back of it melted – and one day soon he'd be quitting the whisky, but not yet. At least with the whisky he could think his own thoughts.

'Dae ye no want me tae get a woman in tae gie the hoose a good clean?' Malky said. 'Gillian'll ken somebody.'

'Can ye she no come hersel?'

'Aw, noo, Christie, ye ken she canna. She's no weel. She's nae energy. Canna dae the hoosework like she used tae.'

Christie knew he was lying. He'd just left off calling her a domestic goddess. Gillian was stuck in the house for the same reason Christie was: fear. And Malky wouldn't let them meet. His own sister. Not without him being present. If they met they'd start talking. Spilling the beans. *And mair than four fuckin cans o them tae.* Those international guys that were supposed to be snooping about, asking questions. Malky didn't want Gillian and Christie getting any ideas about speaking to *them*.

Outside they heard the car engine splutter and die.

'Fuck it,' Malky said, 'I'd better go. I've got frozen food in the boot.'

'Aye, right,' Christie said. 'Thanks for coming by. Wi thon stuff. I can drink mysel tae death in comfort.'

Malky laughed uneasily. 'I think ye'd hae done that by noo if ye were gaun tae.'

'Well, the gas oven then,' Christie said. He had a wee smile in his chest but he kept it off his face. He liked to goad Malky. 'Or the razor blades. *Schff, schff!*' He made cutting noises and swift cutting motions across his wrists.

'Dinna talk like that, eh?' Malky said. 'That's no nice. I'm keepin an eye on ye, amn't I? Ye're awright, eh? Ye wouldna dae onythin stupit, would ye.'

The last sentence was more of a statement, or a threat,

than a question. Christie knew Malky wasn't talking about suicide. Malky was worried about him going to the police. Not the local mob, worse than bloody gangsters they were. The international boys.

'Or the shotgun,' Christie added. 'I could stick the shotgun in my gub.'

Malky snapped. He towered up, heaving like a bull, and pulled Christie in close by a fistful of jersey. Christie could hear teeth grind. He'd got to him.

'That's enough,' Malky growled. 'Stop feeling fuckin sorry for yersel. Jesus, when ye think o aw the folk in the world wi – wi nuthin. *You're* awright. D'ye hear me? Ye're *awright.*'

He let go, and Christie, looking down at his chest, saw the clump of jersey spring open. He found that strangely more interesting than looking at Malky.

'And ye dinna hae a shotgun,' Malky was saying, more gently, as if to a forgetful child. 'We took it away fae ye, mind?'

Christie did not answer. 'Suit yersel,' Malky said after a minute. He banged out of the house. As he got into the car he shouted, 'I'll be back the morn, see if ye're mair fuckin sociable.'

Christie grinned and punched a fist into his palm. He loved it when he put one over on Malky. Fact was, he had another shotgun. Up in the loft. And a full cartridge belt. And a whole box of grenades. And an AK-47 and an automatic pistol. He had the lot. Keeping them for when he needed them. But because he was just a school janitor – had once been a school janitor – nobody took him seriously when it came to that kind of stuff. Nobody believed him.

And the international guys wouldn't believe him either, not just him on his own. He needed more witnesses. He needed Gillian. Gillian must have seen the state of Malky's clothes. She must have washed and dried them. Maybe she'd burnt them. But she knew. She had to know.

The only thing anybody'd ever believed him about was the way the bairns behaved in school. The *other* bairns. In the corridors and in the playground. They liked to hear him go on about that. *The wee tykes. The dirty wee shites. The thieving, treacherous wee bastards.* And they'd laugh and come up with their own stories. Everybody had them, it only took someone to start it off and you were all away. The teachers were the same. Our kids and their kids. You could tell them apart just by looking at them. By their names. By the state of their clothes and the food they ate. Some teachers claimed they could pick them out by smell if they were blindfolded. It was probably true. Christie didn't like them any more than anyone else. And that was just the bairns. The bairns grew into adults and then the trouble really started.

He went to the window and looked across at the field. There were twenty or thirty sheep in it right enough. He might have mistaken them in the half-light of early morning. But that didn't mean the ghosts weren't there. He'd seen them, crawling away from where the shed had been. MacTaggart's brick shed with the corrugated iron roof where he'd once kept an old tractor and trailer. All gone now. Malky had made MacTaggart pull it down. 'Take away the shed,' he'd said, 'and it'll be like nothing happened.' You had to have a scene for something to have happened. Now there was just Brussels sprouts, getting eaten by sheep.

MacTaggart was a nasty piece of work, Christie thought. He used to claim that Auld Sammy only went to the farm to steal tatties. Sammy went up with his dog and an empty plastic poke and came back with enough tatties to feed his family for a fortnight, so MacTaggart said. Finally he'd threatened Sammy with his shotgun, told him not to show his dirty face near the farm again. A nicer old fellow than Sammy you couldn't meet, even if he was a minker and a thief. Always passed the time of day. And the scabby dog was friendly too. Not that Christie would ever have had them in the house, because they weren't his people, but that wasn't the point.

When the fighting started, the school closed and Christie was laid off. It was only supposed to be temporary till the unrest died down, but it didn't, it got worse. You didn't realise till it started how many of the bastards there were. There had always been a kind of undercurrent that boiled up every so often in pub brawls, graffiti sprayed on shop fronts, vandalised cars, but then something changed, people stopped backing down or holding back and it all just escalated. Folk had always gone on about the numbers, how they were going to take over if something wasn't done about it, but it wasn't till you saw them with guns and your own people with guns that you got a real sense that it might actually happen. The bairns had mixed pretty well on the whole, forby a bit of name-calling and a few scraps among the boys, but when everybody retreated into their own houses that was the end of any mixing. Christie lay awake at night and heard pick-up trucks roar past that he knew were full of armed young men. He heard shots at three in the morning, explosions. He looked out into the darkness and saw the houses on the hillside ablaze. In order to sleep, he drank more and more whisky. But when he slept he dreamed. In his dreams he saw the bairns from the school playground running screaming down the road. He couldn't tell which bairns they were. They were like the bairns in the old photographs from Vietnam, their naked skin burning with napalm. In order to stop dreaming, he sat up in his armchair and watched television, and drank till he did not so much fall asleep as fall unconscious.

Malky used to drop in at odd times of the day and night then. He'd wake Christie up if he was sleeping, and they'd sit drinking together: beer, whisky, wine, whatever Malky had with him. He always had drink and he always had money. He talked about the night rides, the gun battles in the towns. He talked about the women they took into the woods and what they did to them. Sometimes they didn't even bother taking them into the woods. Christie listened and he imagined what it would be like. He'd brought his father's old shotgun down from the attic when the fighting started, and kept it handy just in case, because you never knew when somebody was going to come to your door, and sometimes when Malky was talking Christie'd take the gun out of its case and oil it, clean the barrels and look down them as if he knew what he was aiming at. He'd just be cleaning the gun while Malky was talking, that was all. Like a couple of solid guys going about their business. Standing up for what was theirs, for their rights. Christie wasn't stupid. He reckoned there were two reasons why Malky came, and why he talked. The first was that he needed to tell someone, and he couldn't tell Gillian. The second was that he knew Christie wanted to hear.

'I'd take ye,' Malky said, 'but they wouldna allow it. Ye kinda hae tae pass a test. They hae tae ken ye're no gaun tae fuck up.'

'I wouldna fuck up,' Christie said. 'Honest.'

'I believe ye,' Malky said. 'But no everybody does.'

'Who? Who d'ye mean? Folk in the village?'

'Some. They ken what ye're like. And then there's the others, the boys runnin the show. They wouldna allow it.'

It was all shite really. Christie didn't want to go and Malky didn't want to take him. But it was okay talking about it, listening to what Malky was up to. Listening made Christie feel like he could do it if he had to. And it was good drinking with somebody instead of on your own, even if it was just Malky.

Then one morning – a morning when there had already been a lot of traffic up and down the road, which had got Christie out of his bed early – Malky rolled up in his coughing car with two other men in the back seat. Christie came out to meet him – in those days he still used to step outside. Malky said, 'The bastards've done it this time. They've killt young Jock MacTaggart. They're roundin them up noo.' Somebody had tried to set fire to MacTaggart's place in the night, and when the MacTaggarts came out fighting, whoever it was had shot the farmer's son through the head. Whoever it was! They had fled the scene, but MacTaggart, the old bugger, he knew fine who they were.

'So,' Malky said, 'are ye comin?'

'Me?' Christie said.

'Aye. Come on. I've spoken for ye. This is Christie,' Malky said to the men in the back seat. 'My wife's brither. Mind I said aboot him.'

The men in the back seat didn't reply. They were wearing dark glasses and black leather jackets and they were very calm.

Malky seemed agitated. 'Come on, then, Christie,' he said. 'We're maybe ower late as it is.'

Christie went back into the house and got the old shotgun and slung the cartridge belt over his shoulder. He climbed into the front passenger seat and they drove off towards MacTaggart's place. But they hadn't gone more than a hundred yards before they saw a strange procession coming down the road towards them.

There was a pick-up at the front and MacTaggart, in his Massey Ferguson, was herding the procession from the back. MacTaggart's face was like a concrete slab, hard and empty. There were men with guns on either side of the procession. They'd got twelve of them: six men, four women and a couple of bairns. The women were sobbing, and the bairns were sobbing because the women were. The six men, who were all at least fifty, looked quite calm, but it was a different kind of calm from the way the men in the back seat looked. More placid than calm. One of the men on the road was Auld Sammy. He had his dog on a lead, and he appeared to be humming a tune.

Malky reversed the car up onto the pavement and switched off the engine. Usually he left it running but this time he switched it off.

'It canna hae been them. Can it?' Christie said.

'Fuckin right it can,' one of the men in the back seat said. Christie turned round. The one who had spoken had a ring in his right ear. Neither of them was from the village.

'But that's Sammy,' Christie said.

The car filled suddenly with silence.

'Who are you?' Christie asked after a few seconds.

'Fucksake, Christie,' Malky said. 'Ye dinna need tae fuckin ken that.'

'I'm just askin,' Christie said. But he turned round and faced the front again.

'Is he wi us or no?' the man with the earring said.

'He's wi us,' Malky said.

'Cause if he's no wi us, he's wi them,' the man said.

'Christie?' Malky said. He stared right into him.

'I'm wi you,' Christie told Malky.

'Right,' the man with the earring said. 'Nae mair fuckin questions then.'

They all got out. The procession turned into the field and the pick-up pulled over. Now MacTaggart was revving his tractor, urging the people on across the drills towards the shed. Some of them stumbled and the women cried louder. Malky said, 'Aye, ye can greet noo, ye thievin hoors,' and he sounded bolder than he was looking and Christie laughed. Auld Sammy must have heard them because he turned to say something and one of the armed men beside him prodded him in the side with his rifle and he fell to the wet earth. The man kicked him to make him stand up and Christie wanted Sammy to get to his feet and he wanted him to stay where he was. Sammy's dog was running round in small circles trailing its lead, barking and snapping at the legs of the man standing over Sammy. The man pointed his rifle at it and Sammy raised his head and called to the dog and it came and sat beside him. The man pointed his rifle back at Sammy.

There seemed to be a moment when everything might be

different. Everybody – the men with guns, their prisoners, MacTaggart in his tractor – stopped and watched Sammy. Even the two men in leather jackets and dark glasses hesitated. It was as if somebody, with some brave, simple gesture, could change whatever was going to happen. And Christie thought, *I can dae something here, I can really dae something.*

Then Sammy caught sight of Christie and seemed to recognise him for the first time. His eyes flickered with uncertainty. He looked at Christie's face and then he looked at Christie's shotgun. There was a long streak of mud down Sammy's clothes where he had fallen on the ground. It made him look even more of a minker than usual. Christie kept his eye on the streak of mud. That way he thought he could do what he was going to do.

'Wait!' he shouted. He was calling to the man pointing his rifle at Sammy's chest. Christie walked over with the shotgun cradled in his arm, right past the man with the rifle, and helped Sammy to his feet. He felt big and powerful, like a man in a film.

'It's awright, Sammy,' he said.

He took the end of the lead and together Sammy and he started walking towards the shed with the dog between them, and everybody else started moving too. Sammy started to hum again. Up close it was a completely tuneless sound, more of a moan or a whine than a hum. Christie hated it, he wanted Sammy to shut up so he could concentrate. Something big was coming, something so big you needed to focus all your thoughts on it and not be distracted. Christie felt as though by being there some great mystery was about to be revealed to him. It was like a Bible story from when you were a bairn, a story that you believed but didn't understand, and now suddenly, years later, you were about to understand it. And these people, these miserable people moaning and girning the way they always did, they were the key to the mystery. And the mystery was in MacTaggart's shed.

But when they got to the shed Christie didn't go in. MacTaggart stopped his tractor and got down and pulled open the sliding door with a blank expression on his face, as if he might be going to fetch a couple of sacks of fertiliser or something but didn't really care one way or the other if there was none there. They ushered the prisoners towards the door. Auld Sammy looked at Christie and he started to shout, he was shouting, 'Help us! Help us! Why are ye just standin there? Help us!' The man with the earring was watching intently. He didn't seem to see Sammy anymore: he was staring at Christie to see what he would do. To see if he would fuck up.

Christie was still holding the dog's lead. He said, 'I'll tak care o yer dog.' Sammy shook his head. Christie said, 'Sit!' and the dog sat down beside him. Then they pushed Sammy and the rest of them inside the shed and the other men, including Malky and MacTaggart, went in too. The only ones who were left outside were Christie and the man with the earring.

There was a sudden clatter of gunfire from inside the shed, and then nothing.

The man with the earring said, 'Nice work, Christie. But ye canna keep the dog.'

'How no?' Christie said. He searched for the man's eyes behind the glasses, but he couldn't see them.

Malky came out of the shed. His clothes were spotted with blood and so were his hands. His face was very white.

'He canna keep the dog,' the man with the earring said. 'Tell him.'

'But I said I would,' Christie began, and Malky's face flushed up red and he bore down on him so close he could smell the blood on his shirt. 'Ye canna keep the fuckin dog!' Malky said. He flicked his eyes indicating the shed behind him. Christie could hear teeth grind. Auld Sammy's dog was sitting patiently waiting for Auld Sammy to come out. Christie realised that what they were saying was right. He couldn't keep the dog. He pushed the barrels of the shotgun gently against the back of its head, shut his eyes and pulled both triggers.

'Put it inside,' Christie heard the man with the earring say. 'Ye can clear up later.' He kept his eyes closed and stood absolutely still, and he heard heavy breathing around him and wondered what would happen next. He knew with absolute certainty that he could not go into the shed. The only way they'd get him in there would be if they carried him.

A few seconds went by, and each one felt like a minute. Then he heard someone bend down next to him, and give a groan with the effort of lifting something heavy, and when he opened his eyes he saw Malky's gun on the ground and Malky's back as he carried the dead dog into the shed.

Malky came into the house later that day and the first thing he did was punch Christie in the face, sending him crashing into his armchair. Christie sat rubbing his jaw but he didn't get back up, he knew why Malky had done it. Malky took a new bottle of whisky out of a plastic bag and cracked the top open.

'Ye stupit fuckin eejit,' Malky said. 'Ye're lucky tae be alive. Ye dinna mess aroond wi thae guys. Get us some glesses.'

So they sat drinking, and Christie rubbed his jaw and started to talk about what had happened, just the way Malky used to talk about his night rides, but Malky interrupted him. 'Forget it, Christie,' he said. 'Forget it all. Forget aboot Sammy and the dog and everything ye fuckin saw. It didna happen. Awright? It didna fuckin happen.'

And that was the way it had gone on. MacTaggart pulled down the shed and there was nothing inside it and then he planted Brussels sprouts all over the field. Malky would come round and make sure Christie had food and drink, and Christie would try to talk about what had happened and Malky would tell him to forget it. 'Ye're imaginin it, Christie. Ye've been watchin too much shite on the telly. Aw thae news programmes ye watch, the documentaries and aw that. That aw happens somewhere else. Other countries. No here. Ye're away wi the fairies.'

'But I seen ye comin oot the shed,' Christie would say. 'We took Auld Sammy and them inside and ye came oot wi blood on yer claes. I was there, I'm a witness. And I killt thon dog wi my faither's shotgun,' he would say.

'Christie, Christie, ye're makin it up. Ye're no right in the heid. That's why we took the gun aff ye. That stuff's aw aff the telly, Christie. It's got inside yer heid fae the telly.'

'Ye didna tak the telly aff me, though, did ye?' Christie said. He kept quiet about the stash of weapons in the attic.

Let them have the shotgun if it made them feel safe. He had another. Plus the other stuff. A whole bloody arsenal.

'Didna need tae,' Malky said. 'Ye knackered it wi leavin it on aw the time. But I can get ye another ane if ye want. Ye ken that.'

'Naw,' Christie said. 'That ane suits me fine.'

The truth was, he didn't need the television. He looked at the stuff Malky had brought, still sitting on the carpet in front of the fire. He didn't need the bread – the starlings could have it. He didn't need the eggs or the bacon or the baked beans. He looked at the whisky. He didn't even need the whisky, but he needed to think, and the whisky would help him to think. He needed to make a plan. He had to get in touch with Gillian somehow. He had to get in touch with the international boys, tell them about what had happened in the shed. He was a witness. All right, he had shot the dog, but only the dog, and he'd had no choice, they'd have killed him if he hadn't. He picked up the coal-hod and shoved more coals on the fire. He remembered the houses burning on the hillside. Terrible, terrible things had happened. He felt numb with the thought of all that hurt. He went to the window and looked out. It would be getting dark again soon. He wondered if he would see the ghosts again, and how many there would be. He reached for the first bottle of whisky, and started to plan what he would do in the morning.

The Future According to Luke

Luke Stands Alone was the worst prophet in the history of the Lakota people. He went into trances and when he came out of them he would say he'd seen the future. But he hadn't, because nearly everything he prophesied had taken place days, months or years before. Even the century before the last one. He didn't so much see the future as forget the past, then remember it again as if it were still to happen. This wasn't something his friends Dean Liboux and Johnny Little Eagle felt they could really hold against him, but they weren't filled with a lot of confidence when he made a prediction.

Dean and Johnny had discussed Luke's prophetic failings often and concluded that the inside of his head was just a trailer full of junk, with a TV in the corner playing a continuous stream of old Westerns, cartoons, commercials and documentaries. Hardly any wonder he got confused. Again, they didn't blame him for this. The insides of their own heads weren't so different.

One time, Luke said he'd seen white soldiers tumbling upside down into an Indian village with their hats falling off. This meant a great victory was coming, he explained.

'You mean an old-time village, with tepees and everything?' Dean asked.

'I guess,' Luke said.

'You guess?' Dean said.

Johnny said, 'Didn't Sitting Bull dream something pretty much like that before Little Big Horn?'

Luke didn't even blink. 'Yeah, you're right, he did. Man, how *about* that?'

Days went by, and weeks, and Luke wasn't around. Then one day Dean saw him again. 'So when is the big victory coming off?' he demanded.

'It already did,' Luke said. 'They opened the new casino, didn't they?'

'The Prairie Wind? What's that got to do with anything?'

'The first Saturday it was open, a bunch of Air Force personnel came over from Ellsworth and lost two thousand dollars at blackjack. Ain't that a victory?'

'I suppose you're going to tell me they took their hats off when they came inside?' Dean said.

'I guess,' Luke said.

'But there ain't no tepees there. They got a seventy-eight-bed hotel, but no tepees.'

'They got tepees on the website,' Luke said. 'Check it out. Just like in my vision.'

Dean didn't have a computer. He could hardly think of anyone he knew who did. He could think of quite a few who had electricity and even a landline, but computers were thin on the ground on the reservation. Luke himself didn't have one, so he must have seen the website some place else. He used to disappear for long periods, and when he showed up again he would make out he'd been living rough in the Badlands, on a quest for visions, but usually somebody would have spotted him in Rapid City or Sioux Falls. Once even in Denver. Maybe he'd looked at the website in Denver.

There was nothing particularly unusual about the way he took off like that: a lot of folks came and went on the reservation, many of them spent time in the cities, and visions of one kind or another weren't uncommon either. Johnny and Dean had had visions themselves. But these days Dean was trying to avoid them. He wasn't smoking weed or eating magic mushrooms, and although he still liked to drink he was sticking to Budweiser. He'd decided drinking vodka or any of those ten per cent malt liquors was the quickest way to death and he didn't want to go there yet.

As for Johnny, well, Dean didn't know what Johnny wanted. He had a girlfriend who had a baby by another man, and he seemed to like her and the kid but he didn't spend much time with them. He preferred hanging out with his male friends, getting drunk. A lot of guys were like that, whether or not they had girlfriends. Life was difficult and drinking made it easier, at least for a while. Maybe that was what Johnny wanted, just for life to be easier. Maybe that was all anybody *could* want.

Johnny and Dean were good drinking buddies because neither of them was into fighting – each other or anybody else. They tried to stay away from guys they knew who got fighting drunk, because it hurt too much being punched by them and it hurt too much having to accept their apologies when they sobered up. They both liked drinking with Luke, even if he was a shit prophet, because he didn't want to fight either. The three of them would sit around moaning about all the bad things that had already happened to the Lakota, and Luke would foretell all the bad things that were still to come.

Of course you didn't have to be a prophet to be able to do that, you just had to walk around with your eyes and ears open. Luke could tell you, for instance, that in the next three months there would be X number of car wrecks involving Y number of Indians, and you knew that, give or take a few, his prophecy would come true. He could give you similar predictions about how many people on the reservation would die of alcohol poisoning, how many overdose, how many be murdered, how many commit suicide, how many be assaulted, how many be arrested, how many get jobs, how many lose them, how many reach the age of fifty, how many not – until at last, maybe around the fifth or sixth beer, you'd say, 'But Luke, you ain't saying nothing we don't already know.' And Luke would say, 'Yeah, but wasn't I right about the Little Big Horn?' or, 'Wasn't I right about the casino?' And you didn't argue with him, you just laughed, because what else could you do? And anyway, you weren't drinking to argue, you were drinking to get drunk.

Selling, buying or drinking alcohol was illegal on the reservation. So what Dean and Johnny would do was drive over the boundary to Jubal Schele's place, the Buffalo Saloon, and drink there. This one day they had scraped together a few dollars – enough to put some gas in Johnny's beat-up old car – and had set off up the road, and after a few miles they passed Luke Stands Alone walking, so they pulled over and gave him a ride.

It was a cold, clear afternoon in November. When they

arrived at the Buffalo Saloon and got out of the car, Dean saw snow on the distant Black Hills. He drew this to the attention of the others. 'Yeah, I dreamed about that,' Luke said. 'I saw it on the weather report,' Johnny said.

The bar was situated on a rough old back route between Bombing Range Road and the highway to Custer, and the only reason for it being there was to serve liquor to Indians. The big old sign on the roof said INDIANS ALLOWED, which kind of proved the point, but the story was that back in the fifties the words NO DOGS OR had also been up there. Dean asked Jubal if this was true. He asked it in a friendly enough way, but Jubal looked at him suspiciously, like he was trying to start some trouble, even though they were the only customers.

'What if it did?' Jubal said. 'That's an artefact, that sign, a piece of the old days.'

'Them old days,' Johnny said sourly. 'Ain't they over, Jubal?'

'They sure are,' Jubal grumbled, in a way that made you understand he missed them. 'Genuine goddamn piece of Old West memorabilia, that sign.'

'Maybe you should try selling it on eBay,' Johnny said.

'Why would I do that?' Jubal said. 'Might want to sell the whole place some day, and that sign's a part of it. Integral, you know? So I think I'll leave it where it is. You boys wanting some more beers now?'

While Jubal was away Johnny said there could be no greater irony than three Lakota men of warrior age drinking liquor in a white man's bar located midway between a town called Custer and a US Air Force bombing range, and Dean said, oh yes there could, those same three Indians could be laughing about it. So they laughed about it and then Jubal came back with the beers and took the money from the pile of dirty dollar bills and quarters in the middle of the table. Jubal was happy for them to drink as much as they liked, but he didn't keep a tab, not for Indians here in the back room. If there were ever any white customers in the front room, maybe tourists headed for Mount Rushmore, he'd have kept a tab for them, but there never were.

Dean went to the men's room to take a leak. The walls were painted a deep brick red that was almost brown, and there were darker, menacing stains in several places. There had been an infamous fight at the Buffalo Saloon once, many years ago, before Dean was even born, between some reservation Indians and some outsiders, city Indians. Skins versus breeds. The fight had been in the bar and then somebody had followed somebody else out to the men's room, and a gun had been pulled, and a man had been shot and killed. Just thinking about it spooked Dean a little. He seemed to recall that the man hadn't died right there, but later, in the hospital. For a while after that the Buffalo Saloon had had a bad reputation and was always busy. That was when Jubal should have sold the joint. These days it was mostly quiet. There were other places just off the reservation that you could walk to, and where you could get drunk for less – liquor stores, not bars. They were the places most people went to now.

For all that he didn't want to fight, Dean kind of wished he'd been at Jubal's back then. He wished something would happen. It wouldn't matter if it was good or bad. Just if something would happen. He felt like he wasn't fully alive, like somebody had reached in and taken some vital organ out of his body while he was sleeping. It was weird: he couldn't remember ever *not* feeling like that, but he'd only recognised it in the last year. Somebody had stolen something from him, his ability to get angry or even just active. Maybe it was to do with drinking too much. Or maybe, now that he was cutting down, it was to do with not drinking enough. Hell, he was only twenty-five, maybe he'd stop altogether. If he did, would the feeling be there all the time, or would it go away forever?

Back in the bar, Luke had started to tell Johnny his latest prophecy. 'You got to hear this,' Johnny said. 'Start again, Luke.' So Luke started again.

'I had a vision about you guys,' he said. 'The two of you. Only I couldn't tell which one of you was which.'

'I'm Johnny,' said Dean quickly, just as Johnny said, 'I'm Dean.'

'In the vision,' Luke said. 'I couldn't tell in the vision. Do you want to hear it or not?'

They wanted to hear it.

'You're standing on a road. A straight road heading right across the prairie. And a pick-up comes by and pulls over. The driver is a big white man. He's wearing a white hat and there's a rifle slung along the back of the cab. He offers one of you a ride, I don't know which, and I'm saying, no, no, don't get in.'

'What were *you* doing there?' Dean asked.

'I was there but I kind of wasn't, know what I mean? And I'm shouting at you not to get in the pick-up but you don't hear me.'

'So do I get in?' Johnny said.

'What about me?' Dean said. 'Do I?' Because they still weren't taking Luke seriously.

'Neither of you gets in. First he offers you a ride. Then he offers you a blanket. I'm shouting, don't take the blanket, it's full of smallpox. Then he offers you a bottle of whisky. I'm shouting, don't take the whisky, it'll poison you.'

'And what are we doing, just standing around while this guy offers us things?' Johnny said.

'Pretty much. It's like I said, I couldn't see which one of you he was talking to. The other one was facing away from the pick-up, looking out on the prairie. Like he was waiting for something else.'

'For what?' Johnny said.

'Wait and I'll tell you,' Luke said. 'The white guy offers you a piece of paper with a lot of writing on it. He offers you a kettle. He offers you a gun. It's like he has all this stuff on the seat and he keeps showing it to you. A pair of jeans, a TV set, a cell phone. And every time he picks up something new I'm shouting, don't take it, don't get in the truck, let him drive away.'

'I'd take the cell phone and the jeans,' Dean said.

'I'd take the gun,' Johnny said. 'I'd blow the asshole's brains out and then I'd get everything.'

'*Don't take the gun!*' Luke shouted suddenly.

From out front they heard Jubal's voice. 'Hey! Cool it back there.'

'Whatever you do, don't take the gun,' Luke said, lowering his voice. He was out in a sweat, and shivering, like he had a fever. Johnny looked at Dean. Dean looked at Johnny. 'It's okay, bud,' Johnny said to Luke. 'I ain't going to take the gun.'

'The other one of you,' Luke said, 'is still over on the roadside, waiting. And now there's someone coming. It's a rider on a horse. An old warrior, painted up and wearing a war-bonnet and everything. But I can see right through him, like he's made of air. He's a ghost. And he stops his horse and looks down at you and for a long time he doesn't say anything. He doesn't offer you anything because he ain't got nothing to offer. And then he speaks.'

'What does he say?' Dean asked, after Luke hasn't spoken for a few seconds.

'He says a time is coming. All the ghosts are coming back. The buffalo are coming back. The deer and all the other animals are coming back.'

'Oh man,' Johnny said. 'Is that it? Is that your prophecy? We had this a thousand times before.'

But Luke Stands Alone didn't seem to hear him. The sweat poured off him, and he just kept on talking, as if he were the old ghost warrior himself. 'The uranium is going back into the earth,' he said. 'The garbage is all going back to where it was made. The cars are going, and the missiles and the pollution. People don't know how to live in harmony with the earth. The *wasichus* never knew how, and most Indians have forgotten or been killed for trying to remember. But a time is coming. Don't get in the car with that old man. Don't take any of his gifts. Just wait. Don't forget who you are.'

Luke stopped, and for a minute nobody said anything. And then Luke wiped his face and said, 'And he rode off across the prairie. And I looked and the road wasn't there anymore. The pick-up was gone, and so was one of you guys, but the other one was still standing, staring out at nothing.'

'Goddamn ghosts,' Johnny said.

Luke put his head down on the table. It didn't take much to get him drunk, but he looked more exhausted than drunk, as if the vision had taken all his energy out of him. In a minute he was asleep.

Johnny looked at Dean. Dean shrugged. 'Well, just because *he* stopped drinking don't mean we got to,' Johnny said, and he called on Jubal.

Jubal brought them more drink. He jerked a thumb at Luke. 'He can't sleep in here.'

'Looks like he's doing it fine,' Johnny said.

Jubal said, 'I'm saying he can't sleep in here. You can take him out back and he can sleep it off in one of the cars in the yard. Five dollars for the privilege. For that he even gets a blanket.'

'We'll be going soon,' Dean said. 'Just leave him be, won't you? We're your best customers.'

'We're your only customers,' Johnny said, 'and we ain't going yet.'

'He can't sleep in here,' Jubal said. 'Either you take him out to the yard, or you put him on the street, but he can't stay there.'

'It's going to be a cold night,' Dean said. 'He might freeze. He might not wake up again.'

'That's why he gets a blanket,' Jubal said.

'Leave him till we've finished these beers,' Dean said. 'Then we'll move him.'

Jubal retreated, muttering.

Johnny said, 'I'm drunk. Maybe we'll all sleep in one of Jubal's old wrecks.'

Dean said. 'Give me your key, man. I'll drive. We'll buy

some more beers to take with us and we'll get Luke in the car and we'll drive a little ways and then we'll pull over. We'll have another drink and then if I can't get you to my place we'll all sleep in the car. That way we'll keep warm. There's snow coming, Johnny. We ain't leaving Luke alone, here or anywhere.'

'I didn't say we would,' Johnny said.

'We'll have sweeter dreams in your car than in Jubal's yard. Indian dreams.'

Johnny put a hand on Luke's back. 'Do you think he's dreaming about us now?'

Dean laughed. 'Yeah, I think maybe he is. I think he's looking out for us, so we got to look out for him.'

They finished up, and then they hauled Luke through the front room of the bar and out to the street, which wasn't much of a street, just the road with the bar alongside it and a sign that said MAIN STREET. Jubal looked like he'd never seen such a thing in his life, Indians leaving the Buffalo Saloon in a state of semi-sobriety, but he didn't try to persuade them to stay. Maybe he was as tired of it all as they were. Maybe he knew there'd be another party along soon enough.

They slung Luke in the back of Johnny's car and Johnny gave Dean the key and went back in for a six-pack.

Luke didn't stir.

Dean stood in the road, feeling the chill air, watching the snow-lined hills fading into the dusk. Far, far off he thought he saw the lights of an approaching car. Then he didn't, and there was nothing but darkness gathering around him.

The door of the Buffalo Saloon slammed, and Johnny staggered over.

'Hey, Dean,' Johnny said. 'You all right, man?'

'I'm good. You all right?'

'I got some more cans. We're going to be fine. Hey, Dean, what do you see out there? You see something?'

Dean watched a few moments longer. The sky was clouding up. There were some stars, but they weren't going to last.

'I don't know,' he said. 'Maybe I do. What do you see?'

Johnny stood beside him, the brown bag with the cans in it under one arm. He put his other hand on Dean's shoulder, to steady himself, and they peered into the night together for a long time, not saying anything, while, on the back seat of the car, Luke lay sleeping like a child.

Sixes and Sevens

'This is the dayroom,' the woman said. 'You wait here, and I'll see if I can find Dr Muir.'

Everything was dusty. It was cold. There was an enormous fireplace but no fire in it. There were enormous windows too but the blinds were pulled down, making the afternoon light dim and weak and vague, as if it had yellowed with age just like the blinds themselves. I walked from one end of the room to the other, under unlit lamps suspended on long chains from the ornately plastered ceiling. It took me thirty paces. I did it again because I didn't want to stand still. When I walked I could hear the floorboards creaking.

Chairs were scattered about the place, big armchairs covered in faded, heavy, old-fashioned material, and smaller upright chairs with curved backs and tapestried seats, and every one of them was layered with dust. The room was so vast that the chairs looked like they were floating in the sea. The carpet had a pattern that moved like waves. I felt a little sick. I counted seven armchairs and six uprights. They looked as if they might have been creeping towards the fireplace in a game of grandmother's footsteps but had stopped suddenly when someone who was no longer there had turned round.

There was total silence. Not a sound came from outside, not of traffic or sirens or birdsong, nothing. There wasn't even the ticking of a clock in the room, because there wasn't a clock. Only the silence, and the musty, sweetish smells of old carpet and general decay.

The woman had only been gone a few minutes but I felt as if I had been alone a long time.

'Make yourself at home,' she said. I could hear her voice even though she wasn't there, and in spite of the silence. That was odd. Maybe her words were still in the room. Maybe they were part of the silence now. Mrs Jennings, her name was. 'I'm sorry about the state of things,' she said, 'we're all at sixes and sevens here. All of this old furniture is to go. They keep sending a removal van to take it away. The beds, the chests, the wardrobes, the tables – all gone. It's always the same van, back and forth, and the same men in it. I don't know where they take it, to the dump I expect. It's a shame, it was the finest quality in its day. Of course, everything was of a very high standard when we first opened, and I don't just mean the furniture. It was an enlightened place, very comfortable in the public areas, and the staff were excellent. We wanted the patients to be happy. We wanted them to be at peace.'

She made it sound as if she'd been there when the hospital opened, but she couldn't have been. That would have made her about a hundred and twenty. She looked younger than I was. I'd have put her at about sixty. 'I'm Mrs Jennings,' she said when she let me in. 'You're the gentleman who tele-phoned, aren't you? We've been expecting you.' I followed her along the corridor and up the broad stairs. She said, 'I'm managing the place till all the paperwork has been gone through. You wouldn't believe how much paperwork there is. You can't just throw it out, of course. People's lives are in all that paper. That's why you've come, of course.' She was a woman who said 'of course' a lot.

On the dayroom walls were patches where paintings had once hung. I wondered what they had been. Portraits of wealthy benefactors, perhaps? Prints of different aspects of the city? Soothing seascapes and landscapes? I imagined the patients walking round the room looking at them, day after day.

Mrs Jennings noticed me looking at the patches. There probably wasn't much she didn't notice. 'They were the first things to go,' she said, even though she wasn't there. Or the words said it, after she'd gone. 'They must have had some value, but I don't know if they were sold or just thrown away. I don't know where all the patients are now either. Dispersed into the community, poor souls. It's a shame. It was all very grand once, a really grand place. Now look at it. It's done, served its purpose. Take a seat if you like. I'm sorry there isn't a fire. It's very chilly, this room, when there isn't a fire and nobody to enjoy it. We used to have a great big fire here, and a great big fireguard, of course, so that nobody got hurt. But we had very few acci-dents. They were used to fires, the old people, they knew it wasn't safe to get too close. They did love the heat though, and the pictures the flames made. Some of them would sit and stare into those flames all day long.

'Anyway,' she said, 'you wait here, and I'll see if I can find Dr Muir. He should be able to help you.'

She'd not been away long but I didn't like being on my own in that room. I'd only come because I'd read that the hospital had closed, and that they were going to turn it into something else. I'd like to see it before that happens, I'd thought. The university had bought it. But what could you do with such a place? You couldn't knock it down, it was a listed building. Mrs Jennings was right, it didn't serve its purpose as a hospital anymore, but what purpose would it serve instead? I couldn't imagine, but no doubt the university had some plans or they wouldn't have bought it, would they?

'My grandfather was a patient here,' I said. I didn't mean to say it out loud but that was what I was thinking and it just came out, and maybe that was because I wanted to hear a human voice in that great, silent barn of a room, a voice that wasn't Mrs Jennings's voice, I mean. I didn't want to hear her voice, even though she wasn't there.

My grandfather was brought to the hospital during the 1914–18 war. He never left. He died here. My father never talked about him, and nor did my grandmother. My mother didn't know him, and neither did I. Even when I asked about him they didn't say much. They changed the subject. He was a figure of embarrassment, I think, or shame, because he'd been ill and never got better, never managed to get back out into the world again. And mental illness in those days, whatever caused it, whether it was the war or something else, was mostly kept hidden away. There's no point in being sentimental about it. It doesn't matter how comfortable they made the place. Yes, a lot of things are worse now than they were back then, the quality of furniture and buildings in general for example, but one thing we're better at is the way we deal with mental illness. We're more open about it. At least, we say we are, but are we really? Maybe we only think we are.

Anyway, here I was. I just wanted to see the place, and if possible meet someone who could tell me something about my grandfather. That was why Mrs Jennings had gone looking for Dr Muir.

'Here you are,' a voice said.

A man had come through a door I hadn't noticed, in the middle of one wall of the room. It wasn't the door by which Mrs Jennings had left. I hadn't noticed it because there was a lot of oak panelling on that wall, and the door was built into it in such a way that you wouldn't know it was there unless you were very close. The man was advancing slowly through the chairs towards me. He was quite a young man, much younger than me, and he had a friendly smile. Yet when he reached me he didn't hold out his hand to be shaken. He stood at a slight distance, and looked at me rather shyly, but still with that smile, and said, 'Hello.'

If that was his manner I didn't want to offend him. I didn't want to force him to shake hands if he didn't want to. Some people don't.

'Hello,' I said. 'Dr Muir?'

'How are you getting on?' he said.

I said, 'I'm fine. Did Mrs Jennings tell you why I was here?'

'Oh yes,' he said.

'She thought you would be able to help,' I said.

'Yes, well, I often can help, but there is no guarantee.' He gestured with his hand at the chairs. 'Everybody's gone, you see.'

'It's about my grandfather,' I said. 'Did Mrs Jennings tell you?'

'Oh yes,' he said, and he smiled again. 'And how are you getting on?'

'I wondered if there might be some records about him,' I said. 'Mrs Jennings said there was a lot of paperwork. I wondered if there might be some information about my grandfather.'

'I expect so,' he said. 'Highly probable, I think.'

From his looks, I would have said he was in his thirties, perhaps forty at most. He had black hair neatly combed and parted, but I noticed he hadn't shaved for a day or two. Mind you, neither had I. He was wearing a black suit, and a shirt buttoned up to the neck but no tie.

'Well, is there somewhere we could go to have a look?' I suggested.

He looked at me in a puzzled way. 'I expect so,' he said. 'But there is such a lot of paperwork. One forgets.'

I was about to say something about forgetfulness and that being why we kept records, but he made the hand gesture again and carried on speaking. 'People think if something isn't new and modern then it's no use. If only people looked after things, we wouldn't have to replace them. There's nothing wrong with this place, if you ask me. If they looked after it, it would still be standing years after all the modern places had fallen down. But you probably don't agree.'

'I do, as a matter of fact,' I said. 'Then again, there's no point in being sentimental about the past, is there?'

'I'm not being sentimental,' he said. 'Nobody wanted to leave. They liked it here. They were at peace. That's what I think, but nobody listens. And look at the view. Magnificent, if you ask me.'

He wandered over to one of the big windows and stood staring at the blind pulled down in front of it. It didn't seem to bother him that you couldn't see out. There was an armchair beside that window. He looked at it for a few moments too.

'That's my seat,' he said. Then he came back towards me, with the strange, kindly smile on his face, and headed back to the door he'd come through.

I began to say something, to stop him leaving, but it seemed there had been some kind of mistake, so I stopped. I decided that it would be easier, rather than try to explain or apologise, just to let him go.

'Goodbye,' I said.

'Goodbye,' I thought I heard him say as he disappeared, but I couldn't be sure.

When the woman came back, I told her about the young man. I said I felt foolish because I had taken him for Dr Muir, but clearly it wasn't Dr Muir but a patient.

'Oh no,' she said, 'there's nobody here but us. Dr Muir and myself, I mean. All the patients have gone. Out into the world,' she added in a sing-songy kind of voice.

'Well, he certainly knew his way around,' I said. 'He must have been a *former* patient. Perhaps he just came back to have a look at his old home while he still could.'

'Oh no,' the woman said. 'We keep all the doors locked. You can't just walk in and out, you know. It wouldn't be safe. The building's falling down around our ears.'

'Really?' I said. 'It looks sound enough.'

'Oh, it may look sound enough,' she said, 'but underneath the surface it's very unsafe.'

I changed the subject back to the young man. 'I wonder who he was then,' I said. 'He didn't seem quite . . .'

'Quite what?' she said, with her head slightly tilted, as if she were listening for something other than my answer.

'Never mind,' I said.

'No, never mind,' she said. 'I'm Mrs Jennings. You're the gentleman who telephoned, aren't you? We've been expecting you.'

'I know,' I said. 'You told me that before.'

'Well,' she said, 'you wait here, and I'll see if I can find Dr Muir. He should be able to help you.'

It was a crumbling, mouldy room. I didn't like it. It was cold, too. There was a big fireplace but no fire in it. All the chairs were thick with dust. I didn't want to sit on any of them, but after a while my legs grew tired. Everything was silent, but sometimes, away in the distance, I thought I heard noises. A door being slammed, a window being pulled shut. Still nobody came. I found a chair near the fireplace that seemed slightly less dusty than the others, and I brushed its seat with my hand. From there I could look over to the window where the young man's chair was. I was glad he had pointed it out, otherwise I might have sat in it and I wouldn't have wanted to upset him. He seemed a friendly soul, even if a bit wanting.

After a while I woke up. I was very startled when this happened. I hadn't even known I was falling asleep. There wasn't any way of knowing how long I'd been dozing. I wasn't wearing a watch, which was odd because I usually do, and there was no clock in the room. I could tell because there wasn't one ticking. But it was a little gloomier, and much colder, and it was clear to me that nobody was coming.

'This is ridiculous,' I said. I said it aloud because I was angry and because I wanted to hear a human voice. I went to the door through which the woman had come and gone, which was also, I was pretty certain, the one we had used when she first brought me into the dayroom. It was locked. I shook it hard and turned the handle, but it wouldn't budge.

'Hello!' I shouted. 'Hello! Is there someone there?'

I tried some light switches by the door but there was no power. I went to the other door, the one that the young man had gone through. In the gloom it was quite difficult to find amongst all that oak panelling, but I think I did find it, although there wasn't a handle. It too was locked. After I had shaken and pushed at it I tried running at it with my shoulder, but the edges of the panelling made this painful and I stopped after the third run. I tried to be calm. The woman would be back soon, I told myself. She was obviously having trouble finding Dr Muir.

But after another ten minutes I started shouting again. 'Help!' I called. 'Somebody!' The light was disappearing fast now. I negotiated my way through the chairs to the big windows, thinking that I could perhaps open or break one and call out from there. It would be too high to jump. But the blinds were somehow stuck into the window-frames, and there were no strings to pull them up with.

I looked at the chairs. It seemed to me that they had all moved slightly, all crept a little closer to the fireplace. I went to the other side of the room, to be as far from the chairs as I could possibly be.

'Help!' I shouted. I yelled it at the top of my voice. 'Help!' But nobody came, even though I kept shouting and shouting.

And then, between shouts, I heard an echo. Whenever I called 'Help!' I heard it repeated from somewhere else in the room. When I was silent the echo was silent. I said, rather than shouted, the word, 'Help,' and back it came to me, just as quietly, 'Help.' So I yelled it again, and the echo yelled it too. But it wasn't quite an echo, it was an imitation, and I saw that I was no longer alone. The young man was back. He had come into the room with his black hair neatly parted and his shirt buttoned up to the neck, and he was standing by 'his' seat, and every time I spoke or shouted he spoke or shouted the same thing.

'Help!' I shouted.

'Help!' he shouted.

'Is anybody there?' I called.

'Is anybody there?' he called.

At first I thought he was mocking me, and this made me angry, but then I realised that he was not mocking me, he was trying to help. He looked at me after every shout with a silly, encouraging kind of smile as if pleased with his shouting, as if between us we could attract somebody's attention. But then, after a few more shouts, he forgot about me, or perhaps he thought we were in competition, for he began to shout out of turn, and louder, and I shouted back, louder and more often than he. It would have been difficult for anyone else to tell who had started it. I'm not entirely sure myself.

Soon it was so dark that I could hardly see his face. 'Help!' we called, together and separately, our voices strangely intermingling. And then I saw that there were more people in that dark empty place, ten or perhaps even twenty of them, shadowy men and women shuffling around, and those that couldn't walk were rocking violently in their chairs in front of the fireplace. I couldn't see their faces either, and the room was as cold as ice, and 'Help! Help!' they were crying. We were all crying it. It felt as if we had been crying it for years and years, but that can't be right, because I only got here this afternoon.

'Help!'

'Help!'

'Help!'

The woman was there again, I don't know how. She came towards me. 'Thank God!' I said, but I don't think she heard me.

'Goodness me,' she said, 'what's all this noise? Come now,' she said, 'calm yourself. Goodness me.'

I felt very tired. She got me settled in my chair again, in front of the fire, and I thought to myself that I would just sit for a minute, to get my breath back, and then I would leave.

'We were all at sixes and sevens, weren't we?' the woman said. 'But we're all right now. That's it, relax.'

She held my hand and it *was* all right, in a way. I closed

my eyes. I thought I would open them again soon, and have a look at the flames.

After another minute, or perhaps two, I heard her voice again.

'You just wait here,' she said, 'and I'll see if I can find Dr Muir. He should be able to help you.'